By the same author

Rogue Female

NICHOLAS SALAMAN

Rogue Female

HarperCollins*Publishers*

HarperCollins*Publishers*
77–85 Fulham Palace Road
Hammersmith, London W6 8JB

Published by HarperCollins*Publishers* 1995
1 3 5 7 9 8 6 4 2

A catalogue record for this book
is available from the British Library

ISBN 0 00 225007 1

Set in Linotron Janson by
Rowland Phototypesetting Ltd,
Bury St Edmunds, Suffolk

Printed in Great Britain by
HarperCollinsManufacturing Glasgow

For Ilona Household

'. . . The lips of a strange woman drop as an honeycomb, and her mouth is smoother than oil:

But her end is . . . sharp as a two-edged sword.'

Proverbs v.3

One

The front door bell rang – not with a tactful brrrrp but with a long insistent peal – and Duncan, who was steadying his nerves by watching a chat show on television, gave a little start. A fat red teardrop of Crozes-Hermitage (Club Selection of the Month from The Fellowship of Wine, with tasting notes) sprang onto his right trouser leg and sank in before he could catch it.

He put the glass down carefully, trying to reason with the tremble in his hand.

He must have been mad to go in for this, he thought. The whole idea was ridiculous. Who knew where it would end? He wiped the red mark on his trousers with his handkerchief, spreading the stain further. The doorbell rang again.

'Coming,' he called appeasingly and hurried down the little hall.

To his amazement when he opened the door, there was a young woman standing on the 'Oh no not you again' mat his secretary had given him for Christmas.

'Yes?' he asked abruptly, his manners deserting him in his surprise.

'No,' she replied, reprovingly.

'Oh,' he said. 'Sorry. I mean, I didn't mean to be rude. I was expecting someone else, you see.'

'You were expecting Captain Smail,' she said, helpfully. 'But how did you know that I wasn't an assailant?'

She had a pleasant, low, confidence-inspiring voice.

'I'm sorry,' said Duncan.

'Security, Mr Mackworth. The first lesson is awareness. The way you opened the door was asking for trouble.'

'Oh.'

'Yes, it is oh. And it could've been ow and oof and ouch. I could've knocked shit out of you.'

'You could?'

'Definitely I could. No two ways about it.'

'Oh dear.'

He had never cared for the lavatorial expression but she seemed to be respectable otherwise; almost like a nurse.

'Yes, it is oh dear. Now. I'd like you to go back and try that again.'

'Look here. Who are you?'

'Later, Mr Mackworth. First things first. There may not be a next time.'

Duncan had no idea what she was talking about, but she plainly had to be humoured. He shut the door in her face and went back down the corridor. The doorbell rang again.

He approached the door more circumspectly this time. First of all, he put on the door chain, then he peeped through the spyhole. There was no one there. He debated what to do next. His eye lit on a golf club lying in the umbrella stand. He picked it up and crept back to the door; then he flung it open.

The door ricocheted back in his face hurting his nose. The chain – a stupidly long one – was still on. The young woman appeared from around the corner, smiling solicitously.

'Oh dear, Mr Mackworth. We have got a lot to learn.'

Two

All his life he had had the feeling that something terrible was going to happen.

It would be something terrible that would catch him totally unprepared. There would be nothing he could do about it because of his total state of unpreparedness.

He was never quite certain what form this event would take – a car accident, an aeroplane crash, a boating debacle. Or would he perhaps be set upon by muggers as he walked back late from the office? Or beaten by burglars he'd disturbed looking for his watercolours (he had some rather good eighteenth-century pictures by Rowbotham and Beaumont).

When he was younger, he suffered ecstasies of anxiety about the school bully. He later came to realize that Bovinden probably did not even know who he was, but to this day the name Bovinden filled him with dread. Bovinden was a bovine sort of boy, as a matter of fact. He would put his head down and charge at his luckless adversaries, smashing them with his thick skull. Duncan had been too small for Bovinden to bother about him, in point of fact, but that rib-cracking charge filled his nightmares.

Even writing the name made his pulse race. Bovinden asked him to give him a pencil once and he hyperventilated.

Not that he was particularly puny in physique. He was of medium build, neither thin nor plump. He could pass for five foot ten or eleven on a good day; but it was the surge of adrenalin that he found hard to cope with. It made him quite paralysed. Sometimes he thought, it's not because I'm frightened; it's because I'm frightened of what I might do. But that again was fear of a kind.

He had attempted to conquer it, of course. He had tried religion, philosophy, diet, acupuncture, yet nothing seemed to do any good.

It was doubtless all in the mind, but that did not stop it affecting the body.

Perhaps, he sometimes told himself, it all stemmed from some childhood trauma; and indeed he had been a nervous baby. His nurse used to bind him in the cot so that he could not move. He was always twisting and turning, his mother told him later, and the nurse thought so much movement might stop him sleeping. So she trussed him up like a salami. But he believed that this early experience of imprisonment – no, let us call it by its proper name: bondage – must have left its mark upon him.

He still had the greatest dislike of being shut in, of closed places and even of closed relationships. There was, however, another perhaps profounder influence upon the shaping of his phobia, and that was his father. Parents, he understood, are well-known for casting shadows that bend and warp the young shoot, and his particular father had had an obsession. A well-known, indeed famous film-maker and naturalist in his day, it had been his belief that fear not sex was the most important motivating impulse and influence upon the animal kingdom.

He had written learned articles about it, used filmed evidence to prove his point; and, though there were many who disagreed, there were others who tended to go along with him. After all, he had not been the first to suggest the idea. It was perhaps the graphic nature of his films – there was a celebrated sequence of a baboon being caught by a leopard and turning at bay with brave futility on its attacker – that particularly caught public attention and brought him to prominence. Duncan himself used to look endlessly at stills from this sequence, horribly fascinated by the lineaments of fear, the arching backwardness of the baboon's defiance, the grimace of hopeless desperation.

It might have been, of course, that Father's obsession was based on Father's own sense of fear. People often externalize their own alarm in this way. Whatever the cause – parental influence, pressure of circumstance, or the slow music of the genes – something fearful had left its mark on Duncan.

His father's career was regrettably cut short by an insect carrying a fatal disease in a particularly nasty part of West Africa. He left Duncan's mother with a house in Berkshire, enough money for her if not Duncan to be going on with, and his collection of scientific film. His work was carried on by his faithful assistant, a reclusive man called Booth, who shared in some of his estate, inherited all his equipment, and still occasionally flitted in and out of Duncan's life.

Duncan's mother was also an authority, albeit local, on the natural world. She studied flowers, birds and insects, and they kept her perfectly happy in the Berkshire countryside. Sometimes she went on naturalist expeditions exploring the marismas of the Guadalquivir and even the Himalayas. Mostly she stayed in Berkshire while he, a solicitor now with his own small practice (he had read first English and then Law at university), lived in his father's little house off the Old Brompton Road, visiting his mother when affectionate duty or the need for escape dictated it.

This double life suited him, for it prevented any friendship from becoming too close. His profession also was a source of retreat, of concealment. Being a solicitor, he had decided long ago, was like being a doctor. Nobody wanted to know you very well. People first needed to tell you their troubles. As long as you listened attentively and made careful reassuring noises, they were happy. He hedged himself about with a wall of wry, self-mocking humour which the world took at face value, but it didn't deceive him for a moment. Humour, after all, is only another way of looking at pain.

When he was forty his mother died. He was sorry that she had gone but it did not make a great deal of difference to his life. He sold the house in Berkshire and sent the horses to stable. He did not really need two homes. There would always be the fear of burglary.

His existence now settled into a more comfortable mode, but he could not rid himself of his sense of foreboding. In his book-lined office, fronted by his secretary, and at home in his flat, surrounded by all the reassuring trappings of familiarity, his books, his collection of scientific film, he still felt vulnerable. Perhaps, he thought, everyone feels like this. We are all aware of the precariousness of life. But he knew in his heart that most people simply got on with it; they accepted it; they did not let it haunt them.

Who was it said 'We have nothing to fear but fear itself'? How right he was, thought Duncan; and yet how right he wasn't; to speak of fear itself contemptuously; it smacked of little understanding; for fear was the reality. Fear was life. That was the lesson man had learnt from the start, shrinking in his cave from the woolly mammoth and the sabre tooth. Modern man forgot it at his peril.

And yet sometimes, suddenly, just now and then, fear would leave him. There was no particular reason. He might simply be walking to work on a dull winter day and he would suddenly realize that the leaden feeling in the pit of his stomach had gone. He was free.

He would laugh out loud. Passers-by would turn, astonished, for there was little to laugh at in the Old Brompton Road on a January morning. He would twirl his umbrella and swing his briefcase like a schoolboy's satchel. Instead of his usual serious and preoccupied air, his face would register all manner of emotions. Just as the sun occasionally penetrates through the habitual mists of some northern wasteland and lays its beams across the contours of a hidden valley, so did the absence of fear show unexpected interest and warmth in the features of Duncan Mackworth. And, just as suddenly, again for no reason, like that demonic black monkey in Le Fanu's story 'Green Tea' – a favourite of Duncan's for its bearing on his own predicament – fear would be back and the sun would go in again.

The trouble with those feckless, reckless interludes was that they could promote actions which might lead to heaven knew what trouble.

On one occasion he had been on the brink of joining an Amateur Dramatic Society in Fulham; on another (he shuddered to think of it now) he had actually signed up for a Singles Dining Club in Wandsworth!

Women, of course, were a source of anxiety in themselves. He had only to think of them to feel what his mother would call 'agitato'.

It was partly that he had not had much to do with them. It was fear of the unknown. Oh, his mother was a woman, but he did not think of her as such, and besides she was hardly ever around. She was with her horses, proud volatile creatures much more challenging than her diffident son. He had no sisters. At his boarding school there had been no girls.

Not that relations with men were much better. The boys, his peers, considered him a solitary, a bit of an outsider – but strangely, because he had no wish to ingratiate himself or belong, he had been largely left alone. His fears were larger than boys; bigger even than Bovinden.

As for girls, he had been attracted to them, certainly. Just because you have a sense of dread doesn't mean your hormones are stifled. Quite the reverse. In Hitler's bunker during the last days, Duncan had read that there were no end of goings-on. So at university, despite his fears, he had taken a number of young women to the cinema, out to the pub, and it had been like going out with a cross between a madonna and an alien. These creatures seemed to him so delicate, so beautiful, so inscrutable, so infinitely unmanlike.

But when they said (if he were lucky) : 'Like to come up for a cup of coffee?' he was seized with alarm. Half of him wanted to creep inside their blouses and see how it was that bras undid and nipples behaved – to say nothing of the silken mysteries that lay under the skirt – and half of him feared that if he accepted their kind invitations or acquiescences (for he was not unattractive), he would give himself away, he would speak in a careless moment of affection about the dread he had always felt, and it would be known that he, Duncan Mackworth, was like those chocolates that people throw away with a 'yuck!' if they select them by mistake. He was a man with a jelly centre.

Fortunately he was good at his studies, so the girls used to say of him: 'Oh, it's no use talking to Duncan. He's got his head in the clouds.'

It had been cloud cover.

And now, it seemed, if he weren't very careful his cover might be blown.

Three

That last mischievous fear-free interlude of his had endured a little longer than usual; and coming as it did at that particular stage of his life – he had just turned forty-one – it had prompted him to look at himself closely. And of course, after a suitable period of interpretation, he had concluded that he was a mess. It wasn't difficult to see the problem. It was this fear of his, this dread that was always hemming in, making him live like a chicken in a circumscribed wire run because it kept telling him there were foxes outside.

He was able to think quite lucidly about his problem when it was not in residence. He had wondered at one stage whether he should not consult a psychiatrist; but the idea started making him nervous.

'Let me not be mad, not mad, sweet Heaven.'

That would indeed be something to dread. But somehow he knew that madness wasn't his problem. Quite the reverse. To be full of alarm in this violent society, in this uncertain globe hurtling through space round a slowly extinguishing star, surrounded by all manner of threats; some as big as asteroids and others as small as mutating viruses, but most of human dimension; was it not an acutely sane frame of mind to sustain?

But there must be something he could do to make it a reasonable acknowledgement of potential danger rather than an entrail-gripping dread. If only he could be like those SAS heroes – there had been another hijack, on the news recently, resolved by a storming – who did things of appalling risk without turning a hair. There must be something in their training that enabled them to be not as other men – and most especially not like D. Mackworth, Esq. What could it be? The question preyed upon him until suddenly one day, in that stupid dangerous state of fear remission, he had written an advertisement: 'Man (40) wishes to acquire self-defence training at home. No classes. Skilled instructor sought. Write PO Box . . .' etc.

He debated for some time which magazine it should appear in, and concluded that something like the *Spectator* would be respectable. He didn't want to attract undesirables – even though he had preserved his anonymity with a PO Box No. He knew that undesirables have a way of wiggling through.

With this mood of decision still upon him, he sent the advertisement up to the *Spectator*. He paid his money and the thing was accepted. Two days later, he was gripped with panic. What on earth did he think he was doing? The *Spectator* knew his identity. What if an undesirable saw the ad and contacted the *Spectator* – some little clerk who could be bought, who would betray his, Duncan's, name and address, and set in motion that terrible train of events which would culminate in robbery with violence if not mayhem.

His relief had been indescribable when, a week later, he received a polite note from Capt. (retired) Oliver Smail, ex-Paratroop Regiment, listing his credentials and references and suggesting a very reasonable fee for tuition.

This was exactly what he had had in mind. Perhaps he hadn't made such a mistake after all. He contacted Captain Smail by letter and arranged that he should call with a view to describing for him what a series of lessons would entail, also that the Captain might familiarize himself with location (would the flat have a suitable room?) and briefing him on dress, timing, admin. and any questions.

It had all seemed perfectly reasonable. Duncan had felt

nervous, but not unusually so. The Crozes-Hermitage – just an educated glass – would have helped to steady his nerves. And now, here, of all people, impolitely punctual, was not Captain Oliver Smail ex-paratrooper but a woman – and an attractive one at that.

How could a woman make a man of him? It was painful. It was absurd. The best that could be said for the situation was that his normal sense of fear was tinctured with solicitorly pique. This was surely a breach of contract.

Four

There was a further ingredient, he discovered, in his cocktail of emotions when the young woman entered his living room and sat down. (He had to ask her in. He couldn't just leave her there.)

His feelings of dread and annoyance were further curdled by acute embarrassment. His nose still throbbed. He hoped he had not broken anything. He could see its tip lit up like a beacon. At the same time, he felt he could not make any kind of fuss about it in front of this virago who had come to teach him self-defence. And how was he going to get rid of her?

'I was expecting a man,' he said. 'I'm sorry.'

There was absolutely no reason why he should apologize, but some kind of apology seemed called for and she appeared not in the least inclined to come up with one.

'I hope I don't read sexism into that remark,' she said, smiling gently.

He was taken aback at her response.

'Oh no. Not in the least. Simply . . . confusion.'

'That's just as well. Otherwise we might have to call it a day. There's no sexism in self-defence.'

He cursed himself for not having the guts to say his remark had been inspired by sheer bigotry. His problems would have been at an end. Instead, he started stammering.

'Per-per-perhaps we should introduce ourselves. I'm Duncan Mackworth.'

He extended his hand and then hurriedly withdrew it. His exposed wrist looked so vulnerable.

'I know you are,' she said. 'And that was good. You're learning.'

'I am?'

He suddenly felt absurdly, irrationally pleased at her commendation.

'My name is Lindup. My mates call me Jo.'

He looked at her closely. She was, he supposed, in her late twenties; glowing with health from her closely-trimmed topiary of coppery-chestnut hair to the balls of her size 6 Reebok-shod feet. In between, her body proclaimed fitness without fatness. Not that she was slender; she was firmly fleshed and muscled, the skin on her pug-like, slightly rubbery features was blushing peach-gold and her greeny hazel eyes glinted with health. What a picture, he thought – so must the Amazons have seemed – though her breasts (two, unlike the Amazons) were slightly larger than she might have wished.

She held out her arm now and they shook hands. Her breasts shuddered slightly as she did so. With disgust at meeting him, he imagined.

'Oliver Smail has had to leave the country,' she told him. 'He has been seconded to duties in Malawi.'

'Ah.'

'There's a situation developing. He was the man for the job.'

'I see.'

'He'll be back in due course. Meanwhile he asked me to take you over. Any questions?'

'Er. Where did you learn self-defence?'

'My father's a Marine. I learnt it in my cradle.'

'Literally?'

'Literally.'

Jo Lindup, if she had a sense of humour, was doing her best to camouflage it. Her manner as always was polite, professional.

'Good gracious,' he said feebly.

'I work out with Oliver Smail and some of the boys,' she told him.

'Have they gone to Malawi too?'

'That's right.'

'Why didn't you go to Malawi?'

He was surprised to see her blush.

'I don't think it's really your business.'

'Sorry. I didn't . . .'

She seemed to relent.

'They thought it might . . . take their eye off the ball.'

'I see.'

'Two of the boys are . . . you know . . . funny about me.'

Clearly, if not sexism, there was a sex in self-defence.

He was beginning to understand how they felt. There was something mesmeric about her green eyes and her contemptuous breasts.

'Now then,' she said. 'None of that.'

'What? Really, I . . .'

'You're going to need a lot of work,' she told him. 'Forget I'm a woman and I'll forget you're a man.'

It would not be difficult for her, he thought. Something in her manner told him she had found him out already.

'Oh . . . right,' he mumbled. 'Sorry.'

'The course is twelve lessons. That's just for basic training. After that we'll take stock. This room will do if you move back the settee and chairs. Wear something really loose – a jungle jacket, lightweight trousers, T-shirt. Oh, and trainers for the feet. What's that on your trousers?'

She pointed to the stain above his privates.

'Red wine.'

'Is that how you take it? Through your trousers?'

It was, he supposed, her idea of a pleasantry. She was smiling briskly.

'I spilt it when you rang the bell. My hand shook.'

'You're a bundle of nerves,' she told him. 'You contacted Captain Smail not a minute too soon. Same time next week suit you? Good. Mind how you go.'

Five

Accelerated daisies, bees dancing, bees ventilating, drones soaring after queen, thunderclouds forming, kangaroos boxing, meerkat squirting territory with urine, shrews courting, bats mating, snakes shedding skins, cuckoo invading nest, pollen popping, salmon leaping, devil's stinkhorn (glans and shaft) emerging, sundew catching midges, bloodstream catching 'flu . . .

Duncan's collection of original scientific film, painstakingly acquired by his father and his father's assistant over the years, had grown from a mere caretaking exercise into something more central. Perhaps it had always been so; perhaps even when he had been terrified of the pulsing, squashy, tooth and clawiness of nature as a child, he had always been fascinated as well as afraid. Whatever the truth of the matter, the collection filled parts of his life which would have felt bare without it.

Having already converted it to video, more than 1,000 items of it, at great expense, for some time now he had been re-cataloguing. He could now use his computer to find things with a speed that would have been unthinkable to his father. It gave him a certain pride to know this, since the great man was generally scathing about the technological advances of the new generation. He had been generally scathing about a number of things, including his son.

It was strange how the ordering of some of those sequences

that had so scared Duncan as a child had the effect now of laying some of those ghosts – not all, of course, or he wouldn't have been Duncan – but certainly of pushing the fear back into librarianly niches; not to come springing forth with a boo, he hoped, but only in an orderly fashion to be taken out and signed for . . .

Sometimes it seemed a pity to him that he should keep all this material to himself. The tides of time had closed over his father's name. Few people asked for clips of his work now. Just twenty years and it was as though he had never been. And yet, there was so much that was brilliant here. What was it they had said at the time? 'Dickie Mackworth doesn't just know his subject, he loves it.'

Perhaps, Duncan thought, I should give up the law and make a go of it, this love affair of my father's with the natural world. Exactly what sort of go, he could not quite say, but there had to be something – something in television where he could act as consultant. There were, however, problems, fears, unforeseen exigencies that made him pause. Perhaps it was better to keep the collection private, in the family.

And so he catalogued on. Sometimes as he worked, he began to feel there had been more than mere love in his father's eye. Sometimes, it seemed, there was something almost Oedipal in it; lover, yes, but wasn't Nature also the mother? There was something both rapturous and at the same time almost prurient about the way the camera sought out and then lingered on certain subjects: the tumescence of a droplet forming, the cataclysm of its explosion (it had been his father's whim to accompany this sequence with Beethoven's *Egmont Overture*); the sportive tricks of an anopheles larva; the creaky caress of unseasonal frost enfolding a tubifex worm; the deliquescent flanks and hot red lips of an erupting volcano . . .

And then again, it seemed to Duncan, that there was something else coming out of all this. The way his father had crept up on his subjects, teased them out, pried in upon them, whether it were the habits of the slipper-shaped paramecium, or the eerie waltzing of a tornado; mountains, molehills, monsters of the deep, creatures of the microcosmic ooze; all secreted on clips of 16-millimetre film; sometimes it appeared to Duncan like the compulsive recording by a jealous husband of his wife's excursions, to be viewed with sighs and torments, and a measure of regrettable pleasure.

'Were the whole world of nature mine...' Wasn't that how the hymn went? Father had thought it was his – a proprietorship not offered to the glory of the Creator but to the Moloch of the television screen, of a world that was for ever in danger of escaping him.

And when the world was cruel ... ah, how much more excited his camera had become! You could almost sense it growing erect. The death contortions of a bee as it tried to unwind its sting, the futile struggles of a butterfly in a spider's web, the agonizing decoying of a lapwing as a crow attacked its young, the doomed last leap of the snowshoe hare into the paw of the bobcat ... it was compulsive, it was brilliant. It was disgusting.

His father had revelled in showing such sequences to Duncan as a child, pointing out the refinements of the scene, the exquisiteness of the creature's terror.

'Look, boy. He knows he cannot outstrip the panther. Even so, for a short while, the adrenalin in his body forces his legs almost to do so. And so it would yours. You would exceed your design...'

Normally such memories would cause him, even now in his librarianly role, to stir uneasily and find his heart was beating like a baboon's at bay, but it was a measure of his concern about his approaching appointment that the new anxiety, like a fresh wave, erased its predecessor.

He put the catalogue aside and asked himself again why he couldn't have said what he felt to the girl. Like:

'I don't think this will do after all. I was expecting a man.'

He kept repeating it to himself. The next day he said it in the office.

'I was expecting a man.'

'Mr Mackworth? Expecting a man?'

'It's all right, Delice.'

His secretary, a thin, efficient, melancholy woman in her late forties, by no means matched the promise of her name. That was why he had chosen her.

'You were expecting a man, Mr Mackworth. You said so. It's not in your diary.'

'I said it's all right. I was talking to myself.'

'How I'm to keep track of your comings and goings if you talk to yourself is beyond me, Mr Mackworth. It's hard enough when you talk to me. And I'm the one who gets the blame.'

Someone who was so unglamorous should not be such a groaner, thought Duncan – though naturally he did not like to say so. Someone so unglamorous should charm by the force of personality. That had been his mother's view. She had valued personality above looks and said that he would too, but he didn't.

'And whatever have you done to your nose, Mr Mackworth? I wouldn't expect anybody with a nose like that.'

He smiled bleakly but did not reply. He didn't know why he let her speak to him in that way. Loyalty was surely no excuse for brusqueness. He made a note to talk to her tomorrow or sometime.

With unwelcome rapidity, the week sailed round, and there he was with his shirt and jungle jacket and loose trousers underpinned with the regulation trainers.

'I look like a scoundrel,' he said to his image in the mirror. 'I look like someone I shouldn't like to meet.'

The thought rather pleased him, until he reflected that his more aggressive costume could be interpreted as a challenge to someone looking for a fight. At any rate, he comforted himself, he would not be going out in it. He sat and watched a chat show, waiting for Miss Lindup's arrival.

'And what do you think of women priests?' asked the compere of Vernon Prebble, a young fogey whom everyone loved to hate. 'Have you attended a service conducted by a woman?'

'I have. And I should say with Doctor Johnson, it's like a dog walking on its hind legs. It's not well done but it's amazing that it should be done at all.'

There was a pause while the audience divided itself into uproar and downroar.

Duncan wished he could open a bottle of Australian Shiraz-Cabernet, another offering from the Wine Club, but he feared the young woman would find him out.

On the television, the young fogey was explaining that women priests were the least of his problems. The whole fabric of the country was being dismantled. The Church, the Law, the Monarchy, the City – doubtless there would be legalized homosexuality in the Army next – what was a woman priest here or there?

The doorbell pealed with appalling suddenness.

What had got into that bell? It never used to blast like that. He must get it changed. Surely there must be one that crept upon the senses rather than shattering the nerves? Just as well he hadn't been holding the Shiraz-Cabernet or he'd have had red stains on his trews again.

He rose to his feet and slowly made his way towards the hall. Before he was halfway there, the bell pealed anew. This was followed by a peremptory rat-tat-tat on his brass lion knocker. Muffled commands could be discerned outside. What on earth would his neighbours think?

'Coming,' he shouted softly.

Shouting didn't agree with him.

He was so upset, he nearly forgot to put the door on the chain, before he opened it, but just as he had his hand on the lock, he remembered. Phew. Steady now. His heart was pounding louder than the lion.

What else?

Ah yes. Look out through the spyhole. That was right. Damn. He could see nothing. There had been a spate of children putting chewing gum on the outside recently.

Rat-tat-tat.

'All right, all right.'

There was nothing for it but to turn the lock, standing well back in case there was a kick.

Gently, very gently, he eased the door open, pushing it with his stretched-out fingers at arms' length.

There was no one there. Should he go out? Should he go back? It must be her. She would only knock again. His heart pounding, he undid the chain and emerged onto the front step.

'Miss Lindup,' he called. 'Arghh.'

Suddenly she was there behind, those soft capable hands squeezing at his throat.

'I could smell you a mile off,' she said. 'Violets.'

It was the aftershave a client had brought him. He'd put it on that morning for confidence.

'Grey Flannel,' he said. 'I'll stop wearing it.'

'Not on my account. But be aware of it, that's all. I love the smell of violence.'

'Violets,' he corrected her helpfully.

'Did I say violence? There, would you believe it? I always used to say that as a kid.'

Six

'We always start with relaxation,' she said. 'Sit down and make yourself really comfortable.'

Duncan wasn't looking for this at all. His guard was up and he was expecting attack.

'Like this?'

'Never cross your legs. It cuts off the blood supply. Knees apart. Let your arms dangle to the side. Now . . . feel those arms. They're hanging there, Duncan. I may call you, Duncan?'

'Of course.'

'Some people object. But we get the best results if we're name to name.'

'Shall I call you Jo?'

'Of course. Now, Duncan, I'm going to take you into deep relaxation. Let's start with really letting go. I want you to really let go when I tell you.'

'Let go?'

'You find it difficult to let go, don't you, Duncan? That's your education. All that formal schooling. Oh, don't get me wrong. I really admire education. I wish I had had your education, Duncan. I do. I envy your background. But that's why you find it difficult to let go. You have something to hold on to. Me? I'm only too happy to let go, loosen my grip, see? Ready?'

'What sort of, er, background did you have, er Jo?' Duncan asked.

She seemed pleased at the question, but she shook her head.

'Not now, Duncan, if you don't mind. Not in the lesson. We don't want to waste your money, do we? OK, I want you to clench your whole body as tight as you can. Ready? Now!'

Duncan screwed his face up and clenched every sinew he could find.

'And let go,' she ordered.

He sagged prodigiously.

'Very good. Now, Duncan, I want you to imagine that I am taking you down in a lift – in an elevator, Duncan – ten levels, one by one, down to the deepest relaxation we can find. I want you to empty your mind and come with me . . . down, Duncan, to Level 1 . . . You're beginning to be aware of your day-to-day cares receding . . .'

And so she continued the descent. At the tenth level, Duncan was feeling very floppy indeed.

'Well done, Duncan,' she said softly. 'Oh well done. Yes, I think you let go. I think you did. You let go for me.'

He felt ridiculously pleased. Better still, he felt refreshed and relaxed. He realized, with a sense of pleasant shock, that he did not feel afraid.

'Now to business,' said Jo. 'A few exercises first to get you loosened up. Gently now. Nice and easy. No jerking.'

She made him stand opposite her and follow her movements as she stretched her arms wide and rotated from the hip, swivelling the arms to the front and back.

'My,' she said, 'you are stiff, Duncan. You're like an old tree.'

'I have always been stiff,' he told her.

'Not any more. We're going to get you moving as you never moved before. It's going to be like the end of the Ice Age. Legs apart . . . not too much . . . and let's see you touch your toes. Don't jerk, Duncan. No. What did I tell you?'

She was suddenly cross with him. Her eyes, it seemed to him, had now a kind of redness behind the green. Or it could have been the lights from the Bunch of Feathers.

31

'Tell me. Tell me, Duncan.'

'You said not to jerk.'

'That's better. You'll pull a muscle that way. Everything we do must be smooth. Fluency, Duncan, that's what we're after. We don't want you to be like the lobster in the disco.'

He looked at her. What on earth was she talking about? Her eyes had reverted to their normal shade, however, so he relaxed again though not quite down to Level 10.

'He pulled a mussel, Duncan. Where have you been all your life? Now . . . flat on your back and raise your legs in the air after me.'

So the lesson wore on. Exercise after exercise followed, and Duncan – though he was surprised to find he was enjoying the experience – began to wonder where the self-defence came in. After all, he could go to exercises at the local gym and join the aggressive ladies in their leotards if that was all he wanted.

'You wouldn't, you know,' she said to him.

'I'm sorry?'

'You wouldn't find what I'm giving you at the Health Club down the road.'

How did she know what he was thinking?

'You're really transparent, Duncan,' she said. 'D'you know that? Did anyone ever tell you that?'

'No,' he said.

'Well, you are. I could see what you were thinking. You were thinking "Where's the self-defence come in?" Confess, now.'

'Yes,' he said. 'I'm afraid I was.'

'Don't be afraid,' she said, and he felt his heart give a little flip of gratitude as she said it. 'There's no offence. My clients often say that. But before I can teach you to defend yourself, Duncan, I must teach you to move. And when I've taught you to move, I must teach you to be aware.'

'Of course,' he said. 'I'm sorry. I can't run before I can walk.'

'You're not even walking yet, Duncan. You're still crawling. But when I've finished with you, you'll be *Homo erectus*.'

He looked at her quickly. Had there been some nuance in her choice of words?

'You're surprised, Duncan, aren't you? I can see that. You're really a little startled. But I can be educated too, you know, though I had no formal schooling. I've come from a long way behind you, Duncan. You must correct me if I make mistakes in grammar or spelling when I give you notes. Yes, I shall be giving you notes. And now I'm going to blindfold you, Duncan, and you must tell me where you think I am in the room . . .'

The lesson ended with instruction on the ready position, with palms outspread, single foot movements, and rhythms of evasion and retreat, to help him 'get off the line'.

'This is self-defence I'm teaching you, Duncan,' she told him. 'I don't want to see you wilfully get into trouble. We've had lots of weirdos wanting to learn how to work people over, but we don't take them because that's not what it's about. What I'm teaching you is an art, Duncan. It's not easy or else everyone would do it. The life so short, the art so long to learn, Duncan. You see? No formal schooling but I can show you a thing or two.'

'Where were you brought up?' he asked. 'Where did you go to school?'

The lesson was over and she was rubbing her face and hands with a towel. Her combat jacket lay ready for departure on a chair. She paused and looked at him.

'I'll tell you next time,' she said. 'I like you, Duncan. I think you could be good. You worked well, you really did. You have an instinct for the work. But we've probably had enough for today. Don't crowd yourself. Always let experience sink into your learning matrix if you have the time. We have the time, Duncan. Same time, same place, Tuesday. That'll be thirty pounds.'

He gave her the money, which she took with one hand,

undoing her shirt with the other. He was momentarily confused. What could this mean? There was a sudden glimpse of pale pink flesh and white bra top.

'Safest place there is,' she said, tucking the money away.

He could smell the milky sweetness of her, fresh sweat and the cologney scent of clean clothes. Remembering his drill, he peered through the peephole before opening the door for her.

'Good,' she said. 'You're learning. I think we'll make a really good team.'

He liked the way she kept saying 'really'. She turned to go, then stopped and held out her hand.

'Goodbye,' he said.

'Eyes in the back of your head,' she told him, and ran down the steps.

He watched her check to left and right, then make off towards the Fulham Road, keeping to the outside of the pavement.

Seven

The extraordinary thing was, he could feel the fear leaving him. It wasn't like the usual remission. This time it seemed as if a real cure had set in. A healthy pink began to show at the edge of his attitudes.

He found himself thinking about the young woman during the day, her voice, her laugh, her skin, that glimpse of tender bosom he had never expected from such a businesslike exterior – a temperate valley full of figs and flowers, below the snow line.

> *'O lucky Lycra to be prest*
> *Against that Amazonian breast,'*

he wrote in his blotter.

His secretary found it.

'Is this some kind of message, Mr Mackworth?'

Duncan suppressed a sensation of alarm. Not that he had shown it in the past – he had long ago learned that his face could be an expressionless mask even while he himself was undergoing the most acute perturbations. But on this occasion there was no need for a mask. Moving easily on the balls of his feet, he got off the line.

'A message, Delice? It is a clue.'

'Funny sort of clue, Lycra's not a very nice word for a man to be using. I wouldn't have thought you'd know such a word.'

Still moving easily, his weight shifting from foot to foot,

he glided out of reach to her left. Why tell her about the advertisements he read in the magazines she put out in reception? He had sometimes wondered if it were quite done to read one's own reception magazines. He had never heard of a dentist or doctor doing so. However, he wasn't going to debate it with her now – or ever, come to think of it.

'I believe you left the keys of the safe on your desk, Delice.'

He had once almost had an affair with Delice – well, not an affair, a Christmas kiss had nearly been exchanged – but he had remembered reading an article on harassment in the *Solicitors Journal* so he had merely pursed his lips and pretended to brush a little bunting from her shoulder. She had good legs and he had had two dry olorosos. That was the beginning and end of it.

'Please try to be more secure.'

She gaped at him, blushed, and he was gone.

Later he met his accountant Gerald for a drink. It was rare for him to suggest such a thing and Gerald expected news of some kind of financial complexity or crisis as they sat in the bar of Durrants Hotel.

'Something up with the Customs and Excise? The Taxman been at your door constraining?' said Gerald, half whimsical, half anxious.

One did not joke too much about the Revenue.

'No, no,' said Duncan. 'Everything's in order, I just thought we should have a drink. Haven't had a chat for some time.'

'No, er no. Of course we haven't,' said the accountant, raising his glass nervously.

He was convinced that something was seriously wrong. He'd never seen Duncan behaving so strangely.

'Everything all right at home? Investment doing well? The market's going up and up, but I wonder if it can last.'

The fact was that his accountant was almost the nearest thing to a friend that Duncan had. His impassive mask led most acquaintances to judge him a cold fish. Gerald, however, was a kind-hearted fellow who had always behaved towards him with more cordiality than mere accounting would require. Duncan in the past had seen danger in such a relationship, but now he found an irresistible need to confide in someone. He could never have told a woman, or indeed another man, but an accountant was tantamount to a confessor.

'Gerald,' he said. 'Have you ever been afraid?'

The accountant looked at him apprehensively. Yes, whatever it was, it was going to be serious.

'I should think we've all been afraid from time to time,' he said. 'Fear is rather like pain. It's essential for existence.'

'I've been afraid ever since I can remember,' said Duncan.

'What?'

'Except for a few short remissions.'

'But that's impossible!'

One or two heads turned in their direction at the sound of Gerald's expostulation.

'It's true, I assure you,' said Duncan.

'You've never given . . . any indication of it . . .'

'It's not something one wants to go around showing. Not all the time anyway,' said Duncan. 'I learned to dissemble. Most people dissemble other things – greed, jealousy, desire, self-hate. I dissemble fear.'

'Well, I must say,' said Gerald, looking confused. 'You've done very well on it. What are you afraid of?'

'That's the thing,' said Duncan. 'I don't know. Oh, there have been plenty of specific moments – falling off a wall as a child, learning to swim . . . and dive . . . an exploding firework, the Headmaster's study, a car wash . . . But the strange thing is all those specific fears were almost a relief, though I hated them of course.'

'I don't understand.'

'It was a relief to have something real to feel frightened about.'

'I think I see what you mean.'

'Mine was a general apprehension, a sense of dread. I couldn't shake it off.'

37

'Didn't you see a doctor? A . . . psychiatrist?'

'What would they do? Tell me my fear was unreal? Tell me there was nothing to worry about? There's plenty to worry about.'

'Such as?'

'The state of the world, the violence on the streets, over-population, aeroplanes, virtual reality, nurses, infidelity, aster-oids, the greenhouse effect, age, time, the death of grass . . .'

'The what?'

'Have you ever thought what would happen if grass died? There was a book about it.'

'You worry about it?'

'Not specifically. I don't know *what* I worry about. I worry about indefinable things. And it isn't worry, it's apprehension. I just feel that something bad's going to happen. Or, I should say, something bad *was* going to happen. Because now I don't know that it's going to happen any more. The cloud is lifting.'

'This is all very strange,' said Gerald.

'It is strange,' Duncan agreed.

'Why is the cloud lifting?'

'The cloud is lifting because of this strange woman.'

'Ah. *Cherchez la femme.*'

'It's not like that,' said Duncan. 'At least I don't think it is, though she is attractive in her way. No, this strange woman is going to build me up so I can face anything, come what may.'

'"Build you up"? Is she a nutritionist?'

Duncan laughed. He did not, could not often register hilar-ity. But hearing Jo described as a nutritionist sent unmistak-able messages to his smile organs.

'Oh no,' he said. 'Oh dear me, no. She is a self-defence practitioner.'

'She is what?'

Heads turned again as Gerald's voice squeaked his surprise.

'You tell me this woman who has lifted your cloud is a kung-fu wallah? Look here, Duncan, are you feeling all right?'

38

'Never better. And it's not kung-fu. What Jo teaches is self-defence, nothing more nor less. You ought to try it, Gerald. You could walk out of here and get stabbed.'

'You're a damn sight more likely to get stabbed if you try to fight back. That I do know,' said Gerald.

'True. Of course that's true. And that's what Jo says. Never try to fight. Back off, Gerald. Say "I'm just out of hospital with cancer," anything you like. But when the chips are down and we have to defend ourselves, Gerald, I shall be the one that comes through with flying colours while you're lying in the gutter with a knife in your jugular and your lifeblood frothing down the drain.'

Gerald had turned a nasty colour during this recital. He finished his drink with an over-hasty swig sending liquid dribbling from his chin like a statue in a fountain – or a corpse in a gutter.

'Another one, Gerald? You don't have to go yet, surely?'

'Got to catch a train.'

Poor old Gerald, thought Duncan, watching him go, and pausing a while to finish his drink. He'd never do for self-defence. You need to be aware of potential danger all the time. That's what was going to make him so good at it. Jo's genius was to make him see his perpetual sense of fear as a virtue.

He almost skipped out of the hotel, and was just about to hail a taxi when he saw a little knot of people gathered on Marylebone High Street.

He knew it was going to be Gerald on the pavement, yards before he arrived, and he recognized the Mulberry mackintosh instantly.

'Mugged?' he asked one of the onlookers.

'No, he slipped,' said the man, indicating the telltale skid-marks.

'I think I've split my Mulberry,' said Gerald rising slowly from the pavement.

There was clearly nothing seriously wrong with him.

'Eyes in the back of your head,' Duncan told him as the ambulance wheeeeeooooo-whoop-whoop-whooped round the corner. 'That's what we say in self-defence. Always be aware.'

'You know what I say in self-defence? Dogshit.'

And indeed it was that that had brought Gerald low. How Jo would smile when he told her! He left his friend expostulating to the ambulance man, and walked home in the ready position across the park.

Eight

Tuesday at last came round again. Duncan left work early though Delice gave him a serious look and muttered something about it being all right for some, and what about the big conveyancing job for Thursday?

Indeed it was all right, he thought, as he almost ran home. It was all right for *him*. Who was it who had suddenly shed his burden? Bunyan's Pilgrim, that was it, after God knew what perils and dangers, Castle of Despair and foul fiends, carrying the wretched thing. And how Pilgrim had skipped and capered afterwards. He could do a bit of skipping and capering of his own, couldn't he? Pouf! to the big conveyancing job. Had he not conveyed enough for one lifetime?

Careful now, though. He must remember the precepts. Always safeguard your exit. In his new-found freedom, he mustn't become careless. Fear was like pain, remember. It was a useful condition so long as you took remedial action. It was a warning. It was nature's way of telling you something was wrong, something could be round the corner.

These thoughts coursed through his mind as he made himself a cup of tea and sipped it as he changed into something 'really loose'. How he liked that way of hers of saying 'really'. It was an enchanting foible.

No red wine this time. Jo had warned him about that. It could fatally relax him, make him over-confident, trip him up, lay him low.

Perhaps he would make her a cup of tea afterwards. She would like that. He could question her about her own background, with no formal education. Why had she had no formal education? Who had withheld it from so obvious a candidate? Perhaps he could even take her out to dinner . . .

He had always had a particular dislike of taking women to restaurants in the past. There were so many things that could go wrong. Selecting the right restaurant, getting the right table, choosing the right food, ordering the right wine; striking the right tone with the waiter; complaining about the food; sending the wine back; catching the waiter's attention for the bill; tipping the coat-girl; finding a taxi afterwards; getting mugged on the way home . . .

He was always so busy fearing the worst, anticipating the next hurdle, fermenting anxiety, that his face, contrarily, became positively glacial; and any girl who went out with him once would return to her flat, pour herself a stiff drink and say 'never again'. He knew they did, because once he asked someone to go out with him a second time and that's what she told him.

'You're not bad-looking, Duncan,' she said. 'You don't smell and your eyes are nice and you're not a groper. But, my God, you're a bore.'

He wasn't a bore. In fact, sometimes when he looked at himself in the mirror, he found himself really quite interesting.

This face of his, he had thought ever since he had started to consider such things as a youth, looked as though it didn't belong to him. It still didn't. He didn't feel like his face. That was interesting.

In fact, it was quite a pleasant face, as the girl had indicated, midway between a horse and a bun (his mother's classification).

A good straight nose, a well-shaped mouth – rather too long a gap between the two, but never mind, all the more room for raising a glass of South African Pinotage – ears that fitted snugly, chin neither too Punch-like nor recessive, the darkish hair all there, the eyes an interesting mid-light blue the colour of lithospernum (see Bumblebees/Flowers) ... all this was very well. But whose face was it? It gave no indication of being involved with his innermost being, in fact its impassivity seemed to say: 'You worry yourself sick if you like, but don't expect me to get all screwed up about it.'

As a young man, he used to have a little joke with the one or two people he almost knew well. If he went to the Gents, he would say: 'Just going to change my expression.' But it was not all joke. He felt he must look, in case the face had got out of hand, and sometimes, after a glass or two ... there would be something there.

Now, however, they had been together too long for surprises. Face had settled into a habitual, wry, deprecating expression that sat coolly and conveniently on top of his subterranean corridors of fear like a church on a catacomb; telling the world that he was, give or take the odd quirk, like most other men; only, perhaps, a little more restrained.

Restrained, perhaps, but no – not a bore. Indeed, when an American advertising man with a face like a baffled doughnut came in one day for a difficult change of lease, and picked up from his desk, uninvited, a still from one of the scientific film sequences, wringing from Duncan something of his knowledge, he had described him as fascinating.

'In our business,' the man – Reinacker his name was – had said, 'we know a little about a great deal. You are the reverse. You are an authority. Ever thought of getting in on the commercials market? Come out to lunch,' and pressed his card on him.

He was grateful for Duncan's professional advice and his very lenient charge, and he genuinely wanted to help; but Duncan cursed the momentary confidence, occasioned by some quirk of pride. Why could he not keep his mouth shut? Who knew what dangers lay in too open a disclosure?

He had wriggled free from the invitation; pressure of work, meeting at two; the old evasions springing as naturally to

43

him as flight to a gazelle. They were voracious, these people, especially at the waterholes.

But now, yes, after only one lesson, he could actually contemplate taking Jo out to dinner – perhaps, he thought, Il Trovatore in the Fulham Road, where the head waiter, according to Delice, was so attentive. Or would Jo, with her lack of formal education, feel uncomfortable among all those 'buon notte's' and 'signorinas'? Perhaps a Chinese would be more her bowl of noodles?

He started. Somebody was knocking on the door. I am coming, my own, my sweet . . .

Such was his hurry that he forgot the Page One precaution, opened the door without so much as a squint through the peephole, and was rewarded by a thump in the solar plexus, an arm across the neck, and a knife in the throat.

'Hand me yer wallet, fucker,' said a voice he had never heard before.

His first sensation was pain. His second was disgrace.

Oh, Jo, he thought, how I have let you down. It surprised him, even then, that he did not feel any fear. He was just wondering how on earth you got off the line when you had a knife at your throat when he heard her voice.

'It looks as if I wasted my time last week, doesn't it, Mr Mackworth?'

No, 'Hullo, Duncan', no warm greeting, no friendly 'How did your week go?' . . . It was indeed as if last Tuesday had been wiped from her records. He would feel fear returning now like the tide across the sands of Dee; a whispering liquid flicker; runnels of it finding out the channels of his apprehension.

Her face was stony.

'I brought one of the boys along to see how well you were doing, and you do this to me! Did you want to humiliate me, Mr Mackworth? Was that your game? Because if it was, Eddie here will have something to say about it.'

Eddie was putting his 'knife' back into one of his pouches

but managed a cold tutorial nod in his direction. Of course it wasn't a knife, merely a piece of painted wood. Somehow that made the whole thing even more ridiculous. He had failed at the first fence, thought Duncan, as he ushered them into his hallway.

'The only person to be humiliated is me,' he said to her.

'Yes,' she said. 'You're right. And I had such high hopes of you. I'm sorry. I don't like failure. Eddie, will you take Mr Mackworth on?'

'I s'pose I could teach him a few basics. How to open doors and that. Simple security. Personal hygiene.'

'I beg your pardon,' said Duncan.

'Anything wrong?' asked Jo, coldly.

'He said personal hygiene.'

'We always give the really thick ones a course in personal hygiene. Some of them don't know how to keep their feet healthy,' she said. 'Care of the feet is paramount.'

'Some of 'em don't know how to blow their noses,' said Eddie.

'I thought the boys were in Malawi with Captain Smail,' said Duncan.

'Eddie came back on compassionate, didn't you, Eddie?'

'Compassionate?'

'Leave, Mr Mackworth. And now he's here, he could possibly do what I can't. Right, Eddie?'

'Yer, that's right. I could fit him in, I s'pose.'

'Please,' said Duncan. 'Jo. Come on. Please.'

'Miss Lindup, please. Or Operative Lindup if you prefer.'

'Please, Miss Lindup. Don't do this to me.'

He was overdoing it, of course, playing up to her.

'You've done it to yourself, Mr Mackworth.'

'A last chance. Look, I'm getting off the line . . .'

He had started the sequence. Forward, to the side and forward. Back to the side and back . . .

'Get your hands up level with your chest to the defensive

45

position,' Jo shouted. 'Palms out. That's better. Now . . . what do we do when someone comes at us with a knife?'

'We run like hell,' said Duncan, as she nodded approval.

'You'll give me a chance, then?'

'What d'you think, Eddie?'

'He's got a fair glide. He done well on his glide.'

'Very well, Mr Mackworth. A last chance. I hope you won't make me regret it.'

'I won't, I promise you. Thank you, Jo . . . Miss . . .'

He surprised himself at his gratitude.

'Very well, then, Mr Mackworth. Let's begin the second lesson.'

Nine

It was wonderful how quickly he felt relaxed again as she prepared to take him down anew to Level 10. All his tensions, all his fears seemed to float away. There was no worry about the contretemps they had had. Her calm, low-pitched voice carried no trace of affront.

He had worried that he might find the presence of Eddie something of a burden; that he might perhaps be embarrassed to clench . . . and relax . . . with an ahhh! in front of a spectator; but he felt no such thing. Eddie was no more significant than the William Morris wallpaper in his living room. Less significant, for he had not chosen him. He was more like a carrier bag someone had left in the room.

'Here we go, Mr Mackworth,' came her calm, low voice. 'We are going down now.'

Thoughts drifted like pouterfish through his mind, they goggled at him as he descended in his bubble – that was Jo's fancy today. Not a lift but a sphere, perfectly controlled, descending into the depths, the light slowly disappearing and even the creatures of the deep fading away like dreams . . .

Six . . . seven . . . eight . . .

'I want you to empty your mind now, Duncan,' she said, her voice blending perfectly with the gentle whisper of the air that bathed the inside of their bubble.

47

'And there we are . . . Level 10 . . .' she said. 'Feel yourself arrive?'

There was just the faintest sensation of a bump, no more than a reassuring little tremble, as the sphere settled on the sandy bottom.

'Now,' she said, 'you are utterly at peace. Just the gentle flowing of the water around you, deep-sea plants swaying, left and right, left and right, nothing but peace here. Nothing. Can you hear me, Duncan? Left . . . and right . . . Out and in . . .'

He could not speak but he could hear her.

'Answer me, Duncan, without any effort, the easiest thing in the world. Can you hear me?'

He could feel the word welling up like water.

'Yes,' he trickled.

'Very good. You are . . . at peace . . . You are asleep.'

'He's a good subject, isn't he?' Eddie said.

Duncan could hear the words but it was as though they had no meaning.

'He'll do,' said Jo.

'I've to go back tomorrow. Fancy a bite?'

'Maybe.'

'You know I came back because of you.'

'I thought your Mum was ill.'

'Not that ill.'

'Left and right . . . left and right . . .' said Jo. 'In . . . and out . . .'

'Can I stay . . . after?' said Eddie.

'We'll have to see, won't we? Now, don't go disturbing him. He's going to be my prize pupil. I've been looking for one like this.'

'Should I feel jealous?'

'We'll have to see, won't we?'

'Little prat.'

'Don't be so sure. There's more to him than meets the eye. You'll see.'

48

'There'd have to be.'

'I do believe you *are* jealous. Well, well . . . Eddie Parkin jealous!'

'I don't see what's so funny.'

'You won't remember any of this, Mr Mackworth. You'll just feel wonderfully relaxed. And now . . . we're going to come back up to the surface when I say . . . Now! . . . slowly up, no hurry, slowwwly . . . Level 9 . . . 8 . . . yes, we're beginning to see the faintest glimmer of light . . . up now . . . Level 7 . . . fish gently swimming past . . . Level 6 . . . and 5 . . . it's getting brighter . . . 4 and 3 . . . brighter and brighter still . . . the sun is shining on the water . . . and 1 . . . and open wide . . .'

Duncan opened his eyes and looked about the room like a child woken from sleep.

'There. How do you feel, Mr Mackworth? You really went under that time.'

'I feel wonderfully relaxed.'

'Of course you do. That's the object of the exercise. If you're not relaxed to begin with, you can do yourself an injury. Muscles are stubborn things. They have to be relaxed and warm before they can give of their best.'

'Like a woman,' said Eddie.

'Now, Eddie. Don't go inflicting your views on Mr Mackworth. I'm sure he doesn't want to hear all that. But as Eddie says, Mr Mackworth, like a woman. We don't like being tense or started from cold.'

'Like a man too, I should think,' said Duncan.

'Bravo, Mr Mackworth. Hear that, Eddie? Not everyone's as sexist as you are.'

Eddie looked daggers in the corner. Somehow Duncan didn't mind.

'Now to work, Mr Mackworth . . .'

'Please call me Duncan.'

'Very well, Duncan. Let's begin with the exercises.'

And so they launched into the main body of the lesson. By

and large it followed the pattern of the first, though towards the end, Jo called Eddie onto the floor and gave him a large baseball glove to put on.

'Let's see you hit Eddie's hand now, Mr Mackworth.'

'Hard?'

'Hard as you can. And remember . . . don't think of your blow ending where his hand is. Hit through, Duncan . . . at least six inches beyond it, that's what we aim for. Now . . . go!'

Duncan steadied himself and looked at Eddie. No doubt about it, the man had shed all trace of the instructor-pupil relationship. Indeed, destruction seemed much more his bag. Duncan gave him a smile – which Eddie didn't return – to show there were no ill feelings, and launched a blow at the man's hand. It was like hitting a brick wall.

'Ow!' he said.

Only then did Eddie smile.

'That was terrible,' said Jo. 'Like this.'

And she sent a right crashing into the glove, making her breasts bounce like buoys in a rip tide.

Even Eddie rocked back on his size eleven's, though whether at the blow or the breasts it was difficult to say.

'I see,' said Duncan.

'You've got to hit through,' she told him.

He tried again, this time with marginally better results.

'Improving,' she cried. 'Again. Now with the left . . . now with the right . . . move your legs, Duncan . . . legs . . . you can't hit a right with your right leg forward . . .'

Duncan had the distinct impression that Eddie was imperceptibly countering his punches, making the impact much more jarring.

'Left . . . right . . . again,' commanded Jo. 'And again.'

Raining punches, Duncan tore into the glove until he could punch no more.

'That's enough for now,' Jo told him. 'You're coming on. Next lesson we'll do kicking and the vulnerable parts of the body. Rest for a moment, Duncan. Now. I want you to imaging you're asleep upstairs and you hear sounds down here in the night. Right. What I want you to do now, Duncan, when you've got your breath back, I want you to go outside and then, in your own time, come in and show me what you'd do.'

Duncan sat and panted for a while, wished he could sit longer, didn't like Eddie's sneer, and rose to his feet.

'Am I allowed a weapon?' he asked.

'There's no such thing as allow. There could be violent burglars in here, Duncan. Now, what's your drill?'

Duncan went out into the hall, shutting the door. As it happened, he had an old knobkerrie in the umbrella stand. It used to belong to his great-uncle who had been in the Colonial Service. Doubtless it had thwacked a few skulls in its time. Surely now was the time to press it into service again.

Summoning up the litheness of a leopard, he crept to the door, knobkerrie in the ready position, and kicked it open. He was disconcerted to find the room in total darkness. He opened the door further and reached for the light switch. As he did so, a heavy object struck the knobkerrie from his grasp, a horny hand clapped itself over his mouth while a thick arm encircled his throat – with what seemed to be an unnecessary amount of force from behind, bending his whole body backwards.

'Arrrwff,' he spluttered.

At this point Jo turned on the lights.

'All right, Eddie,' she said.

Eddie didn't seem in the least inclined to let go and propelled Duncan into the centre of the room legs first, his feet ridiculously pedalling the ground in front of him.

'I said all right,' Jo commanded.

Eddie let go so suddenly that Duncan almost fell on the floor.

'My knobkerrie,' he cried.

It was lying in two pieces on the rug.

'Sorry about that,' said Jo.

'Must've been rotten,' said Eddie.

'It was my great-uncle's,' said Duncan. 'It's been to Basutoland.'

'Tough,' sympathized Jo.

'Not tough enough,' said Eddie.

'You might at least say sorry,' said Duncan.

'You can't make an omelette without breaking eggs,' Eddie told him.

'Perhaps it was unwise to use an antique,' said Jo. 'The point is, all you lost this time was a stick. Next time it could be your life. You did everything wrong. Show him, Eddie. Show him the right way.'

Eddie went out.

'Now,' said Jo. 'See if you can catch him as he comes in.'

Duncan stationed himself where he imagined Eddie to have been before – not behind the door when it opened but on the other side tight against the wall.

Jo switched off the light and they waited.

They waited five minutes which seemed like an hour. Duncan started to speak but she sshusshed him. The minutes ticked by.

Suddenly, just as Duncan was deciding that the man must have left the building and gone home, a little joke, the door burst open and the lights went on.

There was no sign of Eddie at all.

Duncan waited a while, then deciding some action was called for, left his position and peered round the corner into the hall – at which point the same vicelike grip descended and once more he was unceremoniously flapped back into the room.

'See?' said Jo. 'Thank you, Eddie.'

Eddie had never had a rag doll in his life, but if he had possessed such an item he would have dropped it the way he now dropped Duncan.

'Never come straight into a room where there may be intruders,' Jo explained. 'Throw open the door, switch on the light. Catch 'em by surprise. Be in charge of the scenario. Make it go your way. And above all . . .'

'Get off the line,' said Duncan.

'Bravo,' cried Jo. 'You could still be my best pupil.'

The pride that filled his breast quite eradicated the mortification of being man-handled by Eddie, and Eddie knew it. He glowered.

'Same time next week?' said Jo. 'Kicking and vulnerable parts of the body. Say goodbye to Eddie. He's going back to Malawi.'

Ten

The lessons continued without Eddie, and Duncan found the absence of the mercenary no disadvantage; he actually learned more without him, and the journeys to Level 10 were noticeably smoother.

It was in the midst of these tutorial events that Duncan was surprised to receive a call from Booth, his father's photographic bag-carrier and heir to his celluloid mantle throughout the natural world.

Booth tended to do this; no word for months, and then suddenly, 'I'm in London. Coming round.' Duncan kept open house for him as a matter of habit. Booth was no trouble, coming and going like an owl in a barn.

No one called him anything but Booth. He didn't appear to have a Christian name. As a young man, he had been the Boswell to Mr Mackworth's Johnson. He was a person of incredible patience and unflagging good humour; in stature small and slightly bow-legged, there was something of the Cro-Magnon about him, the brow low and the jaw pronounced. However, there was nothing primitive about his talent. His tenacity in pursuit of a natural story was legendary. Duncan's father had left him a sufficiency to live on and carry on the good work. It was one of the reasons why Duncan had been left less than comfortably off. However, Duncan never resented Booth's small portion of the slender family estate, and when he heard from him – from Spitzbergen where he was investigating the sex life of the snow-shrew, or Paraguay where he was lamenting the passing of some rare parakeet – he would greet him with genuine concern and interest tinged with alarm that he might have caught some fatal and communicable disease.

When Booth finally returned – as now – he would painstakingly edit his work at a studio in Camberwell and eventually embark upon protracted negotiations with the BBC or some other favoured station, depositing the out-takes of his work with Duncan, who kept them, along with his father's collection, in the workroom in the attic.

Duncan liked the man, but now for the first time he felt an embarrassment. He was expecting Jo a little later. It wasn't that anything was going on between him and Jo, worse luck; it was just that, if something did go on – though of course it wouldn't – he would be hopelessly put off. He couldn't say it on the telephone, of course; that would have been too crass. He had to wait until Booth arrived. How he hated himself for what he was going to have to say!

And there Booth was now, climbing out of the taxi with that low, simian swing, as if he were crawling out of a hide.

Duncan went to the front door to greet him, keeping warily at an uninfectious distance.

'Hullo,' he said, picking up one of the cases with ginger fingers – he had a horror of leprosy – and bringing it into the hall even though he was shortly going to have to carry it out again.

'Good of you,' panted Booth, submerged under the usual tide of camping gear, lens cases, film boxes and what not.

'Good shoot?' enquired Duncan. 'Where was it, now?'

'Outer Mongolia,' said Booth matter-of-factly. He could have been talking about Cockfosters.

'Ah.'

'Though I was in Inner Mongolia too. And Siberia of course.'

'Of course.'

It was really prodigious. The man must be at least sixty and he treated the world like the Home Counties. It was going to be difficult to refuse him a bed.

What he couldn't refuse him at least was a cup of tea, which the little man drank with quick furtive sips like a marmot at a gap in the tundra.

'What next?' asked Duncan at last, hoping to steer him towards the subject of 'where now?'.

'That's the question at the moment,' said Booth. 'I've finished the BBC commission and I'm looking at one or two offers.'

He was quite celebrated himself in his own way; not as famous as Duncan's father, of course – his character was not as large, his learning not as profound – but his experience in the field was second to none.

'What sort of offers?' asked Duncan, encouragingly.

'The Brazilians want me to do a rainforest, but to be honest I'm up to here with rainforests.'

'They're in the news at the moment,' said Duncan, not wanting him to miss any opportunity of going away again. 'I don't think they're going to disappear. I mean, not in terms of interest,' he added hurriedly.

He had seen Booth's face assume that crusading look which phrases like 'fur trade', 'global warming' and 'fox hunting' tend to elicit.

'I didn't mean I wasn't interested in rainforests,' said Booth earnestly, 'one has to be. It's just that I did the Indonesian one last year, and the Tasmanian one the year before . . .'

'Quite,' said Duncan. 'I understand. Of course I do.'

'The rainforest situation is critical.'

'Right.'

'Three-quarters of the air you breathe comes from the . . .'

'Absolutely.'

Duncan didn't need reminding. The erosion of the rainforest was part of the old endemic background dread. It went along with things like the death of grass and the low male sperm count, perpetually hanging over his horizon like the fogs of Newfoundland.

There was a ring at the door. Duncan got up.

'Am I in the way?' asked Booth.

It was a strange question. He had never said anything like that before, in fact he often seemed oblivious to social sensitivities. Perhaps his instinct for animals had at last, after all, graduated to humanity. Duncan looked at him curiously. He had never really got to know the little man, seeing him merely as part of the landscape of his life.

'In the way?' he asked.

'Well, you know. You may have women you want to see.'

'Women?'

This was getting to be like a sex talk. He hoped Booth wasn't going to launch into the birds and the bees, to say nothing of the gilded fly and the red-bottomed baboon. Perhaps he thought Duncan, as an only child, subsequently orphaned, needed such instruction; but it turned out that Booth was thinking of himself.

'It's time I had a woman.'

The doorbell rang again, saving Duncan from registering shock.

'Sorry,' he mumbled, retreating. 'Door . . . must talk . . .'

It was Jo. In his hurry, he almost forgot to open securely.

'Hurry up slowcoach,' she said. 'I thought I'd give you a surprise and come early. I was in this part of town.'

Duncan felt stupidly confused. For some reason he wasn't keen for Jo to meet Booth.

'There's someone here,' he said.

Jo stopped and looked at him searchingly.

'Someone?'

'A man I know. Used to work with my father. He shoots wildlife films. Very good . . . I take some of his work for my collection, Father's really . . .'

He spoke fast, his pulse racing; it was partly the shock and pleasure of seeing her early, partly something he couldn't

57

quite fathom, like not wanting the old part of his life to meet the new. She marched along the passage to the kitchen. Booth stood up quickly, spilling his tea as she came in. Duncan had never seen him so impressed. It irritated him rather; more irritatingly, Jo seemed to be impressed as well. She mopped the table and dabbed at the film-maker's trousers with a J Cloth.

'There,' she said. 'That's better. Really pleased to meet you. You do wonderful work, I'm told. Nature and suchlike.'

Booth blushed with pleasure, but he couldn't cope with it. He started gathering himself together.

'Going?' asked Jo. 'Not on my account, I hope.'

'Got to see someone,' he told her. 'Next job.'

'I'm really sorry.'

'Got to go.'

'I'll see you out,' said Duncan.

At the front door, Booth stopped.

'I was going anyway,' he said. 'I just didn't want you to think I was ducking out. I came straight here, you see, because that's what I always do. But I do have somewhere to go.'

Duncan felt touched and guilty. He picked up some of Booth's bags, then put them down again. A thought had struck him. He didn't know when he would see Booth again.

'Would you mind if I sold some of the film sequences for use in TV commercials?' he asked.

Not that he had to get Booth's permission if the films weren't shot by him, but it seemed a politeness. The American, Reinacker, who had expressed interest had been in touch again. Duncan supposed it was the sort of enterprise Americans would make a business of; his mother had called it their can-do tendency.

Did he really want to make a business out of it? His attitude to the archive, he recognized, was equivocal. On the one hand, it reminded him of his father and filled him with ancient stirrings of anxiety. On the other, he knew it was a rare accumulation of material with considerable historical (and natural historical) interest. He wanted to keep it to himself, a private thing like the pains of childhood, but half of him recognized the incongruity of having a collection which nobody ever saw.

He knew he was not really an expert. He had no wish to be. He was not besotted with the notion of scientific films, nor did he even spend much time on the collection, apart from his re-cataloguing activities which were more of an extension of his tidy mind than an undertaking of love. He was not a film-maker. He left all that kind of thing to Booth. He was simply the thing's keeper; and yet he could not altogether ignore it.

It lay inexorably on its racks in the attic conversion overhead, as if waiting for some inevitable but as yet undisclosed opportunity.

Perhaps this TV-commercial idea was the opportunity it was waiting for. The question was, was he waiting for it? Was Booth waiting for it?

'Can do?' he asked, Americanly. 'What d'you think?'

'I'll think about it,' said Booth. 'Do you mind? I have to think what your father would say.'

'He's dead, for heaven's sake. What do *you* say?'

'I don't know, to be honest. I'll think about it.'

Duncan could get no more out of him. Not that it was urgent. His can-do phase was already burning out; there were bound to be dangers; besides, he had a business already.

'That girl, I like her,' said Booth as they stood surrounded by his luggage at the bottom of the steps.

'Where will you go?' asked Duncan.

Booth hesitated.

'I've got a little house in Colliers Wood SW19, to be perfectly frank.'

He had a habit, when imparting a confidence, of speaking with a hand cupped in front of his mouth.

'I didn't know you had a place of your own.'

'After my last trip, it was. I was saving up for it. I thought,

59

I can't go on doing this for ever. I must slow down, find a place. Find a woman. Settle down, that sort of thing.'

He was Papageno, the bird man, looking for a mate.

'I was going to tell you, actually, today,' he continued. 'I thought you might be upset if I just walked off without saying anything. Oh, I know I've been hardly here at all, but . . . I thought you might be upset. Now I see you've got a woman of your own, I know you're going to be all right.'

'She's not exactly of my own,' said Duncan. 'She's a friend.'

'Taxi!' shouted Booth.

He had an eye for the opportune. A black cab stopped and purred tractably by the gate.

'That woman of yours,' he said. 'You want to hold on to that one. Wild though. Like a panther.'

He said it seriously, palm cupped to mouth again, as Duncan handed in the luggage. Booth did not joke about wild things.

Eleven

A change in Duncan was beginning to be noted by his acquaintances. He had been asked to a drinks party at the weekend which normally he would have skipped. But because of his new-found confidence he went along and became quite its life and soul. He found himself describing his self-defence course and demonstrating getting off the line to a rather pretty researcher from the *Economist*.

'One, two and aside, one, two and aside. That's getting off the line.'

'And how d'you get *on* it?' she asked.

There were peals of laughter.

'Sounds great, Dunc,' said an Australian moneybroker who had met Duncan once or twice before. 'Can I come along? I nearly got mugged the other day.'

It was the last thing Duncan wanted. He could have kicked himself. Other people learning with him would only confuse things, take Jo's attention away. He could be her star pupil; she had said so. She wouldn't want to muddy the waters with someone at a lower level. It was bad enough having Eddie watching. Having a fellow-student would be a disaster.

Besides, he hated being called Dunc. He'd had enough of that at school where they called him Donut.

'I'm afraid not,' he said.

He shook his head regretfully, playing for time. Come on, he told himself, think of a reason. Full up, yes, that was it.

The Australian was already looking baleful. He'd better put it to him.

'The class is full unfortunately,' he said. 'Alas.'

'I'll take the number, then.'

'Oh, er. I don't have it on me. I think it's 734 783 . . . something . . .'

He made it up as he went along.

'I'm pretty sure it's that. Ask for Harry.'

The Australian was putting the number in his electronic notebook.

'I thought you said it was a woman.'

The fellow had been listening earlier. Damn. Think, man. Get off the line.

'Harriet,' he said, 'known as Harry.'

Thank God he hadn't said Bruce. It had been close. He didn't like the look of that Australian. There was a certain Eddie-ness about him.

He moved across to a quiet corner, nursing his drink. He had nearly got into a confrontation. He could feel his heart thumping. He mustn't think, just because he'd had a few lessons, that he was anything more than a novice. Here he was, beginning to behave as though danger was a thing of the past or to be flirted with. And yet, he had to admit, he *had* thought quickly when trouble loomed. There was a time, not so long ago, indeed two weeks ago to be precise, when he would have frozen.

The pretty researcher came over and stood next to him. She was not quite so pretty now he saw her under the light. Her complexion owed a great deal to Max Factor, and she smoked. He couldn't help comparing her with Jo. It was chalk and cheese, and Jo was the Brie.

The researcher – she was called Anna – flashed off-white teeth at him.

'Why don't we go to my place?' she said. 'I'm fed up with this lot. We'll buy a bottle of wine, I'll cook something, and you can tell me more. I'm fascinated.'

This time, he was cornered.

He opened his mouth once or twice but nothing came out. He started to make gliding motions with his feet.

'Well?' she said.

She was an impetuous creature but his behaviour would have tried the patience of a film editor.

'Is this your party trick? Fish impersonations?'

'Level 5,' he managed to say.

'I beg your pardon.'

'Relaxation's part of the course,' he was thinking well at last. 'You go down in a glass sphere deep into the ocean.'

'My God,' she said. 'This is extraordinary.'

'You go down and down to deeper levels of relaxation. And as you go, you see the fish, like this against the glass.'

He opened and shut his mouth again for her.

'Come on,' she said. 'Let's go. I must hear more of this.'

It was useless to resist.

'When attacked,' Jo said, 'when you can't run away or get off the line, don't waste your energy pulling away. Go with it. Then make your move.'

They made their goodbyes – their host, a distant relation on his mother's side of the family, opened his eyes wide in a gesture whose significance Duncan failed to catch – hurried into the street and hailed a cab.

'Where to?' asked Duncan.

She gave an address in Battersea. Duncan's heart fell. Saturday night in Battersea . . . who knew what violence might not walk the streets. Only the other month an innocent stroller was killed by a man wielding a baseball bat, hit so hard his skull caved in like a cracked egg. Was he ready to face Battersea on a Saturday night?

'Hop in,' said the driver.

It seemed there was nothing for it.

In the cab, the researcher sat close, pressing her Lycraed knee against his. She smelt of Opium, a scent he particularly resented on the impregnated pages of the magazines in reception. At the same time, there was something undeniably exciting about her knee. It seemed to have some incandescent quality about it, both slippery and inflammatory at the same time, a conjunction that seemed almost against Nature.

If she wants advice on self-defence, he thought, one couldn't do better than start right here. Was it prudent to ask a complete stranger home to your flat? Oh, they had met at a respectable party, but he could be any kind of debauchee or pervert. He could be a kleptomaniac. He could have pubic lice. The truth was, she didn't know where he'd been.

And where had she been? He didn't know, but he would damn well find out. Still, there couldn't be any harm in showing her the on-guard and the anti-burglar drill.

The flat in Battersea smelt faintly of gas. It was chilly and cheerless as only flats in Battersea can be. There were a number of coats and umbrellas in evidence in the hall.

'You share with someone?' he said hopefully.

'Oh those,' she said dismissively. 'People leave them. Don't worry, we won't be disturbed.'

She took him upstairs to a sitting room. The smell of gas was pervasive. Perhaps the whole place would blow up.

'Damn,' she said, 'we forgot the wine. Would you go round the corner?'

She led him downstairs again and pushed him out into the street. Round the corner turned out to be five minutes' walk away. The roads were badly lit round here and it was a moonless night into the bargain. A fine drizzle was falling. Duncan was so keen to use the outside of the pavement that he slipped and half-fell into the gutter. A couple of black men passing by laughed. His fragile confidence began to disappear. It was all he could do to remember the ready position. Only the thought of Jo kept him going. How proud of him she would be if he could maintain street discipline.

The off-licence finally came in view. He bought his Vieux Telegraphe Châteauneuf-du-Pape (he had once read that however bad you felt, it would always make you feel better) from a taciturn Pakistani – and who wouldn't be taciturn keeping an off-licence in Lavender Sweep? – and returned to base, always walking on the outside of the pavement but not quite so extremely.

Halfway back, two ominous shapes appeared round a corner. He fanned out into the road, using a gliding motion. They turned out to be two old women carrying returnable brown-ale bottles revealed under a rare street lamp.

'Mind yourself, sonny,' they cackled.

When he returned, Anna was cooking something absolutely disgusting.

At least the odour was a change from gas. But it was a change for the worse.

'What is it?' he asked.

'Monkfish,' she told him. 'It's been in the fridge three days. D'you think it's all right?'

Visions of food-poisoning assailed him. How terrible it would be to be ill in Battersea.

'It smells a bit,' he said.

'The other thing is, I'm not much of a cook. What d'you do with monkfish?'

Throw it in the bin was the retort that sprang to his lips, but he choked it back. He felt it was too extreme for such a shallow acquaintance. Perhaps a more diagonal approach was the best policy.

'The thing is,' he said, 'I'm a vegetarian. D'you mind? I don't eat fish. You get like that when you see them goggling at you.'

'Of course,' she said. 'How silly of me. I should have asked. Let's have some bread and cheese, and drink the wine.'

The fish was thrown out and the bottle broached. Duncan began to feel cheerier.

'Do you smell gas?' he asked.

'No.'

So that was the end of that. How ridiculous it would be to

end up scattered in little bits over SW11, just when he was in sight of his new freedom.

'Sometimes I think I can hear time escaping like gas,' he said, giving it one last go, thinking he might at least lift the occasion onto a higher plane.

'Too morbid for me,' she said. 'And pretentious. That's your trouble, if you ask me. All gas and gaiters.'

She put on some music: it would have to be the ghastly Rodrigo Guitar Concerto. She asked him about his job; his replies provoked no excitement, as well they might not. He asked her about hers. It seemed to be something to do with compiling statistics.

'There are lies, damned lies and statistics,' he said.

It appeared that she had heard that one before. Her interest in the defensive art also seemed to have waned. She spent some time tapping her fingers. The end of the bottle being reached, Duncan thought it was probably a good moment to go. He noted that there was still quarter of an hour before closing time (at which point of course the streets would be loud with the noise of skull-crunching).

He looked at his watch and stood up.

'I think it's time . . .' he started.

'Of course it's bloody time,' she said, and started taking her dress off.

In a flash, she was in her bra, stockings and suspenders, towering over him.

'Now,' she commanded. 'Take me to Level 10.'

Twelve

How he extricated himself from the situation he could never exactly tell. It was touch and go. More go than touch, thank God.

He forgot all his training – that much was certain. Good old-fashioned panic took over. It wasn't helped by the fact that part of him was intrigued by the situation. Absurd though it might be these days, he had never seen a young woman undressed. So that was how soft and white the inside of the thighs were! How neatly, sweetly the straps of the bra hugged the shoulders! But curiosity is not the same as desire. Half of him wanted to stay, the other half needed to be far off. *Procul, procul, abeste profanes.*

He was startled and cold, that's what it was. He was like a muscle. Jo had said women needed a warm-up and he had suggested – to Eddie's derision – that for men it might be the same. Now here he was to prove it. There was something so peremptory about Anna's approach. How scathing she might be about his performance! He knew what you were supposed to do, of course. He had read magazines which he never took to the office and stowed away carefully lest Mrs Fobbs his cleaner should stumble across them. But as he knew only too well in other walks of life, there is a world of difference between manuals and machinery.

What if (as Ecclesiastes has it) desire should fail? Anna would seize him roughly, give him a furious and fruitless rubbing, fling his member away like a piece of broken window sash, snort contemptuously and expose him to the world as an unman.

All these considerations jumbled in his head and led to his leaping up with a strangled cry and heading, without explanation, for the stairs.

As he clattered down, he could hear shrill, vituperative noises coming from the room he had vacated. Anna appeared at the top of the stairs, railing at him, while he wrestled with the front door.

'Call yourself a man,' she yelled. 'You're not even an animal.'

At last he was out into the rain; darkness closed about him, with the sound of a thousand gutters.

What now? The pubs would be closing. He had stepped from the frying pan into the line of fire. Figures lurched past shouting and cursing. Someone threw up in front of him. A temptation to panic again swept over him; a blind urge to run down Latchmere Road and over Battersea Bridge, not stopping till he reached the safety of Chelsea. Not that Chelsea was safe any more. Nowhere was safe.

Then, at that moment of despair, he heard Jo's voice; the calm tones, the reassuring competence.

'Keep to the well-lit roads, be aware, walk as if you mean business. If attacked, run like mad. If you can't escape, say you've just come out of hospital, you've got cancer, a triple bypass, anything. And if you have to strike in the last resort, strike to inflict maximum damage.'

Where maximum damage might be inflicted she hadn't taught him yet, but you didn't need to be an Einstein to think of one or two places to be getting on with.

Having guidelines to follow helped soothe him. He tried to hail a cab but they were all full. Closing time on Saturday night was not a good moment. More fool he for going out, he thought, but he couldn't regret the confidence that Jo had started to bring him. It was the way he used it that was wrong. It was like a betrayal of Jo herself.

He waited for a long time near the police station at the top of Latchmere Road – it seemed a sensible vantage point and one very much in line with all the best precepts – and at last a bus came by.

It was bound for Kensington High Street and he thankfully climbed aboard, taking one of the cross-bench seats near the platform. As the bus trundled forward, he made sure that he was fixing his eyes on the trodden-in chewing gum on the runnelled floor; difficult while maintaining constant all-round vigilance but essential. Duncan knew all too well the dangers of eye-contact on public transport. It could result in anything from a stream of abuse to an invitation to something either erotic or narcotic to a gruff demand for your wallet, though the latter could be elicited even if you kept up an almost tree-like impassivity.

What a strange thing it all was!

His thoughts, with something in them of the distress of the transmission-weary double-decker, ran on the changes in London during his lifetime. When he had first come up to town to work as a junior in a family friend's office in Holborn, it had been the '70s. It wasn't wonderful then – of course it wasn't – but there had still been some semblance of that English reticence and cheerful, innate decency which his mother used to talk about, perhaps a touch of the spirit that had pulled the country through the dark days of the war, the Blitz spirit no less.

Where was it now? Scattered like the litter that festooned the central aisle; denigrated and lampooned on a million walls and walkways; ripped off, scammed, squatted and squandered at every level from the insider-trading nabobs of the City to the financial satyromaniacs with a degree in accountancy and a burning desire to screw everything in sight, to the little boys of twelve who regarded the appropriation of other people's property not as a crime but as a birthright.

Call him a fogey, but these things needed to be aired.

His mother used to say that the wretched state of the world

was the fault of men. If only women ran things, there would be much more sense in the ordering of affairs, she said. But now that they did run the world, or at least had equal shares and a louder voice . . . what had happened, Mother? Things had got worse! And they themselves now appeared to combine the worst traits of both sexes. Not quite all of them, thank God. Jo, of course, was an exception; she shone, and not merely by comparison. But when you looked at the shrill, cigarette-puffing, enflamed-with-lambrusco denizens of Pistons ('get it?') Wine Bar down the Brompton Road, you had to see Jo as a goddess among the goblins . . .

His reflections continued in this vein while the bus pursued its course down the Latchmere Road.

Somewhere around Battersea High Street he became aware that the people sitting opposite and beside him – two young yobs who looked as though they should have been in bed, a very large woman who sat with her knees apart, a peroxided prostitute and her pimp, as well as the West Indian conductor – were all laughing. Nor were they just laughing. They were laughing till they cried . . . at him.

At first he tried to ignore it but they laughed all the more. Next, he tried to smile with them, but that produced near hysteria.

He looked at himself. Was there some ghastly bogey glued to his chin? A sticker of some kind that someone might have applied without his noticing? A bird-mess on his head? He began checking himself all over, which induced fresh explosions of mirth.

The object of their hilarity seemed to be nearer the floor, come to think of it. An enormous dog-turd like the one that did for Gerald, on his shoe?

He glanced down as surreptitiously as possible and saw that, neatly wrapped around his right ankle, was a pair of small lace panties. The effect was rather like the frill on a lamb cutlet. He must somehow have got entangled in them when Anna was undressing, and walked them halfway round Battersea.

70

They were no longer the little wisps of delight that doubtless once they had been. They were sodden, they were mud-splashed; but what they were was unmistakable.

'Elastic went, did it, dearie?' asked the prostitute. 'And what sort of stockings are you wearing?'

Smiling, to show it was the most natural thing in the world, he leant down, picked the knickers off his foot with a flourish and stowed them in his pocket.

Strange words came into his mouth, stemming from some Level as yet unknown to him.

'There,' he said to the yobs. 'Let that be a lesson to you. Never take up ventriloquism.'

It was satisfying to see how their laughter turned to respect.

When he finally reached home, he felt his life had reached a watershed. He had been tested and not been found wanting. Oh, he had made mistakes. Going out with that girl had been the greatest mistake of all. If that's what people do with their confidence on Saturday nights, he thought, give me my feeling of dread; but he didn't mean it. He meant Jo. He wanted Jo. She had accelerated him from sprat to shark in less than three weeks. Well, not quite shark yet. Mackerel, perhaps. Nevertheless, an extraordinary transformation.

As he switched on the security alarm and climbed into bed, he wondered what Jo had been doing that night, and what sort of knickers she wore under her tracksuit. It was an unworthy speculation, he knew, but sometimes a man cannot help himself.

Thirteen

Wednesday came round, and Duncan could hardly contain his excitement. At last it was half-past four.

'I'll be off then,' he told Delice.

'Someone's got to do the work,' she said. 'But I'm sure we don't get paid overtime.'

'You know what to do if you don't like it,' he told her.

Even as he said it, he was amazed at himself.

'What?'

Delice stood up. She was quite shocked. He had never spoken to her like that before. Her mouth gaped like something at Level 6.

'You heard, Delice. I must have willing helpers. If I choose to go and take lessons in personal security, I should have thought my loyal staff would be only too pleased.'

She burst into tears and disappeared towards the Ladies. That's her sorted out, he thought. He should never have brushed those silver pine needles from her dress.

An irritable man with a pointed head came in.

'I want to swear an oath,' he said.

'Sorry,' said Duncan. 'We're closed.'

'No, you're not.'

'Yes, we are.'

'You're certainly not.'

'We definitely are.'

'How d'you know?'

'I'm the owner.'

'Oh well, then.'

'That's right.'

'But I'll report you to the Law Society.'

'You do that.'

'Well, fuck you.'

'There you are. You swore your oath. What are you complaining about?'

There was no argument with that.

Pointed Head stormed out; Delice re-entered chastened. Was it really he? Duncan wondered. This was indeed a brave new world. Was it his new training? Or was it . . . love? It was a serious question.

He went home and prepared himself. Most people shower after exercise. He showered first, splashing on just a little Grey Flannel Cologne because she loved the smell of violence – not too much or she would find him too easily in the dark.

The appointed hour came; and then it went. She was ten, twenty, thirty minutes late. He was in despair. She had had an accident, he knew it. Even her all-round awareness and street security wasn't proof against some idiot mounting the kerb, some joyrider running her down as she crossed a zebra.

He was about to call the police and ask if there had been an accident when there came the familiar ring at the door. Trrrrrr trr. It was her call sign.

He rushed to open it, remembering in the nick of time to practice the proper drill. And there she was all pink in the face. She had been running.

'Forgive me,' she panted.

He smiled at her. A thousand times, he thought.

'Let me take your backpack.'

She slipped out of it with one graceful motion.

'Come in. I was worried about you. Can I get you a drink? Tea? Juice?'

She shook her cropped chestnut hair.

'Just water, Duncan, please.'

He handed her the glass.

> '"Drink to me only with thine eyes,
> And I will pledge with mine"...'

She drank deeply before she replied.

'That's beautiful, Duncan. That's what I like about you. You've got education. I never had the education. I had to teach myself as I went along.'

'I don't pride myself on it,' he told her. 'It was just assumed that I would go to that school, go on to this university. It was the order of things. I had very little to do with it.'

'Ah, but you've a brain, Duncan, too. Education's no good without a brain. It's like a good egg in a broken cup. You have to have the means to hold it. But we mustn't stand here talking. Level 10 calls.'

'Just one thing. I don't mean to pry but...'

'Yes, Duncan?'

'Well, I wondered whether you had far to come, a bad connection, bus trouble ... whether I could collect you next time.'

'That's very kind of you, Duncan, but it's all right. I have one or two other engagements Wednesdays. I teach the kids football down Notting Hill way before I come to you. Usually I do, anyway. Today I promised to see Eddie off. He stayed an extra day or two, see? Anyway, his plane was delayed, so we had a good talk.'

'Ah,' said Duncan, torn between jealousy and relief that the man had gone.

'I told him it was no good, him and me. You've got to be straight, haven't you? Funny thing was...'

'Yes?'

'He thought it might've been something to do with you, Duncan.'

'Me?'

74

Duncan could have shouted with joy.

'I know it was silly, but there it was. He thought I was impressed with your learning and education.'

'And . . . aren't you?'

He raised his eyes and met her own. He could lose himself in those seas if he wasn't very careful, and he didn't want to be very careful.

'Why, yes, Duncan as a matter of fact I am. But don't let that spoil our relationship.'

'I don't think it does spoil our relationship. I think it improves it. And I'd just like to say that I . . .'

'Yes, Duncan?'

He was about to tell her that he couldn't stop thinking about her, that she'd transformed his life, that he loved her, when he remembered. Muscles. They mustn't be startled. He would warm her up, perhaps over a meal – that was it – and then there'd be no strain when he told her, no strain at all.

'I wondered whether you'd care to join me for dinner,' he said, 'after the lesson.'

Fourteen

It had come on to rain again and a cold wind was blowing from the east. They huddled into their coats and walked out into the night, keeping to the outside edge of the pavement.

Because she had no special clothes with her, and didn't want to go anywhere smart, Duncan decided to take her to the little Italian round the corner.

'I like dressing up, I really do,' she had said to him, 'but I'd let you down tonight if we went up-market.'

'I'm sure you wouldn't,' he told her. 'But I'd like to see you dressed up. I'd have to look to my heart, though.'

He said it whimsically but he meant it right enough.

'Your heart?' she asked quickly. 'Anything wrong with your heart?'

'Nothing physical,' he told her. 'Just a figure of speech.'

She relaxed again.

'I was worried for a moment. We don't take people with bad hearts, you know. There'd be legal ramifications. I'm glad, though. About *your* heart, I mean, being a figure of speech.'

With that, she disappeared into the spare bathroom, and Duncan took his second shower of the day.

As he did so, he reflected on the session: another good one. Best of all had been the descent to Level 10 again. He really looked forward to that. It was like a sort of bath; all strain, all impurities were removed by that deep water. After that, anyone would move well, and he had, skipping off the line when she lunged at him like a gazelle. They had recapped on hitting the glove, though he hadn't liked to do it with quite the venom he had unleashed on Eddie.

And then she had taught him the vulnerable parts.

'Eyes, nose, ears,' she had said, 'they're the obvious targets . . .'

'Nose?' he had queried.

'Palm your aggressor against his nose and you can drive the bone into the brain.'

'My God. And ears?'

'Clap your hands, hard and fast, over his ears and you'll burst his eardrums.'

'Eyes?'

'Don't splay the fingers and stab. Gouge with your thumbs.'

'Ough.'

'Listen, Duncan. I'm only talking emergency here. Only if you can't get away. Better to kill than be killed. Right?'

'Of course.'

'Now for the seventh vertebra . . . here . . .'

She pressed the backbone below the base of his neck.

'Give that a smart blow and it'll break the spinal cord. Now . . . square your shoulders . . .'

She hit him with clenched fist on his back, somewhere behind the collar bone. It gave him a tremendous jolt as if he'd been kicked by a mule.

'Nerve centres each side. It'll give you the chance to get away.'

'Anything else?'

'The sternum if you can find it. The Adam's Apple of course. The testicles, that goes without saying. Kidneys. But one of my favourites is the knees. You can do a lot of damage to a knee, completely incapacitate a man. I like a knee. One good kick, Duncan, and the kneecap shoots right out. Lovely! We haven't done kicking. We'll do kicking next week. With kicking you'll be getting close to what it's all about . . .'

Yes, a good session, and now it looked like being a good

evening. Jo seemed really pleased to be going out with him, and with her beside him, how could he not be confident?

Luigi, the owner, received them attentively. Sometimes he could be off-hand but tonight he was almost obsequious. His was an old-style Italian restaurant, none of your Apicella vaulted ceilings and arches, but wood and Chianti bottles in straw fiascos and appalling pictures of donkeys and wide-eyed moppets. It was quiet, unpretentious (apart from its essentially Italian pretensions) and it glowed softly with electric candle-light behind Chianti-coloured shades.

'Take your coat, signorina?'

'Grazie,' she said.

'Ah, la signorina parla Italiano?'

'Poco, poco,' she said. 'Piccolo.'

'Ah, la bella,' Luigi told Duncan. 'You are lucky man.'

'Indeed I am,' he replied.

How lovely she looked! Her complexion was that wonder-ful, almost magical, peach-blush golden pink that looks as though it has never had a spot in its life. Her hair, short but not severe, curled like treble clefs around her ears and the nape of her neck – ah! the nape of her neck, it was the most kissable place in the world. Her hands were strong and cap-able, yes, but the fingers were well-proportioned and graceful, unlike his own chipolatas. And her eyes, lustrous in Luigi's candlelight, seemed to acquire new depths and richness of green not seen before by man.

Luigi handed them the menu.

'You'll have a glass of wine?' Duncan asked her.

'Just a glass. I don't drink really.'

Duncan ordered a bottle of Barolo.

'We'll think about the food awhile,' he told the Italian.

'Si, signor.'

Luigi hurried off.

'Tell me about yourself,' asked Duncan. 'You promised to.'

'I was born in Barnard Castle,' she told him. 'D'you know Durham?'

78

So, she was a North Country girl. He had thought he'd detected a flatness in her A's.

'I'm sure I've been there once or twice. I can't say I know it.'

'It's cold,' she told him. 'But it's a lovely place. Middleton-in-Teesdale, the River Greta . . .'

> '"Oh Brignal Banks are wild and fair
> And Greta Woods are green,
> And you may gather garlands there
> Would grace a summer queen",' he said.

'There you are. It's just like that. I love it when you quote things. You've got a quote for everything.'

'Not for you,' he said, half-jokingly. 'You are above quotation. Others abide quotation, thou art free.'

She gave him a long look when he said that; searching, appraising.

'Sorry,' he said. 'Go on.'

'I was brought up by the aunts,' she said. 'They were old-fashioned. They thought children should be thrashed.'

'Where was your mother?'

'She was there too. She was the younger sister. They kept an eye on her.'

'And your father?'

She blushed.

'I didn't have a father. That was why they kept an eye on her. In the end she escaped to Leeds, then to London.'

So the Marine story was a fabrication – justifiable under the circumstances, of course.

'Didn't she want you with her?' he asked.

'No.'

There was pain in her reply.

'Did you have an uncle?'

'One of the aunts was married. That was the problem.'

She blushed again. The implication was clear. The man had abused her.

'Oh Lord. Did you do anything about it?'

'I left as soon as I could.'

'When was that?'

'When I was fourteen. I was quite big for my age. I said I was sixteen and I learned typing. So I got myself a job.'

'In Barnard Castle?'

'Oh no. In Leeds. I thought I might see my mother.'

'Did you?'

'No.'

There was a short silence while he took it all in. Luigi poured the wine, Duncan gesturing that he did not need to try it.

'It must have been tough for you,' he said to her.

'That's why I never finished my schooling, see. That's why I have to teach myself. It's meeting people like you makes me realize how little I know. You're a walking university, you are, Duncan.'

Duncan thought about his previous way of life – how sheltered he had been – and yet somehow he had continued to be afraid! Jo had lived in the thick of things and still come up smiling.

'I couldn't begin to think how I would have managed in your shoes,' he said.

She looked pleased with his reply, giving him a long shining look which made him feel quite fidgety under the table.

'Signor, signorina?'

Luigi was hovering over them again.

'Oh . . . you order,' she said to Duncan.

'What about insalata tricolore, and an escalope milanese with zucchini,' he suggested.

'And a little green salad for the signorina?'

'Sounds fine,' she said.

Luigi bustled off again.

'The thing is,' he said, 'we both find things to admire in each other – though in my case I know just how unadmirable I am.'

'That is a good thing,' she agreed. 'And I'm sure you're too hard on yourself.'

They gazed at one another, smiling.

'So you stayed and worked in Leeds for a while?'

'I worked for people who didn't ask too many questions,' she said. 'I was underage, see. I worked for a Pakistani in the importing business. He used to import cousins, mainly. Then I worked as a book-keeper for a nightclub. That's when I started going to the gym daytimes, you see, and met Eddie.'

'You've known Eddie since then?'

'Off and on. Anyway Eddie got me into the self-defence game and taught me all he knew – after which I learnt a bit more – then, when I was eighteen, I came down to London.'

'To look for your mother?'

'I'd given her up. No, it just seemed a good idea. Change of scene and all that. Funnily enough, I met my ma when I wasn't looking for her. She was on the game. Does that shock you? She's dead now.'

'Nothing about you shocks me, Jo.'

She looked at him carefully.

'I wouldn't say that too quickly if I was you.'

He laughed.

'No, I'm serious,' she said.

'Very well,' he told her. 'I'll walk on the outside of the pavement.'

'That's better.'

The food arrived. It was a pleasure to see her tuck in. Her teeth were so ridiculously healthy.

'Mmm. This is good,' she said. 'What's it called?'

'Insalata tricolore.'

'I had no idea what it was going to be.'

He laughed again. He could not remember ever having been so happy.

'Your teeth are like Good King Wenceslas's snow,' he told her. 'White and crisp and even.'

That made her giggle.

'Crisp and even's all right,' she said. 'But I'm not sure about deep teeth. It's not white, it's deep – in the carol, that is. You see, I do know something.'

'All the better to bite me with,' he said.

She shuddered.

'Don't. My uncle used to tell that story.'

'I'm sorry.'

'It's all right. You weren't to know.'

She smiled at him. There was a pause while they ate. He topped up her glass with some more Barolo.

'So,' he said. 'We're nearly up to date.'

'I took a job as secretary at a gym in Kensington, I was there for five years, then I moved around a bit, got a job on a cruise liner, and now I'm freelancing in Notting Hill and one or two other places, and working out with Oliver Smail. I've stopped being a secretary now, of course. It's PE and sports instructing. I got my diplomas at night school. And of course now I'm doing hypnotherapy.'

'Is that the Level 10 thing?'

'Deep relaxation, Duncan. That's right. You like that, don't you?'

'Love it.'

He pondered a little.

'I don't go right under, though, do I?'

'You're a good subject,' she said, 'but people are mostly awake all the time. You can't put anyone to sleep against their will. There's a lot of mumbo-jumbo talked.'

'But do I?' he persisted.

'You are a good subject, Duncan. I really enjoy taking you down. You have a lot of tension to get rid of. I'll be taking my diploma in hypnotherapy very shortly. There's a professional body, you know, because of the abuses. No, you don't usually go right under. You just give up the will to be tense.'

'And does anybody take *you* down?'

'I've a lot of resistance, Duncan. The old man I study with, Stefan – Hungarian he is, come over after the uprising – he tried several times but I can't let go as easily as what you do.'

Luigi took away their plates, substituted the escalopes, zucchini and salad.

'Everything all right, signor?'

'Fine, fine.'

Jo studied him with amusement over her glass of wine.

'There's five hundred years of knowing what's what behind your "fine, fine",' she said.

He laughed.

'I believe my great-grandparents' family were timber merchants,' he said. 'Nothing particularly wonderful.'

'I bet they were,' she said. 'I bet they had silver on their table and Sèvres potties under the bed. You will correct me when I make mistakes, won't you?'

'Mistakes?'

'Mistakes in speaking or spelling. Just like I correct you when you snatch or jerk. I know I shouldn't have said "as easily as what you do" just now.'

'You're a strange girl,' he told her. 'Of course I will if you want. But I like your mistakes. They're . . . endearing . . .'

He knew that was the wrong word. A little frown crossed her face.

'And don't be condescending with me, will you?'

'I'm sorry. I didn't mean . . .'

'I know you didn't, Duncan.'

She put her hands on the table in an impulsive gesture of friendship, and Duncan took them in his own, and held them.

Luigi beamed directly from the back. He liked his restaurant to be romantic.

Jo let him hold her hand for long enough to make him know that she returned his feelings, even giving him a little squeeze by way of endorsement. They looked at each other without speaking.

'Yes, signorina, and to follow? Tiramisu, how we say, pull me up? Zuppa inglese?'

Business was business. If they wanted to spoon, let them

83

spoon something from the sweet trolley. But they declined. Love was not always the best appetizer, he knew.

'Just coffee, please, Luigi. Two cappuccinos.'

'Due cappuccini. Certainly, signor. And a little liquore for the signorina? Sambucca? Strega? Make her sleep well,' he leered.

'Nothing for me,' she said. 'I've had more than my usual already.'

They were quiet over their coffees. They both had a lot to think about. Jo kept lifting her face to his and looking him deep in the eyes. Duncan noticed that the place had become quite full. He simply hadn't taken it in until now.

'The bill, please, Luigi.'

'Certainly, signor.'

'When am I going to see you again?' he asked.

'Next Wednesday,' she told him.

'Not before?'

'Not yet, Duncan. I have to think. Nothing too sudden. I don't want to rush things. There's something happening, though, isn't there? We know that.'

'Yes,' he said. 'There's something happening. Next Wednesday it'll have to be.'

He paid the bill, Luigi fetched the coats, and they started to go out.

'Grazie, signor, signorina. Oh, signor, you've dropped something. Your handkerchief . . .'

Luigi stooped down and picked the thing up before his Latin discretion could be properly brought to bear on the object.

It was a pair of panties, Anna's panties as it happened. Luigi's face was a picture, graduating from surprise to alarm, then to embarrassment and, last, to hilarity. He stood there, holding them out, laughing.

Jo turned on her heel and walked into the night.

Fifteen

'Jo ... wait ...'

He ran after her, but by a stroke of bad luck, she had hailed a passing taxi and was climbing in.

'Jo ... I can explain ...'

'I expect you can explain the moon out of the sky,' she said, 'that's what education does for you. But if that's education, I'd rather be pig ignorant.'

He had never seen such a change come over someone so quickly. She was implacable. It was almost as though she were a different person. Her whole face seemed longer; her hair darker; her eyes closer together; her lips compressed. She was breathing fast and her skin had gone an extraordinary vivid white. Her breast heaved and she held a hand to her throat.

'Drive on,' he heard her say to the driver, and he thought he heard her say Great Portland Street.

Why hadn't he asked her where she lived? It was a criminal omission.

'Wait, Jo,' he cried despairingly. 'It's all a mistake.'

'Too right it is,' she said. 'Get out of my sight before I ...'

'Sorry, chum,' said the driver.

And the taxi disappeared into the darkness.

Luigi came up full of apologies.

'I belabour myself, signor. I had no idea. She is jealous, mm?'

'It's finished,' said Duncan brokenly.

'I am so stupido.'

'It's not your fault. I should have got rid of the wretched things.'

'You lead a double life, signor?'

He had gone up in Luigi's estimation. It was scant consolation.

'No . . . no, of course not . . .'

'You are a dark horse. You have girl here, another girl there. Panties in your pocket. Bra in your briefcase. You are a cavaliere . . . Bravissimo.'

'I love her,' said Duncan brokenly. 'I'll never see her again.'

'She will come back, signor. I see her look at you like she want to eat you with her leetle white tooths.'

But she didn't come back.

She didn't come back for the lesson on Wednesday. She didn't come back to Luigi's as, in grasping-at-straws mode, Duncan thought she might have done. She didn't reply to the letter he wrote to her explaining the whole incident, addressing it care of Captain Smail. She didn't answer the advertisements he put in the agony columns of the various Martial Art papers. She wasn't in the telephone book.

She had dived off the edge of his world.

He couldn't sleep. He went off his food. He couldn't concentrate. His half-made plans for Mackworth Scientific Films were set aside despite renewed encouragement from the persistent Reinacker, who had adopted him, he said, as an example of what could be done in this country. It didn't have to be a third-rate ex-world-power with a population of no-hopers . . . Well, that was Reinacker's problem. As far as he, Duncan, could see, no hope was the name of the game. He stopped cataloguing his collection, drawing a firm line in front of PARASITES and all the promise of the Ps.

He was almost too unhappy to be nervous, most of the time.

Delice, who had been regarding him with something

approaching awe since he had shouted at her, worked with unflagging energy, but even this couldn't disguise the fact that some of the clients were getting less than one hundred per cent for their money.

There was a falling off of business while Duncan scoured Notting Hill looking for gyms that might employ Jo's services, but every time he drew a blank. He took to loitering in Great Portland Street because that was the name he'd heard her give to the taxi driver.

It is a long street which, even if he'd heard her right, makes loitering a hit-and-miss affair. Several times he was made to move on by the police. Once he was arrested on suspicion of having a bomb in his bag.

He took to drinking rather more red wine than he should have done, and forgetting to shave.

He made a mistake with a conveyancing job. He should have queried an unsatisfactory reply to a search enquiry from a local council, but somehow his heart wasn't in it. All he could think about was the ache in that organ. No more would he see the dear features, the reassuring arms would no longer lock around him, the gentle strife, the wise instruction would never be his again. Oi moi potapoi! The lead in the stomach was unbearable.

Debates about a possible bypass that might result in an enforced purchase order seemed not so much trivial as completely irrelevant.

Luckily, the situation was saved by Delice who went and interviewed the elusive Councillor, became suspicious of collusion and persuaded the vendor that, although contracts had been signed, he might be sued for false declaration. There was more to Delice than met the eye, it seemed. But anyway Duncan's client was not to be placated and removed his business with dark threats of complaint to the appropriate bodies.

Booth dropped in one day, and even the film-maker – who never noticed anything about humans, whom he considered

87

to be outcasts of the animal kingdom – even Booth commented on Duncan's appearance.

'My God,' he said, 'you look like an albino meerkat I once saw in the Atlas mountains.'

'You in town? I thought you were in Greenland or somewhere,' said Duncan wearily.

'Burning the candle at both ends, I suppose,' said Booth. 'Lucky fellow.'

Booth was thinking more and more about women, but the conduct of his life as well as his advancing years made his search for happiness as yet seem doomed to fruitlessness.

'What happened to that idea of yours to sell out-takes to advertising?' he asked.

If Duncan could have been surprised at the moment, he would have been. It was unlike Booth to remember such a thing.

'Oh that,' said Duncan, dully. 'I don't know. No interest.'

'You surprise me,' said Booth. 'I keep being told nature's hot. As a matter of fact, I quite like the idea. Got to make cash while we can, especially when we're thinking of settling down. Ah well, see you whenever. Just off to the Rift Valley. 'Bye.'

''Bye,' said Duncan.

The man could go to the canals of Mars or the incandescent sulphuric Mountains of Venus for all he cared; in fact, the latter seemed particularly appropriate.

'We can't go on like this,' said Delice one day in March, five months after Jo had disappeared.

'No I can't,' said Duncan dully.

'Oh dear, Mr Mackworth. I do wish I could help you.'

Delice had guessed, of course, at the source of Duncan's misery.

'*Cherchez la femme*,' she had told her girlfriend Janet who worked for an insurance broker.

It was perfectly obvious to Janet that Delice was in love with her boss.

'Now's your chance,' she had told her.

But Delice had shaken her head.

'He doesn't see me.'

'What a cock-up the world is,' said Janet, who was something of a philosopher.

And things went from worse to awful. One week Delice couldn't even pay herself.

'We'll have to shut up shop if this goes on, Mr Mackworth. I've got to live even if you haven't.'

Duncan looked at her as though she were a deep-sea creature, out in the waters beyond his bulb.

'Yes, Delice, if you say so.'

'Don't you care? Don't you mind?'

'Going home now. Not feeling too good,' he said.

He was down to cheapo Côtes du Rhône now, but the sun gave it a lovely garnet glow in the glass. He sat not looking at the television, letting the wine do the work, watching the unmoving clouds pronged on the bare silver birch in the back garden – like marshmallows on a toasting fork. He wished he were a cloud.

Then, suddenly, unmistakably, the front doorbell went Brrrrr brr. He gave a great shudder, spilling wine in a great wound down his trouser leg. Dabbing himself frantically, he rushed into the hall and flung open the door.

There was no one there. Oh God, how cruel. Someone was playing a trick on him. It was boys, no doubt, just chancing on *her* ring, halfway up the street by now. He went down the steps, looked left and right, peered across the roadway. Nothing.

Slowly he mounted the steps again and closed the door behind him. As he did so, a hand came over his mouth, an arm closed over his throat, and a voice – the voice above all voices that he wanted to hear – whispered in his ear:

'Have you forgotten everything I taught you?'

His knees sagged. She had to hold him up for a moment.

'Oh Jo,' he said. 'Oh Jo.'

She held him to her like that, only slowly relaxing her grip. He could feel her body pressed against him, the gentle cushion of the breasts, the hard little pincushion of the pubic bone. She turned him round at last and they began to kiss.

This wasn't hungry kissing. It was famine. They kissed as though terrified to let even a scrap or peel of desire escape. They gorged love from each other until they had at last to stop and breathe.

'Why?' Duncan said. 'Why didn't you come before? Why now?'

'I only got your letter yesterday. Oliver Smail came back for a couple of days and called me.'

'Don't go without giving me your telephone number. I never want to go through that again.'

'You poor old thing. I must say, you don't look too good.'

'I'm not too good. At least I wasn't until I saw you. Now I'm cock-a-hoop.'

'Yes,' she said. 'I felt that. And there's wine all down your trousers.'

He blushed and she laughed at him.

'You are a silly old thing,' she said. 'Your story about the panties was so crazy it had to be true.'

'Where have you been?' he asked.

'Oh, around and about. A spell in South London, Wimbledon way. I went up to Barnard Castle for a while. One of my aunts died and my uncle was ill. It's better there now. I don't take any nonsense from them.'

'Did you . . . see Eddie?'

'Him? Once or twice, but he's been away too. Mozambique, I think.'

'Oh?'

He didn't want her to see Eddie.

'You're jealous! You shouldn't be. I told him about us. I think he'd like to kill you.'

'You'd better teach me some more self-defence.'

'What? Now?'

'Maybe not now.'

'What then?'

He looked involuntarily towards the ceiling.

She shook her head.

'Hmhm. Not that.'

'But why?'

'It's all too sudden, Duncan. It's all too much. Remember the muscles.'

'But you're not cold.'

'It's just . . . I'm fond of you, Duncan. But I'm not ready.'

'I've never slept with a woman,' he said. 'I'm a virgin. Pathetic, isn't it?'

'Don't say that.'

She was really cross with him for a moment.

'Sorry.'

'It's one of the things I love about you. You're not dirty or second-hand. You've kept yourself just for me. Some people . . . it'd be like eating out of a dustbin.'

He didn't ask her if she were a virgin. He would have liked to, but he had the feeling that she might react badly. An instinct for kid gloves was beginning to develop.

'What would you like to do?' he asked.

'I'd like to take you down to Level 10 – deeper, Duncan. I'd like to take you down to Level 20.'

'I didn't know there was a Level 20.'

'Oh there is, Duncan. Level 20's a beautiful level.'

'And afterwards?'

'We have some brushing up to do. And then perhaps some kicking . . .'

Sixteen

The next few weeks were the happiest in Duncan's life.

His strange past, blighted by foreboding, was left behind. It was as if he had grown up under the vast shadow of something nameless, never perfectly described, a huge hogweed of a thing that had kept the sun off him, made him grow up etiolated; nerve-wracked, old before his time. But now miraculously it was gone. With one hand outstretched in the on-guard position and a palm-hit up the nose, she had laid its root cause low.

Oh, she might not have been aware of what she was doing, but that was the effect all right; and when he told her of the miracle that she had achieved, she smiled and said:

'It's a two-way thing, you know.'

'I? What have I done for you?'

'I've had my problems too, you know.'

She meant the uncle who had abused her as a child, he thought. God, he would like to have been alone with that pig for five minutes. He'd have given him abuse. What sort of abuse would he be up to after a kick to the kneecap – right through, not a dainty prod nor yet a jerk, but smooth, totally crippling – followed by a palm to the chin, snapping the head back, kick in the balls with a good follow-through and, as he doubled up, a thump like a ton of bricks on his seventh vertebra? He wouldn't lift a finger against her after that; in fact, he wouldn't be lifting anything at all.

Even as Duncan thought it, of course, he knew he couldn't do it; she wouldn't have wished it. She said it again in her concluding lecture at the end of their tenth session.

'Always remember, Duncan, that what I'm teaching you is for defence not attack. Any yob can attack, Duncan. It's not clever. It's basic. Bang! Wham! Caveman stuff. What I'm teaching you is subtlety. It's movement. It's timing. It's turning their energy against them, using their strength to overthrow them. What they don't expect is for you to be prepared. Don't let me ever see you attacking, Duncan. I can see there's some aggression in you . . .'

'In *me*?'

He had laughed.

'I'm getting to know you well, Duncan. Better maybe than you know yourself. Yes, there's aggression. Not that it's bad. It would be bad if you had none. I wouldn't respect you if you had none. But it's been repressed, Duncan. That's what makes it dangerous. Didn't you tell me once that some of your fear has been fear of what you might do? It's a genie in a bottle, aggression, Duncan. You've got to let it out carefully. Channel it, control it, use it as energy – but only in defence.'

'Very well,' he smiled. 'I submit.'

'Only if you agree, Duncan. Not just to please me.'

They would often go out to Luigi's after training – Luigi had given him a big 'I told you so' look when they had first appeared together again. Then they would stroll back to his flat, listen to some music, talk or watch the news.

One day she said:

'Choose a book for me, Duncan.'

'What sort of book?'

'You've got all these books here. Have you read them all?'

'Most of them I suppose.'

'I want you to educate me, Duncan. I teach you. Now you teach me.'

'What d'you want to learn?'

93

'I want to learn everything you know.'

He laughed.

'There's no point in two of us knowing the same things.'

'What then?'

'You must first learn what interests you.'

She began to get cross then. He could read the signs. Oh, oh, kid gloves.

'Just give me a book, Duncan, for goodness sake.'

'I'll give you the book I most enjoyed reading in my life,' he said.

That did the trick.

'Oh yes,' she told him. 'That's the one for me. What's it about?'

'It's not a novel. It's a history. Do you mind?'

'If you enjoyed it, of course I don't.'

He took Barbara Tuchman's *A Distant Mirror* down from the shelf.

'"The Disastrous Fourteenth Century"?' she said. 'Very well, I'll read it. By the time I see you next week, I'll have finished it.'

'Does that mean I'm not going to see you tomorrow?'

'Not if I'm going to finish it.'

'But I'd rather see you than have you read books.'

'I have to be worthy of you,' she said. 'You'll have to share me.'

It became the pattern of their life.

In his own time, after and sometimes during office hours, he set about finishing his catalogue and even drawing up a draft for a prospectus he might one day send out. He dug out the American's card and called him up, arranging to visit his office the following week to pick his brains about the advertising world and commercials.

'Sure, I look forward to it,' said Reinacker. 'Anything I can do to help. You helped me, I'll help you. There aren't enough people in this country doing anything new.'

'It's difficult here,' Duncan told him. 'It's an old country, over-populated, thick like treacle. Difficult to get anything moving . . .'

It was one of the reasons why he hadn't quite made up his mind to launch Mackworth Scientific yet. Did he really have the will, the energy, the conviction? And could he run it at the same time as the practice, or was he going to have to put all his eggs in this unknown quantity of a basket? It was a problem he debated with himself, though not with Jo. She wasn't ready for life talks yet, their relationship was not sufficiently advanced. His relationship with Jo was the most important thing, more important than getting things moving in this old country, but he could not speak of it to the American.

On Wednesdays she would arrive, give him his lesson – he was on to ways of dealing with knife-pullers now, and breathing exercises to quell the effects of adrenalin – and they would go round the corner to dinner. Then they would come back, she would give him back the book she had borrowed, and he would give her another one.

To his surprise, she didn't just finish *A Distant Mirror*, she enjoyed it, even pointing out things that he must have missed or forgotten.

'That young Duchesse de Berry, she was brave, wasn't she – when the king was dressed as a wood demon, in a tarry suit with all those leaves stuck on, and he caught fire – she put it out with her dress. And that chap de Rosnay, treading on the peasants and making them say "bark, dog". When he died of burns, they all lined up and shouted "bark, dog" at his coffin.'

'You're amazing,' he told her. 'Quite the academic. I believe you really could be if you wanted. It's not too late.'

She didn't believe him, but she was ridiculously pleased. So pleased that she allowed him to take her upstairs to his bedroom where she kissed him passionately and, to his surprise, ubiquitously. So much so that he couldn't stop himself when she had him in her mouth, and he thought she would be furious, but she kissed him all the more and cuddled him all night. Night-long he smelt the freshness of her and touched the skin that had an extraordinary velvety smoothness, felt the breasts which had occupied so many nights of sleepless dreams, and the undreamt-of tenderness of her stomach and her thighs. Only the one place remained concealed.

He tried once or twice to take her knickers off, or to make *her* take them off, but she immediately stiffened and took his hand away.

'No,' she said. 'No! Don't.'

And then:

'I'm sorry.'

'It doesn't matter. Nothing matters. I love you, Jo.'

'Do you? Do you really?'

'I do. Can't you feel I do?'

'Yes. Yes. I can.'

He wouldn't ask her if she loved him. Let her say it in her own good time.

He had never before been a very carnal person. The erotica of the schoolboy had, of course, crossed his path – the black and white starkness of *Health & Efficiency*, the sugary nipples and candyfloss bushes of *Playboy*, the capering orifices of *LicketySplit* – but they had never really deserved, he felt, the fuss and droolery devoted to them by boys like Bovinden. For boys like Bovinden, even Latin declensions became an opportunity for grossness.

'Bim, bum, bottom, arse in the grass . . .'

He could hear them now – the songs, the jokes, the limericks, the dirty stories, the evermore inventive foulness. You would think these boys sprang into the world wrapped in a caul of filth from which they never escaped; without the benefit of gentle mothers or pretty sisters; engendered solely by some awful male parthenogenesis.

So sex of this kind, talked-about sex, left him as cold as the fear that went with it; apprehension that when he met the untalked-about kind, he might not be able to do it; fear of ridicule; fear of rejection; fear of fathering a baby; fear of catching a disease and his dick dropping off . . .

His diffident organ, then, had lain there (at any rate in his waking hours, for there were dreams which confirmed his vision of something better than the Bovinden version) with the switch turned to 'Off', the keyboard locked, waiting as it seemed for an endlessly postponed Evensong.

By some extraordinary kindness of fate, right against the run of things, the service, inaugurated and invested by Jo, was now held on a weekly basis. Darling Jo – he did not call her darling to her face for it seemed hardly self-defensive – but he thought of her as darling – darling Jo, he thought, I am frightened to, I do not dare to, tell you quite how much you mean to me.

Seventeen

Duncan regretted his decision to visit the American almost as soon as he had made the appointment, but when he saw the huge brass nameplate as big as a man and the tall glossy bossy girl at reception, he knew that he was in dangerous waters. The place reminded him of his first employment as a junior in a big City law firm which itself in a curious way reminded him of school. More glamorous than school, of course; but the pecking order and the privileges seemed much the same. You could keep your flies half undone/date the secretaries provided you were in the school team/a partner. Indeed you could probably do both if you were a partner. (This was in the days before harassment, of course.)

The place was full of pretty girls: girls who tripped through, looking preoccupied; girls who stopped and talked about last night to the girl at reception; girls who seemed to have nothing to do but come and stare out of the front door in an important way and then retire to wherever it was they'd come from; girls who sat reading the magazines – a richer haul than the old *Cosmo* and *Country Life* that his own office sported; girls who sent shivers of harassment writs running down his spine; girls whose desirability even the image of Jo, held up like a silver cross against a vampire, could not altogether expunge; but girls in the end who looked like a media person's idea of a girl, not a heroine who could break a knifeman's arm with a flick on his wrist and a smash on his elbow.

Oh Jo, sorry for coveting my neighbour's maidservants.

'Wanting?' said the maidservant behind the desk, who would have scratched your eyes out – and got away with it – if you'd called her a maidservant.

Wanting to look up your micro-skirt, ducky, an ugly croaking little voice inside him wanted to say. Surely not. That was surely not his real wanting? He looked at his face in the huge mirror that flanked reception and was reassured to find it was having nothing to do with his nasty thoughts. It was looking questing, if a little withdrawn. Why did this place affect him so, make him feel so dangerously, misleadingly excited? He felt like an ugly croaking little worm among all these glossy girls, he felt like a serpent among the Eves. Or were they the clever maid-serpents, learnt to walk at last, and he the old Adam?

What were they all doing here? What conceivable job could justify so much – what did the Americans call it, what was the word?

'Ass,' that was it.

'I beg your pardon.'

The receptionist was used to all the crudeness of the young creatives in the agency, the FODFOMs as they were known (Feet On Desk, Foul Of Mouth), but as it happened she was an evangelical Christian, though she still dressed like a high-class escort girl.

Duncan was covered with confusion and tried to get off the line.

'I mean, ass I'm new to this place, ass I'm a little early, I'll just sit here if I may, look you,' he said.

'Name?'

He spoke before he thought it through.

'Evans,' he said.

He suddenly realized that the receptionist would phone the name to Reinacker's secretary, who would disclaim all knowledge of him or, worse, Reinacker would come down and think he'd gone mad.

''Eavens,' he exclaimed, looking at his watch, 'is that the time?'

The receptionist had started to write, stopped, and gazed at him bleakly.

'Name?' she asked again, crossing out what she'd written. 'You've spoiled an identity clip.'

'Er, Mackworth. That's with an A-C-K.'

'I'm afraid you'll have to sign in. Wanting?'

'Mr Reinacker.'

She gave him an absurdly large, pendulous name-tag, ignored him for a few minutes while she dealt with a messenger and massaged her switchboard, then breathed Floris rosewater mouthwash and a couple of diphthongs into a telephone, and asked him to take a seat. He thumbed through the magazines in a desultory manner, taking note of the latest fragrance impregnations, until finally another beautiful girl, blonde this time, arrived and led him into a lift. He would have preferred her to have led him into a small anteroom and removed his pendulous name-tag with many an alluring dance, but he could not explain this to her or indeed to himself. There were strange potential infidelities rising in him like impurities.

Shocked at himself, he wondered why an advertising agency should have this effect upon him. The smell of money? The glamour of pseudo-showbiz? The razzmatazz of presentation? He concluded that, after all, this was the cutting edge of dreams. Those entering this world, like himself, for the first time, unconditioned as it were, might find the air too rich, the appetites over-stimulated.

Or perhaps he just felt like this because Jo wouldn't sleep with him.

The lift continued its gently-mewing upward course. Arriving at the top, the girl ushered him along a corridor. She too was wearing a very short skirt and wonderfully liquid-looking tights so that her legs shimmered deliquescently as she walked in front of him, sending Duncan into a dither of unrequited lust.

Finally, she stopped in front of a large door and showed him into a boardroom where Reinacker (Duncan recalled his name was Tom) sat with a very large pink-faced man looking at body-spray commercials. At this point she retired, both aware and careless of the agitation she had caused.

'Thank you, Zeugma.'

Hands were shaken all round.

'Excuse me,' said Duncan, he had to ask. 'Did you call her Zeugma?'

But Reinacker was already plunging into the meat of the meeting.

'Tony here is our TV producer, er Duncan. I thought he could answer some of your questions.'

If they didn't want to talk about the girl's name, they didn't want to talk about the girl's name, but it seemed a pretty silly name to him; however, obediently, since he was here to ask questions not talk about girls' names or even their deliquescent legs, he got out his list and weighed in. He asked the producer, Tony, who he thought his customers might be, whether agency or commercial film company; what sort of competition was there already; what sort of fees he should be charging; what kind of insurance he should have; how agencies responded to publicity for such ventures . . .

Tony, though large, had small eyes. He appeared guarded, as though he didn't want to be dragooned or compromised artistically in any way, or made to give up his already cosy arrangements just to gratify a director from head office on the way out. But he replied with what seemed to be experience and authority, and the meeting at length drew to its close. They all stood up.

'You'll let us know when you decide to start?' asked the producer. 'I'm sure we'll be interested sooner or later.'

'You'll stay to lunch?' asked Tom.

They took his ludicrous name-tag off him and walked him round the corner into Dean Street where one of the big new media restaurants had just opened. Duncan was experiencing considerable feelings of dissociation by now, though his face maintained its customary sangfroid. The place was crammed with pretty girls lunching with media men. The producer drank wine and ate prodigiously. Tom drank water and nibbled a Waldorf salad.

'This country reminds me of the French army in 1940,' he said. 'More interested in wining than winning.'

'Why win when you can eat?' asked the producer, tucking in. The intensity of his enjoyment was beginning to elicit pimples of perspiration around his temples.

Duncan drank a little wine, an Australian Marsanne that Tony had ordered, interested because Marsanne had not yet appeared on The Fellowship of Wine's list (with tasting notes). He ate a little fish because it is the dish of love. He did not drink too much because it was a Wednesday. Jo did not mind wine in moderation, otherwise The Fellowship of Wine would have had to look for another customer, but she disapproved of it before a session. Duncan hoped she wouldn't notice the Marsanne – bags of fruit, melon and apricot, almost fulsome, with a long dry finish – but you had to be on your toes to fool her.

The American chatted on as he pushed the walnuts round his plate. Tony polished off a mountain of moules. Every now and then someone would wave, or stop at the table for a chat. Duncan was confused. This was life, this was gloss, this was style – and, yes, it would rub off, if that was what you wanted. It was another world. It was an escape. It was like a door in a high wall into a sunlit park. But was it a park? Or was it a set made up to look like a park to tempt the unwary?

'So when are you going to start, Duncan?' asked the American.

'Not sure,' said Duncan. 'I have to do a feasibility study.'

He was pleased with himself for dredging up a media phrase.

'Can do,' said the American. 'That's the only feasibility study you need.'

Tony polished off the last of the Marsanne and hitched himself about in his trousers.

'Let me know if I can help,' he said. 'Nature's hot right now. Nothing like nature for selling nappies and Sanpro items.'

'We have a lot of Sanpro,' agreed the American.

'Sanpro?' asked Duncan.

'Sanitary protection.'

'Ah.'

The noise of the restaurant was very loud under the low vaulted roof. Duncan suddenly had a feeling of oppression, as though he must get out. Waves of laughter hit the ceiling and bounced back, mingling with the splash of wine and the crash of crocks. All he wanted was to be back in the quietness of his house where the afternoon moved on soft shoes. This place was some kind of attack.

'Would you mind awfully?' he said. 'Just realized the time. Got a meeting five minutes ago. Thank you so much.'

He offered to pay his share for the lunch but they'd have none of it.

'Goodbye. See you. I'll be in touch.'

Eighteen

He put the visit to the advertising agency behind him. Well-meaning though Tom Reinacker was, the whole thing had been only partly productive. He was going to have to take this advertising thing slowly, acclimatize, pause in the passage before throwing the door open. How could he have been unfaithful to Jo even in thought? It was a travesty to compare her with those creatures. And yet . . . something had been let in . . . It was like lifting a stone and finding yourself under it.

Assailed by guilt, fear's first cousin, he applied himself to Jo's instruction all the more. And, not surprisingly, his skills advanced, if not by leaps and bounds, at least in a rapid, gliding, forward motion; and, thanks to the exercises she gave him, his body was growing stronger too.

She gave him hypertension practice – contracting his back with his feet under the bed. There were sit-ups, contracting the stomach; press-ups off the knees to strengthen chest, shoulders and arms; and the robustly named straddle-squat to tone the legs and buttocks.

'Exercise can be a powerful psycho-therapeutic tool,' she told him. 'You need to use your body more, Duncan. Learn to wind up your body like a spring and launch a strike. Learn from the cat. Faced with sheer aggression it usually runs. Only when cornered will it strike with speed, precision and commitment.'

He loved her when she talked like this to him after a grappling session, the light perspiration on her upper lip a reminder to him of other deliquescences; the breasts' lift and fall recalling to his mind the perfect picture of their nakedness. He admired her that she seemed able to commit her mind totally to instruction without letting it wander into tenderness.

He had tried a little stroke of the hand once, but she had almost struck it away.

'While we work, we work,' she had told him. 'There's no emotions in training.'

But usually, at the end, as now, she would soften and encourage, praising the progress of the day.

'Good hard work today,' she told him. 'Strong low kicks and good mental reactions, like when I produced that knife; good confronting of weapons. That was a quick wrist-lock. Mind you, it's different if it's cold steel and not a bit of silver wood. You have to be very skilled to take a weapon. You'd be better with a head or throat take-out.'

'Have you ever . . . been attacked?' he asked her.

She smiled.

'Oh yes . . . I've been attacked all right.'

But she wouldn't tell him more.

'Have you ever . . . killed anyone?'

'Blood-thirsty, aren't we?'

'No, but have you?'

'If I had I wouldn't tell you. You're a solicitor.'

'Not as far as you're concerned. I solicit only your affection.'

It was a weak joke but it seemed to convince her.

'Well, then perhaps I have.'

'Killed?'

'When? Where?'

'Never you mind. This is self-defence, remember. Getting out of trouble not into it. Maybe one day I'll tell you. Nothing to be proud of, I'll tell you that now. Meanwhile here's something to remember. The person with less than three years' intensive unarmed combat practice is likely to come off worst in a physical contest with an attacker. Be aware. Keep out of trouble. Peel your eyes. Keep another pair in the back of your head.'

'Three years?' he complained. 'Can it really take that long?'

'For many people it does, sensitive people who don't like to gouge eyes or rip testicles – people who still feel squeamish when they're cornered. They have to cross the barrier. They have to be prepared to do the unthinkable to save their lives. It takes a lot of training. People freeze when they're about to be attacked. They can't believe it's happening. That's why I'm giving you exercises, breathing exercises next week, Duncan, what the SAS do – I should say which – to help you switch on in a crisis . . .'

He was still a long way off three years. Even so, three months had made him more confident than he'd ever been – and confidence, of course, meant happiness.

It resulted, as happiness so often does, in an improvement in his business. He started to cultivate long-neglected friends and associates, not for the work they might give him but because happiness, like a cat, wants people to rub its head against. In consequence, people had once again started to bring him their legal matters. Meanwhile his plans for Mackworth Scientific Films, in spite of his misgivings about the advertising world, were slowly moving ahead, and other useful acquaintances were being made.

He would have liked to have introduced Jo to these friends, but she was reluctant to share him in public, she said.

'Later,' she told him. 'We're still discovering each other. I don't want to waste the little time we have together.'

He had wanted her to see him every evening, but she said she had to train as well as study.

'I've got to keep fit,' she told him, 'otherwise I'll lose my job. Then there's Stefan. I'm taking a new course. And I've got to keep my learning up, otherwise I'll lose you.'

He assured her that this would never be the case, but the pattern of their relationship continued – with the added dimension of one further scene following the dinner at Luigi's.

At his flat, afterwards, they would make love – never the final consummation but wonderful all the same – upstairs on his four-poster. Then, in the morning, she would slip away, before he woke.

He had offered to take her back to her flat, of course, but she always refused.

'Go on,' he would say. 'I'd really like to. It's no trouble.'

'I'm a private person, Duncan,' she told him. 'I value that. I learned long ago not to trust anyone too much. I don't want to get too fond of you, see. I really like you, but I need my space. I don't think you'd thank me for going all the way.'

'But I would, I would,' he protested.

'We have to keep on the outside of the pavement, Duncan. Relationships are like everything else. Never let yourself be boxed in. There's always something you shouldn't give away.'

Nothing he could do would change her mind; and indeed he had an instinct that he should not do so; that if he in his turn discovered that inner key of hers, as she so signally had discovered his, it might be an unkindness, even a danger to use it. There are secret rooms that contain treasure and others that hold skeletons. But of course he knew the matter was out of his hands.

Nineteen

Sometimes she would come and see him on a Sunday and, in the days of daffodils and the springiness of things, they would drive out into the country for lunch.

She loved the countryside around Henley – 'I can't live without hills,' she used to say. (The Cotswolds beyond Woodstock and the Berkshire Downs near Newbury were other favourites.) They would walk after lunch along flint-strewn bridleways, looking for fossils; or in woods six-o'clock-shadowy with bluebells; or up hillsides where primroses defied the gloomier prognostications of the environmental lobby.

And then one day it happened – among primroses, as it turned out, where they walked on an afternoon of breathless blue. He was as happy as the first butterflies which dithered about among the flowers, hardly knowing where to start.

> '"*Primroses deck the bank's green side*
>   *Cowslips enrich the valley,*
>   *The blackbird warbles to his bride,*
>   *Let's rove the fields, my Annie . . .*"' he sang.

The ditty came from an old book of his mother's, and lent itself well to his light baritone, but Jo had shaken her head.

'Don't you like it?' he asked her.

'I like it very much,' she told him. 'I like it too much. What do they sing now? Not words like that. They sing violence . . . mugger's songs.'

'So what didn't you like about it?'

'I didn't like the last word, Duncan,' she told him, eyes shining.

'What?' he said, stupidly. 'You mean? . . .'

'Annie,' she told him. 'Who's that?'

He laughed.

'It's no one. Just a song.'

She threw her arms round him and kissed him hard. They were standing under a great beech tree, and his heels crackled on the mast as her embrace pressed him backwards against the trunk. All around him he could feel the world of nature fizzing and popping, algae multiplying, pollen rattling, worms thrusting like earthmovers.

'What was that for?' he asked, dazedly, when they stopped at last.

'I think I'm in love with you,' she said.

It was what he had been waiting to hear and he grinned like Humpty Dumpty.

'Darling,' he said. 'I'm so happy.'

'You'd better watch out, though,' she said, walking on. 'It's back-to-the-wall time now. There's no way out.'

'I'll watch,' he said, 'don't you worry.'

She lay down suddenly on the warm grass and pulled him down – he sometimes forgot how strong she was – on top of her. There was no one about. They had walked for miles. They threw off their clothes, the sun curiously hot on those places where the sun never shines, and made love where they lay. It was the first time she had allowed him to penetrate her, and she came with a cry that was at once triumphant, plaintive, and despairing, in the manner of peacocks.

He lay back exhausted, happier than he had ever been, smiling at the thought of silly headlines like 'SOLICITOR STRUCK OFF FOR LOOSE BRIEFS' or 'LAWYER CAUGHT BARE-CHEEKED ON PRIMROSE PATH' should they be caught.

But when he looked at her, he saw she was weeping. He reached out a hand and caressed her shoulder. Women sometimes do cry after intercourse, he had read in a book on women. It helps release excess emotion.

When she raised her eyes to his, however, he was surprised to see that redness behind the pupils which he had noted that fatal night in Luigi's.

'You bastard,' she said.

Twenty

The look in her eyes said hate, and it made him think. However, he didn't need a book on women to tell him that love is akin to hate. He had even made a joke recently in a fish restaurant on the subject, substituting (rather wittily, he thought) the letter K for T, so he dismissed it from his mind and addressed himself to soothing her, assuring her of his love and respect.

She was not easily appeased.

'You knew,' she said furiously, 'you knew I didn't want to do that, but did you stop, did you consider my feelings for one moment? Did you hell!'

It would not have been tactful, let alone gallant to tell her that she had more or less forced him to make love to her; his lawyer's experiences at dealing with excitable clients stood him again in good stead.

'I'm so sorry,' he told her. 'It's just . . . I love you so much.'

'Love? Love?' She cried, 'Love's no bloody excuse. Love's cheap. Love's in every grubby little song, every dirty little film.'

'You don't mean that . . .'

'Don't tell me what I mean.'

'Of course. Sorry.'

'And don't keep saying sorry. At least Eddie didn't say sorry.'

This hurt him. Why did she mention Eddie? Had she been

seeing him again? Perhaps that was what she did all week: she went out with Eddie.

At least when she had been away she had gone to South London, not to Archway where he knew Eddie lived. But was she telling the truth? And did she sleep with him? She couldn't be doing that. Or could she? It was not an edifying thought.

He fell silent while his happiness lumbered away through the woods like a startled pheasant.

'And for heaven's sake, don't sulk,' she told him.

He opened his mouth to deny the charge but shut it again, knowing it was useless, and applied himself to putting his clothes on. It was one of nature's miracles that women could get dressed so quickly. Why did men have to have all these lace-up shoes, these socks, these fastenings?

'And for heaven's sake, get a move on,' she said. 'I want to go home.'

He walked beside her in silence while she railed at herself. Fastening's a bad word, he thought. Slowerings, they should be called. Don't rush me, I've got to get my slowerings done up.

'I must be mad,' she said. 'Mad. I should never have let you do it. Never.'

Every now and then, he tried to get her off the subject. At last, a deer ambled across their path.

'Look at that,' he said. 'Roe deer.'

It was followed by a tiny fawn. That did the trick.

'Ah,' she said. 'Sweet little thing.'

'"*A troop of hunters riding by
Have shot my fawn and it will die,*"' he told her.

'They'll do no such thing,' she said. 'It'd be a kick in the groin, a palm to the nose and a kneecap sailing away through the trees like a discus if they tried any of that. Couldn't you eat that little thing?'

'You mean venison?' he asked, happy to introduce a lighter note.

'I do not mean venison. I mean I love it.'

'Ah. That grubby word.'

'Don't you twist everything I say, Duncan Mackworth, just because you're a lawyer. And ask that doe where the man in her life is, will you?'

But it had done the trick, and by the time they had reached the car, she was herself again. As they drove back, she explained why she had been so upset.

'My uncle, auntie's husband, used to do it,' she said. 'He used to come into my room at night. My aunts were downstairs watching telly and he had a little study place along the corridor past my bedroom where he'd enter competitions. He was a competition enterer. That was his hobby. But instead of entering competitions, sometimes he'd come to my room and enter me.'

She'd told him about her uncle before, of course, but only in passing reference. He hadn't realized the man had gone the whole way.

'My poor Jo,' he said. 'What a terrible thing. Frankly, I think castration's too good for such people. Couldn't you say anything to your aunts?'

'They were hard women, Duncan. He swore he'd tell them he'd seen me doing things with the boys and...'

'Go on.'

'And doing things ... to myself. That I'd shown him what I did, and that I was begging him for it. You know the way men talk?'

'Not all of us,' he said mildly.

A car flashed past, hooting wildly, full of gesticulating orcs.

'Some of us,' he told her.

'At any rate I believed him,' she said.

'How long did this go on?'

'Three years. Until I left home.'

'You were lucky he didn't make you pregnant,' he said.

'Who says he didn't?'

'Oh my God. You poor girl.'

113

'He tried it on a year or two back when I came home, but I tell you one thing. He won't do it again.'

He drove on for a while in silence. He could feel a question forming in him like a boil.

'I suppose . . . you wouldn't like to marry me?' he broke out at last.

'Marry you?'

She leant across and kissed him lightly, almost insultingly, and sniggered.

'What's so funny?'

'Me marry? The boys would laugh their heads off if they knew.'

'I don't see why.'

'I'm not the marrying kind. Independent, that's me. Sweet of you to ask, though.'

He could feel another change had come over her. She had pressed a different key: brittle, bright, one of the boys. It disturbed him that she should change moods so quickly. It was like watching one of his stop-frame weather films with the camera locked onto the same location through the changing seasons: clouds, rain, sun, wind, ice, snow, tempest, and little April showers . . . She loved watching those. Like the eye of God, she called it.

'Stop,' he said suddenly.

'You're driving.'

'I mean, stop it.'

'That's nice. That's very nice.'

'I mean, we made love an hour or so ago. Now you're talking as if the boys meant more to you than me.'

'Maybe they do.'

He could feel the pain of it in his stomach – like going back to school when he was nine, but sabre-toothed. He concentrated on not letting his features fall apart.

'Just because I let you make love to me,' she said, 'doesn't mean you own me, you know.'

'I never said it did.'

114

'Just because I tell you about myself, doesn't mean you know everything.'

'I didn't think I gave that impression.'

'Just because you're a lawyer doesn't give you the right to judge other people.'

'I never suggested it would.'

'Well. How's this for a suggestion? I suggest we call it off right now. I suggest you stop the car and let me out this minute. What do you think of that?'

He drove on.

'Stop the car.'

They were going over the Hammersmith flyover now. There was no possibility of stopping.

'Stop the fucking car.'

It was shocking to hear her swear.

'I can't stop here,' he said.

'If you don't stop the car, I'll break all the fingers in your left hand,' she said. 'Then you won't be able to change gear.'

He knew she wouldn't have done it, of course, but he stopped the car to show her that he too could throw surprises.

To pull up on top of Hammersmith flyover in Sunday evening traffic is to invite considerable derision if not down-right hostility, and so it was now. Horns hooted, arms waved, faces that had been white as bottoms, now reddened with the spring sun, grew redder as the temperature mounted.

In the other lane, a police car pulled up and its passenger, a sergeant, asked what the hell they thought they were doing.

'I'm getting out,' said Jo. 'This man's abducting me.'

'I can't be abducting her if I'm letting her out,' said Duncan.

'You'd both better follow me to the station.'

Twenty-One

At the station, she changed her mood again. She explained it was a lover's tiff and looked vulnerably at the Station Sergeant with her big green eyes. They were let off with a caution.

Outside, she did not speak to Duncan, and while he stood on the pavement, wretchedly, knowing that he should let her go her way and screw up somebody else's life but hating it to end, she hailed a cab, climbed in and disappeared towards Kensington.

The back-to-school feeling had once more reasserted itself in his stomach. If only he didn't love her so much! She was one of those people, he thought, with whom life seems sharper, stranger, more intriguing; the very swing of her moods was dangerously exciting, like the bump and lurch of a speedboat; when she wasn't there the world was black and white; with her it was dazzling Kodacolor.

No wonder people killed themselves for love. The adrenalin it engendered was a drug as strong as any in the peddler's pharmacopoeia.

He returned, sorrowfully, to his flat and poured himself a glass of Californian Pinot Noir which only served to liquefy the lead in his stomach – by no means the promise of the tasting notes. How dreary the place seemed, how limited his life, how futile it all was. He went to bed rather drunk, and in the morning it was worse, and attended by a headache.

The only thing he could do, he felt, as Delice scurried around him with hope again wafting her own hopeless aspirations, was to wait until Wednesday. On Wednesday, Jo might come round again. On Wednesday she might burst into tears and beg his forgiveness. On Wednesday, that was the day, the bus of love might arrive once more at the desolate By Request where his world had stopped.

But Wednesday came and went, and there was no sign of her; nor did she come the following Wednesday; nor the Wednesday after that. May turned into June, and the surge and bloom of summer left him dry and promiseless as a dud tuber.

This time, however, he managed to pull himself together. He didn't let himself go, he kept working. The catalogue was finished, the plans for Mackworth Scientific Films were complete. They only wanted a launch date. He even managed to go out a little. His old fears – advancing, retreating – seemed to have been to some degree banished by his martial education, for Jo had managed to make him, if not expert, at least adequately proficient. Trained soldiers, she had said, don't cower under a threatening sky, and he was more trained than most. (On the other hand, she had also taught, it is a foolish soldier who doesn't feel some fear, so it was as well he kept a foreboding or two in reserve.)

He met a woman at one of these parties. She was called Monica and she worked in public relations; a jolly girl, she took him under her wing and introduced him to her friends. He became fond of her – it wasn't the same as it had been with Jo, nothing could be – but it was colour of a kind. One evening after dinner, worked up by wine, they made love. It was not a success. Duncan had the curious feeling that Jo knew about it; she had this peculiar knack of knowing what he was thinking, even what he was doing. Eerie, really. It was a kind of sixth sense, or telepathy she supposed you could call it, and it was one of the things that made their relationship so strange, so important.

117

'I've always had it,' she had told him once. 'Don't ever try to hide anything. I'll know when you're lying.'

It had been one of the things, she said, that made her good at self-defence. She could anticipate; but it made her vulnerable because she knew too much.

At any rate, it upset Monica, who also sensed that Duncan wasn't with her.

'You're going away from me,' she told him as he tried to oblige her.

But like Cynara, Jo and her shadow kept falling on his memory in the darkened stranger-smelling bedroom and, at last, he had to give up.

It is a galling moment for a man. You feel hungry, you eat. You feel thirsty, you drink. You can do both, even if you feel neither. To induce erection in an unresponsive penis, however, is beyond anything except injections of papaverum, which are not always to hand, and would be ludicrous even if they were. And it requires a degree of understanding and self-confidence in a woman if she, too, does not feel in some way diminished at the response.

Monica was a nice girl. She did not casually sleep with men; but when she did she expected, she hoped, she prayed for some recognition of her attractiveness. None being forthcoming, she blamed herself as many women do; and wept. To try and soothe her, Duncan told her a little about Jo, but this was another bad move.

'What!' she cried, affronted. 'You mean you went to bed with me when you were in love with someone else? But that's disgusting. What did you want to do? Humiliate me?'

He denied the charge, of course; it was the last thing he wanted to do, yet he couldn't but agree with the general sentiment.

So that was the end of Monica. It was perhaps just as well.

In July, scientific films came to the rescue. Booth called up. Working and living alone, he had no idea of the patterns of other people's lives, so the hour of his call was entirely arbitrary. On this occasion, it was midnight.

He told Duncan that he was speaking from Pembrokeshire. Duncan received the news with sleepy surprise. Not that there was anything surprising about Pembrokeshire in itself; in fact, that was the point. It didn't have the ring of the more exotic locations which tended to be Booth's norm.

Duncan must have indicated something of it in his tones, for Booth answered almost defensively that there was nowhere better to watch the Atlantic grey seal. He was doing a recce for a documentary he was planning. 'A Year on Seal Island – the Resident and Tourist Seals of Selsey.' There was a programme (at least) or perhaps even a series on the subject, and some useful bird footage to be had as well, razorbills chucking out their young and so forth. He indicated, however, as he sometimes did, that he might need some kind of bridging finance. Would Duncan be interested in putting up a little money against the day when the programme was sold?

Duncan reflected. Booth's needs were by no means extravagant. Since he tended to do most of his filming by himself, there was no question of an expensive crew. It was simply a matter of stock and living expenses. On the other hand, his own financial situation was tight enough . . .

Still, all things considered, he felt he should help out; besides, there might be useful material for his film company which, encouraged by recent enquiries and more gee-ups from Reinacker, he had, yes, decided to start. Indeed, he was even thinking positively of giving up his practice and running it full time. The question was when, not if. He'd had enough of legalities. There was no law in love and no love in law. Nature was the thing.

And there was another reason. Pembrokeshire was where Duncan's grandparents had lived, and where he had spent his holidays as a child. He had hardly been back since they died. It was probably little changed now; he remembered a county of stony moors, bent trees, bare hills, desolate headlands, dangerous waters and dizzying cliffs . . .

He decided he would go to Pembroke himself. The change would do him good – he had made no plans for a holiday that year. The very thought of lying in bright sunlight on a beach without Jo beside him filled him with the most corrosive dismay.

No, Pembroke was the place. At least there would be other memories there, memories full of the mysterious bittersweetness of childhood, strong as love in their way, to supplant the images of Jo.

'All right,' he told the little man, 'I'll come up and have a look. Maybe I can find some cash. Where are you exactly?'

'Just outside St David's.'

'I know it well. My grandparents used to live near Tenby.'

'It'll be good to see you. Great if you can help out. There are seals everywhere . . . it's just asking for a programme . . . you know seals are at risk? They had the phocine virus last year. There's heavy metal in the North Sea. And now there's all this plastic – some beaches on the east coast there's more panty-liners than seaweed. But this place out here, it's perfect for 'em . . . hundreds of islands, storm beaches, sea caves . . . I went to a lighthouse fifteen miles out yesterday. Just a slab of rock sticking out of the Atlantic. It was awash with seals . . .'

'When are you planning to shoot?'

'I should think very early next year, mating time. I met this man they call the Captain. He says there's a particular female on Selsey Island. Hauls up on her own beach. Won't let the males near her. And, if she can, she drives them away from the other cows . . . Even tries to drive away a boat!'

'Formidable creature,' said Duncan. 'I'm surprised they haven't signed her up for a television chat show.'

'That's just what I mean. Isn't she a symbol or something? Sign of the times? An icon?'

Booth must have been reading up on contemporary topics

in order to further his connubial interests, thought Duncan. He'd never heard him use such terms before.

'You're talking like a media man,' he joked.

'I am a media man,' Booth was quite serious. 'This seal could be the making of us.'

'Our seal of approval,' suggested Duncan.

'Joke if you like, but I need the money. I'll be married soon.'

'Married?' Duncan was amazed. 'Anyone I know?'

There was a slight pause.

'She hasn't said yes yet,' Booth confessed. 'I haven't asked her yet.'

'"If you go in, you're sure to win",' said Duncan. 'Down on your knees. Give it a try.'

'It's different when you're sixty,' Booth told him. 'Still, I really think she likes me.'

He paused again. There was silence for a minute. Duncan thought they'd been cut off, or that Booth was working up to telling him her name.

'Hullo. Hullo . . .'

'I'm here.'

'Was there something else?'

Booth spoke very carefully, as if explaining something to a child.

'Did you know seals will do anything for crayfish?'

Twenty-Two

As he was poring over his map that evening, going over the old, familiar ground, working out where Booth would be shooting, there came a ring at the door.

He was not expecting anyone. Indeed, he was annoyed at being disturbed, for he intended to drive down to Pembrokeshire next day, and he had various pieces of business still to attend to. Grumbling, he pushed the map aside – he had a habit of grumbling to himself – and made for the front door.

'No peace for the wicked.'

He tended to grumble in platitudes which are the vernacular of grumbling.

Something, he did not know what, made him remember the drill for door opening. It was a habit that he had neglected of late; indeed, Monica had teased him about his caution and perhaps he had dropped it at the time; but now he peered through the spyhole in the recommended way, vigilant for assailants. There was nothing to be seen.

On the alert now, he put on the chain and opened the door, standing well back. Still there was no one in evidence.

'Who's there?' he asked firmly in the prescribed manner.

A tall man of military bearing stepped into view.

For some reason, prompted by optimism, he thought it might be the elusive officer who had first replied to his advertisement all those months away – it seemed almost a lifetime.

'Captain Smail?' he asked.

'Detective Inspector Hathaway.'

'Ah.'

The man showed his identification.

'May I come in?'

'Oh. Very well. I'm rather busy at the moment.'

'It won't take long, sir.'

Duncan fiddled with the chain. He always had trouble with it, especially if people were watching.

'Security conscious, are we, sir? Very wise these days.'

He led the policeman into his drawing room and offered him a chair.

'Ta, very much. It's about a Miss Lindup, sir. I believe you knew the young lady.'

He proffered a picture which was recognizably Jo but must have been taken when she was fifteen. Even that slightly out of focus, immature, thumb-printed image had the power to open the trapdoor of love again. Duncan could feel himself falling like Alice into Wonderland.

'What's . . . what's happened to her?'

'Nothing that we know of, sir. She just seems to have disappeared. We know that you knew her, because you both came into a police station three months ago about . . .' here the policeman looked at his notes '. . . about a parking offence.'

'Ah,' said Duncan, relieved and yet distraught. 'Yes. That was the last time I saw her. We had a bit of an argument and she went off in a taxi.'

'A taxi, sir. I see,' said the policeman, taking notes. 'Which direction did she go in?'

'Kensington.'

'I see, sir. Anybody else see her go off in the direction of Kensington?'

'No, of course not. I was outside a police station. Look here, Inspector, I'm a solicitor. You're not suggesting I . . .'

'We're suggesting nothing, sir. There's no suggestion of foul play at the moment. But you were seen having an argument. That's all we have to go on. Knew her well, did you?'

'Very well.'

'Having a relationship, were you?'

'She was teaching me self-defence.'

'Self-defence, eh? Well, well, well. Quite violent I should think that gets.'

'I was taught to avoid confrontation if possible.'

'But it isn't always possible is it, sir, to avoid confrontation – whether in the direction of Kensington or otherwise.'

'No,' Duncan admitted, 'no, in your job I suppose it isn't.'

This seemed to mollify the man a little.

'Sorry to ask all these questions, sir. Just routine.'

Duncan took the opportunity to ask a question of his own.

'How did you know she was missing?'

'She was reported missing.'

Ah, thought Duncan, her aunts no doubt. She had told him they sometimes asked her for money.

'Come to think of it, sir, if she was your teacher, why didn't you report her missing when she didn't turn up?'

'Because,' Duncan told him, 'because we *were* having an affair. I was in love with her but she just walked out. I tried to get in touch with her but . . . I thought . . . she didn't want to see me. Love's like that, you know.'

An idea struck him amidst his candour.

'There is one thing.'

'Yes, sir.'

'She did it once before. I finally managed to contact her by letter.'

'Letter, sir? You have an address?'

'Yes. Here it is . . .'

He gave the man Captain Smail's poste restante.

'And who's this Captain Smail? You asked me if I were he.'

'I've never met him. A friend of hers . . . colleague, I believe . . .'

'I see. Well, thank you very much, sir. I won't take any more of your time. You will let us know if she turns up?'

'I will.'

He showed the policeman out, but as he turned to go, he paused and turned again.

'Just one other thing, sir.'

'Yes?'

'How do you feel about the young lady now?'

'I love her with all my heart,' said Duncan unhesitatingly. 'The world seems completely pointless without her.'

'Thank you, sir,' said the policeman. 'That will be all. Good evening to you.'

As Duncan fiddled with the security chain, he peeped once more through the spyhole. The detective's black-mackintoshed figure, inflated by the lens, looked like a plumply-robed demonic pallbearer as he walked slowly down the steps.

'Carrying away my happiness,' Duncan thought. 'Come away, death.'

It was terrible to be still in love.

Twenty-Three

He woke with a start in the night. Something was banging somewhere. A window? A . . . burglar? Was this the crisis so long delayed? He sat bolt upright. He should be ready for it now.

To still the panic-state, there were formulae, patiently instilled. 'This is happening, it is real.' Breathe deeply. In, one-two-three. Hold, one-two-three. Out, one-two-three. This was what the SAS did before an operation.

Tap, tap, tap. It wasn't as loud as he had thought .

Trying to imitate the action of a tiger, he got out of bed, felt underneath it for the stout club he kept there – successor to the knobkerrie – and moved cautiously across the room. Surely no burglar would make such an obvious noise? The strange thing was, the sound seemed to be coming from the first floor, not from below. There could be no question of barricading the stairs in the prescribed manner, or of hurling furniture down on the assailant. The danger was already up on his level.

He trod softly out into the landing and saw with horror a dark shape spreadeagled nightmarishly against the outside of the window like a man-bat out of Bosch. Six months ago, he would have frozen, his mind refusing to believe what his eyes told him; but now, thanks to Jo's precepts, he felt able to control his alarm. All the same, he had the strongest instinct that there was something evil outside, vampire-like; something that could destroy him.

Come, come, he told himself. The SAS don't go jelly at the knees and talk about unearthly visitants. They get on with the job. They relax, they count one-two-three in, one-two-three hold, one-two-three out, and then they pounce. He thought about Jo and how she would be mistress of the situation, and it gave him strength.

He could make out a white face now, and an arm raised to strike the sash. Grasping his cudgel firmly, he sidled up to the window along the darkened wall. The distant streetlight only illuminated one side of the landing, and from outside he knew he would be invisible.

At the critical moment, he sprang out, club raised, and the figure gave a muffled cry, swaying perilously backwards. The noise he heard seemed to echo in his heart. Jo? It couldn't be Jo? The figure, as far as he could see, was dressed like a man; but there was no mistaking the tone.

'Jo!' he called.

'Let me in, stupid. I nearly threw a seven when you stepped out like that.'

He opened the window and she clambered in.

'Jo! What the hell are you doing?'

He wanted to take her in his arms and kiss her, but something held him back. He put down the ridiculous cudgel and looked at her. She started to peel off her woollen hat and tracksuit. The sweet light fragrance of her was making his head spin. Under the suit she wore nothing but a blue shirt and very short shorts. Fain would I kiss my Julia's dainty leg, which is as white and hairless as an egg.

'I need somewhere to stay,' she told him. 'I wouldn't have come to you if there had been anyone else.'

'Not come to me? But you must've known . . .'

'Must've known what?'

'That I . . .'

He hesitated. He didn't want to force the situation or make declarations of love too soon; better to wait and see what she wanted. Half of him was thrilled to see her; all the old hormones were charging round his bloodstream. Half of him was alarmed; hadn't he managed to live without her? Wasn't he going back into the tunnel?

'That you what?' she repeated.

'That I'd always be happy to help you. You're a friend,' he told her.

'A friend?' she smiled ruefully. 'Some friend, after the way I treated you.'

'Oh Jo,' he said, weakening and stepping towards her.

'No,' she told him, stepping back. 'None of that.'

He kicked himself for being too impetuous.

'Come downstairs to the kitchen,' he said. 'I'll make you a coffee. Then you can talk about it.'

Over coffee she told him that the police were after her. Her uncle had reported her for violence and she was on the run.

'Surely it's only his word against yours?' said Duncan.

'The aunts are on his side. They always were.'

'I'll represent you, of course,' he told her.

'I don't want representing. I just want to keep my head down for a while.'

'Wouldn't it be better to face the music?'

'You would say that, wouldn't you? I mean, being a lawyer. You're on the side of the law. It's different if . . .'

Her voice trailed off. If she were what? He didn't press her further. She was obviously under pressure of some kind.

'Why did you climb up like that?' he asked. 'There's a perfectly good bell. You might have killed yourself.'

'I didn't want to be seen, did I? They'll be looking for me and they know we were together – once.'

She said the word once so dolefully it gave him hope.

'There was a policeman round last evening,' he told her.

'There you are,' she said. 'I knew they would.'

'I think I persuaded him that I hadn't seen you for three months. I don't think he'll be round again.'

'I was reckoning on that,' she said. 'That's why I came here. But you can't count on anything with that lot.'

'I thought you were on the side of Law and Order.'

'So I am. But there's times when you have to take the law into your own hands, and the order too.'

'What d'you want to do?' he asked her.

There was no point in arguing legalities at this time of night, although he knew he would be in grave trouble with the Law Society if he were found to be harbouring a fugitive. Not that that need be a problem for much longer. The Scientific Film Association – if there were such a thing – would hardly strike him off the register.

'I wanted to say sorry,' she said. 'Sorry I ran away, sorry I didn't get in touch, sorry for letting you down. You must have hated me. Sorry, sorry, sorry.'

'Never,' he told her. 'Though sometimes I hated myself.'

She put a hand on his. It was cool and light as it rested on him; cool and light as a sundew which ate its visitors. The feel of it startled him out of all his good intentions.

'Jo,' he said suddenly.

Tears had started to his eyes. It was as if he were in pain.

'Don't,' she said. 'Not now.'

He swallowed.

'Not now? You mean . . . sometime.'

'I don't know, Duncan. Honestly. We should never have started it, never. Captain Smail, he give me, gave me such a hard time. It was unprofessional, Duncan. No wonder I was all confused.'

'What do you want?' he asked once more.

'I want to start again, Duncan. Do you think we can? I was happy when we started out. We both had knowledge to exchange. Do you think we can go back to that?'

He shook his head, doubtfully.

'You want to stay here, don't you?' he said.

'I've nowhere else, Duncan. I need to keep my head down for a bit. I wouldn't be no trouble.'

He didn't correct her although she used to tell him to. It was too late for corrections.

'I'll have to think about it,' he said. 'You put me in an awkward position.'

She smiled and started to put on her tracksuit again.

'What are you doing?' he cried.

'It's all right, Duncan. You don't have to spell it out. I'm an embarrassment to you, aren't I? I might get you into trouble.'

'It's not that. Really. It's just . . . I don't think I could bear to have you here and not . . .'

He stopped and waved his hands.

'And not what, Duncan?'

'And not have you here.'

She put her tracksuit down and came and sat beside him.

'Let's give it a try, Duncan. Hm? Just for a bit? Give it a try and we can review the situation. You would like me to be here, wouldn't you, Duncan?'

'Oh yes,' he said, 'I would, yes, very much indeed.'

'The trouble was,' she told him, 'do you know what the trouble was? The trouble was that I think I loved you. I warned you, didn't I? I find love very hard. It's very hard, Duncan. It's a room, like I said, without an exit. That's what I was afraid of. Very hard to cope with, that. No time to get off. It's grappling with an adversary what's bigger and stronger.'

'You don't mean me?' he asked incredulously. 'Not your adversary?'

'Of course not. It's love itself. It's something in you – I don't mean you, in me, that's bigger'n I am. And so I had to leave you. Oh, that hurt, Duncan, believe me. It hurt me as much as you. Do you know what I did when I was away? I read one of the poems you gave me, *The Ballad of Reading Gaol.*'

'Did I give you that?'

'Short memory, Duncan. I read that *Ballad* and I thought, fantastic. It really moved me. "The little tent of blue we prisoners call the sky." We're all prisoners, Duncan. We all have that little tent of blue, something to look up to and yearn for. You were my tent of blue, Duncan. And what did I do? When

I got my tent of blue, I tried to pull the bloody tent down, pardon my French. And that was the other thing I liked. For each man kills the thing he loves. You remember?'

Duncan nodded. He had never seen Jo like this. She was wound up, almost as if she were high on something, though of course she wouldn't be, it was anathema.

She read his mind.

'It's seeing you again, Duncan, makes me like this. Now listen.

> *"Yet each man kills the thing he loves,*
> *By each let this be heard,*
> *Some do it with a bitter look,*
> *Some with a flattering word,*
> *The coward does it with a kiss,*
> *The brave man with a sword."'*

'I remember it,' said Duncan. 'I once won a prize at school for reciting it. It's good. I love it.'

He had never seen the kitchen so bright, so absolutely awash with colour. The very bills on the mantelpiece sparkled like something out of an icon, and not a contemporary one either.

'I love it too, Duncan,' she continued. 'Thank you for showing me *The Ballad of Reading Gaol*. But it seems to me that poem's only got half the truth. If I were to rewrite that poem I'd say something like this: "For each man kills the thing he loves, but a woman does it quicker". You see? Please forgive me. Let's try and take the pressure off and see if we can't enjoy each other again.'

Later, as he was making up the bed in the spare room, Duncan remembered his projected visit to Pembroke. The trip, of course, was now out of the question. He must remember to call Booth. Then, just for a moment, he wondered whether Inspector Hathaway might not have been Captain Smail after all.

Twenty-Four

So began a sequence of days in which Duncan found himself, like Prometheus, in possession of his flame, but chained, and with his heart pecked out by the eagle of frustration.

Even so, it was a very great deal better than no flame at all, he told himself. Pain at least tells you you're alive. It is better than numbness.

Jo was busy round the house. He had not realized how obsessively tidy she was. It pained her to see towels not properly folded or his clothes not put in a drawer. She was fastidious about her own garments. Duncan secretly hoped he might find tights, bra, knickers, delicate whatnots draped across the racks in the drying cupboard, but there was no vestige of such things. It would have heartened him. He could have pressed them to his nose, questing for the tender aromatics of her body. He could have done with such associations and comforts.

The other thing that pained him was that she kept her door locked. Did she not trust him? He never mentioned it to her and tried to explain it away to himself by reference to her unfortunate childhood; but it hurt.

She seemed to be less worried about the police being after her; nevertheless she did not venture out much by day as far as he knew, except to go to Stefan, her coach in hypnotherapy, whom she saw once a week for a session. Soon, she said, she would be taking her diploma. She had said that before, he recalled. Stefan was a slow coach.

'Why don't you bring him round?' Duncan suggested one day. 'We could give him dinner.'

Jo immediately went on the defensive.

'I don't think it would be suitable,' she said. 'He's just a Hungarian.'

Sometimes she went to the gym for a work-out, but most of the time she spent reading from his library, or going through his film collection. From these researches, she would throw comments in the evening.

'I'd no idea sperm had such a hard time. It just shows, doesn't it?' or 'The pod of a fuchsia explodes pollen at speeds of up to seventy miles an hour.'

Some of these things he already knew but he evinced pleasant, even startled, surprise on being given the information.

'Really? Seventy miles an hour? It seems incredible – even unnecessary.'

He had delayed the launch of the film company for a little while longer to concentrate on her – she was a very energy-absorbing presence – but of course he would have to do something about it soon.

Meanwhile, twice a week now, they would train – always preceded by the relaxation session, which became more and more necessary for him as his tensions mounted.

'You *are* tense tonight,' she would say. 'Poor old Duncan. We'd better talk you below 10 again. You'll pull a muscle with tension like that.'

And down they would go, under the sea. These days she would feed in variations, doubtless learned from Stefan himself and, as ever, Duncan would find her voice overwhelmingly soporific.

One memorable night she had a new variant which wasn't Level 10 at all, nor even Level 20.

'You are lying on a beach, Duncan, the most beautiful beach in the world. You are lying on white sand, fine white sand, no more than powder but so soft, Duncan. You are naked. The sun gently warms your body. A warm sea stirs nearby

133

with waves that are no more than ripples. A warm breeze ruffles your hair. It's so gentle, Duncan, you can hardly feel it. There is nothing else except me, Duncan. I am with you on the beach. I lie down beside you, Duncan. It's so warm, so peaceful. We can feel the sun heating us so gently, on our arms ... our legs ... our chests, Duncan ... our stomachs ... our groin ... it is so warm there, Duncan ...'

Even in his drowsy state he could feel something stirring and it wasn't a hermit crab.

'Feel the sun there, it is like a soft hand stroking you, making you full of its gentle heat ... I am warm too, Duncan. I can feel the sun warming and stroking, and the rise and fall of the stroking, warm sea. I lean over, Duncan, and take you in my hands. I am caressing you with the gentle heat of the sun and the sea ... up and down ... so warm and full and up and down and ... gentle and ...'

He came with what seemed a fuchsia-like explosion and started up from his chair, mopping at himself in chagrin.

'Oh my God ... I'm so sorry ...'

'Don't be silly, Duncan. I wanted that to happen. I wanted to do it for you with my voice. I know it's been difficult for you. Just sit and relax. Take out the tension. Deep breaths. Take a spot on the wall and concentrate on it. That's right. Cut out all noises when I stop talking. You are feeling calm, heavy and peaceful. You can feel calm, heavy and peaceful whenever you feel like it. Later we will do Colour Codes to help you gauge degrees of danger. But now, Duncan, there is no danger; we are calm, heavy, and very, very peaceful.'

Twenty-Five

Some days now he did not go to work at all.

Delice, if her heart was heavy, was by no means calm and peaceful when he finally appeared. She muttered all morning and when he came back late after a long business lunch with a neighbouring lawyer, she could contain herself no more.

'I thought you were better,' she told Duncan, 'but now you moon around just letting everything go. I wonder I put up with it.'

He had made up his mind to tell her he was closing the practice.

'We're shutting up shop,' he said to her. 'I'm setting up in scientific films.'

He had made up his mind about it last night, having put out one or two more feelers. Jo was all for it. The costings were right, the business plan soberly hopeful. Without her encouragement he would never have done it, even now. There were too many pitfalls; but here he was winding up his business. He called Reinacker to tell him the news.

'Great,' he said. 'I'll pass it on to Tony. You, uh, don't need any backing? I'm kind of looking around.'

So that was what the American had been up to! The skids were under him and he'd been looking for options. Duncan had thought the producer had been less than deferential. Well, he did not need partners. He had a partner already, even though he felt sorry for the American.

'I'm all right at the moment,' he said. 'But I'll let you know.'

As for Delice, he knew there was a job waiting for her, but he still felt guilty. Still, what could he do?

Her face had dropped like a scone.

'What can I do?' he asked her.

She started crying. He did feel bad.

'I'll pay you compensation,' he said.

She shook her head.

'It's not that.'

'What is it?'

'It's you. I can't bear to see it happening. You've changed.'

'Changed?'

'You used to be so nice. Gentle.'

'Gentle? It was a front I put on because I was afraid of something.'

'Afraid? Afraid of what?'

'Something I dreaded happening.'

He was able to tell her now. It didn't matter. He was past all that.

'Everybody's afraid of something.'

'They are?'

What a terrible thought! All these years he had thought it was only him. No, no. They couldn't have felt the same way. The way he felt was acute. If everybody felt like him, they'd all be taking up self-defence.

'Mine was acute,' he said. 'A sense of foreboding.'

'Oh, Mr Mackworth. If only I'd known.'

This was dangerous. At any minute now she might become sympathetic.

'I'm sorry,' he said. 'I'll tell my friend Mr Burgeon at Burgeon and Dulcimer. He always said he wanted to steal you. I'm giving them all my business.'

He had had lunch with Burgeon and concluded the arrangements.

'I don't want to be stolen.'

She mopped her eyes. Her distress moved in him, perversely,

a spark of desire, evoking the Christmas near-miss. She wasn't a bad-looking woman. Pretty brown hair (now going a little grey), neat features behind the inevitable glasses, and of course the legs, good legs which she didn't make enough of. But she was like a fire that has been too long laid, although laid was perhaps not the best word in the circumstances. And she dressed badly. She wasn't plain but that was the impression you received.

He had overheard once a couple of electricians who came to fix their wiring, discussing her in a pub. Inevitably, one of them wondered if she was having it away with anyone.

'Christ, no. It'd be like opening an old book,' said the other.

It was a disgusting image. There were times, Duncan had thought, when he could understand the feminist point of view. But then of course there were women like Jo who could fend (or defend) for themselves. He wished he were with her now and wondered what she was doing. Strange that she hardly spoke to him of what she did by day. How secret, how cat-like she was in some ways. How exhilaratingly open in so many others . . . He forced his mind back to what Delice was saying.

'I fear for you, Mr Mackworth, I really do. You're going down the primrose path.'

His mind went back to that day in spring when Jo had let him make love to her on the flowery bank.

'Yes,' he said, 'I probably am.'

'Don't let things slip, Mr Mackworth, Duncan. Keep me on. I have this feeling . . .'

'Yes, Delice?'

'Foreboding really. You might be getting into deep water. Your whole life might just . . . fall apart . . .'

'I assure you, Delice, quite the reverse is the case. For the first time I feel a real centre. A firm centre, Delice, not a soft one.'

Her fondness for chocolates had often been a subject of reference. On this occasion she was not amused.

'I know it's a woman, Duncan. We women have an instinct

about these things. Let's just hope, though, it's not a hard centre. Let's just hope you don't crack up on it.'

'I don't see why I should. I have enough money to survive. The film company will help. The outlook seems particularly rosy.'

'Let's just hope you don't burn your boats,' she said.

'Well, I hope not, Delice,' he said as judiciously as he could. 'My boats, such as they are, I feel are non-flammable.'

He wanted to get back to Jo. If he had a whole Armada, he would burn it for her. However, when 5.30 came around, Delice was still at her desk, slumped over it like a ragdoll. He would not have been human if he hadn't sat her up, and given her a large drink of the sherry that he kept at the back of his bookcase. This seemed to revive her a little, especially when he filled her glass again; but when he talked about going, she drooped once more.

Finally, in despair, he suggested that they should go out to a pub. At least it would get her out of the office. She perked up again at this, and they walked down to the Anglesey Arms where they sat in a corner and drank champagne to the delight of the landlord. Duncan felt it might cheer her up.

'I dunno why we're drinking champers,' Delice said. 'Nothing to celebrate. Cheers!'

Her normally dusty meticulousness was beginning to fray at the edges but at least she was smiling. She smoothed her skirt, crossed her knees, showing her good legs at last to advantage, and asked for a packet of crisps.

'I don't want to get tiddly, do I?' she said.

Duncan thought she probably did, yet there seemed absolutely nothing he could do about it. He would have liked to have called Jo, but every time he looked at the telephone box there was someone in it. She would doubtless be cooking dinner for him as she normally did. He liked her cooking; simple, wholesome, with no 'wiggly bits'. She hated shellfish and offal.

He sipped sparingly. Delice gulped it down, looked at the

glass longingly until it was refilled, then gulped again. Finally, the bottle was finished and he stood up. Delice stood up too and then sat down again.

'Oops,' she said.

Her legs seemed to have lost their bones like the wives of some nineteenth-century king of Buganda. What on earth was he going to do? The telephone was now occupied by a gesticulating Iranian who looked as if he might be disputing a finer point of Zoroastrian theology, or it could be the price of Semtex; either way, there seemed no possibility of it ending.

Delice sat and giggled.

'I don't drink that much,' she told him. 'Much.'

One or two people began to look in her direction.

'You'll have to put me in a taxi,' she said. 'I'll be all right, really I will. It's my legs have turned to cotton.'

Duncan got up and walked to the road. At last luck was with him; a cab was passing. It stopped and he spoke to the driver.

'I'll just get my friend,' he said. 'She's inside.'

When he returned to the pub, there was pandemonium. Delice was sobbing hysterically and crying out like Rachel weeping for her children. A group of people were trying to comfort her.

'He's gone,' she kept shouting. 'He's left me, the bastard.'

The landlord, seeing Duncan, approached him sternly.

'You'll have to get her out of here double-quick,' he said. 'I can't have a disorderly house.'

Delice now spotted him and became extravagant.

'Don't leave me,' she shouted. 'Don't ever leave me. Comfort me with apples for I am sick of love.'

She floundered about like a sea lion on the ice floe. Some of the women turned on Duncan as he tried to lift her to her feet.

'You bastard,' one hissed. 'What have you given her?'

'Trying to get her drunk so he could have his way. Pathetic!' said another.

'Left her in the lurch, have you? Hope she cuts your balls off,' said a third.

Half dragging, half carrying, he propelled Delice towards the waiting taxi while she tried, not altogether unsuccessfully, to smother him with kisses.

'I can't take her like that,' said the driver.

'Oh come on,' said Duncan, producing a tenner. 'She only needs to go to Earls Court. She's just a bit jolly, that's all.'

'You'll have to come too. She'll never get out otherwise.'

Duncan had to agree there was some justice in what he said.

'Oh very well,' he said. 'What's your address, Delice?'

'Thirty-four Earlth Court Thquare.'

Rather surprisingly, drink had brought out a lisp instead of a slur. As they went on their way, Delice started to become fulsome in the back.

'Not thafe in takthis, that'th me,' she said, pressing her thin chest against him as the taxi went round a corner and fingering his thigh remorselessly.

'Please don't do that,' he told her.

'I wath only playing inthy minthy thpider,' she said petu-lantly and started weeping again.

The journey up to her top-floor flat was a nightmare, but at last they toppled through the front door, and Duncan was able to stretch her out on her sofa.

'I'll make you some coffee,' he said. 'But first I'd like to use your telephone if I may.'

'Where am I?' she suddenly shouted. 'Help!'

'You're at home,' he told her. 'Everything's all right. You just had rather a lot to drink.'

She seemed to quieten down while he went to the telephone and dialled. The number rang and rang but there was no answer. He dialled again. Still no reply. He turned to speak to Delice but she had gone. A sense of nightmare gripped him.

'Delice?'

'In here,' came the reply. 'Come and find me.'

Her voice suggested she had recovered a little.

He walked across to the open door of the bedroom. She was lying on the bed dressed only in bra and stockings, striking a travesty of what might be taken for a seductive pose.

He suddenly felt a terrible sadness, not just for her or himself, but for the whole condition of humanity. It was the absurd suspender belt that touched his heart. She must have been wearing it all day.

'I'm so sorry,' he said.

'What will you think of me tomorrow?' she asked, gathering up bedclothes to hide herself.

'More than I thought of you this morning,' he said. 'Goodnight, Delice.'

'A kiss,' she said. 'Just one.'

He leant over and kissed her cheek. She smelt of champagne, smudged lipstick and loneliness.

'Poor Duncan,' she said. 'I hope you'll be all right.'

Twenty-Six

'You smell of champagne and smudged lipstick,' said Jo when he at last reached home. 'What sort of time d'you call this?'

She was sitting in his drawing room reading *Jane Eyre*. This in itself was a relief. He had been half-expecting her not to have been there at all.

'I've had a ghastly evening,' he said. 'Let's not have a row.'

'Oh that's good, Duncan. You come home late, supper's ruined, don't even telephone and you say let's not have a row. I wasn't going to have a row as it happened. I was relaxed and peaceful. Why should you think I might want to have a row?'

He took a deep breath. There was no point in saying he'd called.

'Well, the trouble with you sometimes, Jo, is you can't see a handle without experiencing an irresistible desire to fly off it.'

There. He'd said it. He'd been saving it up for some time.

'What?'

She was looking at him with sparkling eyes. There might almost be a tear in them.

'You can't see a handle without experiencing a desire to fly off it,' he repeated.

To his amazement she was smiling.

'That's good, Duncan. I like that. You can't see a handle without experiencing an irresistible – don't leave that out, that's very Duncan – an *irresistible* desire to fly off it.'

'You like it?'

She laughed.

'Oh, Duncan, you are a funny old thing. Do you really think of me like that?'

'You can be a bit . . . volatile . . .'

She laughed again.

'What? Volatile? Do you really think so? I must tell that to Captain Smail.'

'Not in your work,' he said quickly. 'You've always been absolutely professional. But in your private life . . . perhaps it's just with me . . . perhaps I make you tend towards the labile.'

'Labile? I don't like that word, Duncan. What's it mean?'

'It means volatile.'

'Well why use another word when volatile's so good? Labile's rude. The Victorians didn't give the ladies sal labile when they fainted. It would be disgusting. They gave them sal volatile.'

'Well, perhaps that's what I make you tend towards.'

'I do get migraines sometimes. But that's not unusual. People get migraines, it doesn't mean they're volatile.'

'Of course not.'

'I think it's because I've never been with anyone like you before. It throws me sometimes. It's a whole new world. Living like this; books, science, art, music . . . You ought to see the place I grew up. No wonder I'm volatile. But never call me that other word, Duncan, because that's absolutely revolting.'

'I'll make a note of it.'

'And now, Duncan, I expect you're wondering why I'm not cross with you tonight, even though I *am* just a lodger . . .'

'You're far more than a lodger,' he told her. 'You're my guest.'

'Lodger's more independent,' she said. 'I'm paying you with lessons. I give you far more time than you pay me for.'

There was some truth in that, although the extra time was spent in other ways than training.

'Anyway,' he asked, 'why aren't you cross with me?'

'It's your house, Duncan, it's your life . . . I would have no right to be cross . . . except of course for the spoilt dinner which *did* get me a little volatile at the time but it soon passed. No, Duncan, the reason I didn't get cross . . . even though you *were* late and did turn up with lipstick all over your collar . . . was . . . guess . . .'

He laughed.

'Because . . . you trust me . . .'

'Not absolutely, Duncan; but I have no right to, remember. We happen to share the same roof, that's all. I'm jealous, you see, so I find it difficult to trust absolutely.'

'I should like to have you jealous about me.'

'That's unkind, Duncan. You don't want to make me jealous, do you? Jealousy is a terrible thing. It's like a band round your chest. It's like a fever in your brain. Don't make me jealous, Duncan.'

'I won't. I'd just like to be in a position to be able to.'

'Put that away, Duncan. Put it away where you put that word I didn't like which I can't bring myself to say. Where were we?'

'I was querying.'

'You were wrong with that last guess. One more. Go on.'

'You weren't cross because . . . you don't care what I do.'

'Oh, Duncan. Now that was mean. That was below the belt. That was a palm-punch to the nose. I do care for you, but it has to be like you were a friend because it doesn't work the other way and we need to be together. We do need that, Duncan. I know these things.'

She held out her hand and he took it. He wanted to kiss her, touch her, but he knew the initiative would have to come from her – though, as she had taught him in the classroom, some initiative must reside with him. He mustn't be an object.

'Well,' he said at last, breaking the tension, being a subject, 'I've had my two guesses. Why weren't you cross?'

She smiled.

'I've been following you, Duncan.'

144

'Following?'

'I've had you under surveillance.'

'You're joking.'

He was genuinely shocked.

'You mean . . . following me?'

'I been doing it for days. There's hardly a moment of your day I don't know about. I even come into the office when you're not around.'

'Come into the office?'

'I sometimes stop the bikers. It's two floors up. I say I work for you and they give me the envelope or whatever.'

'But that's outrageous. I'll speak to their . . .'

'Don't speak to anyone, Duncan. It's all down to me. I do it because I care for you as a friend. I do it to be of potential assistance if you was to get mugged or something. And I do it to check up on your street awareness. You see? I hardly let you out of my sight, Duncan, and that's a fact.'

'But I've never seen *you*.'

'Ah.'

She smiled a secret smile.

'That's training,' she said. 'That's down to Captain Smail. He's got a jungle warfare bloke who teaches tracking and disguise. Fellow called Croucher. Gives me the creeps. Suitable name for a man in his line of business. I've noticed people have suitable names. I call it Lindup's Law of Names. Feel like a lesson now? I could teach you surveillance.'

'No, thank you,' said Duncan, crossly. 'I . . . I don't know what to say. I'm disturbed.'

'Who's flying off the handle now? Just because I take an interest in your welfare doesn't seem to me to call for disturbance. Gratitude would be much more what I would have expected.'

'How would you like it if I followed you?'

'I would be flattered. And you'd be lucky.'

'Lucky?'

'My senses are honed, Duncan. You've probably noticed.

They are; I have a sixth sense. I would know if you were following me.'

'I suppose I should have known myself. I tell you, I'll look out for you now. Mind you, you won't need to come to the office much more. You know we spoke of it the other day? I told Delice today we were closing down.'

'I know.'

'How on earth? . . .'

'I was in the pub, Duncan. She was telling the world about it when you went to get a cab.'

'I didn't see you,' he said, hopelessly.

This was all too much.

'I know. I was dressed as a bystander. When you got the taxi, I came home and cooked dinner. It's only cheese-and-potato pie, Duncan. Would you like it now?'

Twenty-Seven

'These wonderful places are at our back door,' said Booth. 'I bet you're sorry you couldn't join me.'

He was just back from a rush job in the Camargue, but he was speaking about his recce on Selsey Island. Duncan gave Jo a look. He wasn't sorry, considering what had happened, but his face framed a suitable expression, and after all he could have been sorry if it hadn't been for Jo.

'Very sorry,' he said. 'Something came up at the last minute.'

Jo started to giggle.

'Birds,' Booth continued. 'I've travelled a bit but I've never seen such colonies. Kittiwakes, razorbills, guillemots . . . the cliffs are almost white in places . . . in summer the young are ready to fly . . . and from these ledges, three inches wide sometimes, one hundred, two hundred feet up, the parents just . . . push them off! If the young are flying before they reach the sea, they're fine. If they're not, they drown.'

'They don't have any mature students living with Mum?' asked Duncan.

Jo kicked him under the table.

'Certainly not,' said Booth. 'As for the seals, there's a resident population through the year of about thirty, and at pupping time – between September and January – it can go up to two or three hundred. Now that's a fascinating thing. It's like trippers invading Cornwall. There's quite a drain on the resources. Each seal eats at least ten kilograms of fish a day. There's lots of human parallels here.'

'And when do they mate?' asked Jo, who didn't like fish.

'Just a week or two after pupping.'

'That's not very human. And not very nice either. You'd think they'd be more dainty.'

'That's what this odd female reckons. Not that she's pupped, we think. But she won't have any of it. The Captain says she drives away the bulls when they come near. Of course, I haven't seen it because they're not pupping now. That's why I want to be there, soon as I can, in early January. December would be best.'

'Why can't you go there now?'

'I have to finish this World Wildlife project in Lapland. The Russians have been really fouling it up. Mining, nuclear waste . . . it can't wait.'

Booth had called in from Colliers Wood where he was staying en route for the North Cape.

'How much more do you need?' Duncan asked.

'Oh, I don't know. About £5,000 should cover it. I'm already over the overdraft limit on this other job.'

'I've just sold my business,' said Duncan. 'You can have the money. But I'd like exclusive rights to the footage once it's been shown.'

'You've got it,' replied Booth.

'Hold on a minute,' said Jo.

Booth looked at her curiously.

Duncan had told him that Jo would now be acting as his part-time assistant and, knowing how protective Booth was about anything that affected his work – even out-takes that might be used commercially – he was rather expecting some close questioning about her qualifications. But Booth seemed to take it very calmly, almost as a matter of course; as well he might, thought Duncan. Jo could be exceedingly efficient when she chose, and already she had made herself useful, busying herself on the administrative side in areas which he himself found tedious: VAT and income tax, book-keeping, dealing with photographic houses and print shops, compiling lists of potential customers . . . and now here she was querying the financial arrangements!

Booth looked discomfited at having his deal interrupted. Funny, though, thought Duncan; he himself is looking sharper these days; smarter too. Did he have some pretty Myfanwy or Angharad tucked away in St David's? Was that why he was so keen on staying a year in Selsey?

'What is it?' Booth asked her. 'What's the problem?'

'How much have you budgeted for the job?' Jo enquired.

'About £15,000.'

'But it'll be useless if you don't get the extra £5,000.'

'Not useless but . . . not as sensational as it could be. We need the mating season. I want to see what effect this female has on the males' harems. Could be fantastic, red hot.'

'Then I think we should have a share in the television sale.'

'Jo!' exclaimed Duncan.

'Yes?'

'I think that's fair,' said Booth hurriedly.

'Fifty per cent of something is better than a hundred per cent of damn-all,' said Jo.

'So I've always been led to believe,' said Booth. 'What about twenty-five?'

But it had been fifty in the end.

When he had gone, Duncan remonstrated with her.

'That was uncalled for.'

'Uncalled for? I was making us money.'

'Yes, but . . . I have money, he hasn't. He's as poor as a churchmouse in a multiple parish.'

'Don't be afraid of hurting, Duncan. You mustn't be squeamish. Eyes and testicles . . .'

'He's not an assailant, for goodness sake. He's a friend.'

'Anyone who wants money off you's an assailant in my book,' said Jo. 'You ought to be glad you've got me on your side. You ought to be glad I've developed an interest, even if I draw the line at your creepy-crawlies.'

Arachnids and orthopters had been one area of knowledge that Jo had jibbed at. Playing around one day, she had unfortunately started on 'Arachnid Trapping Fly'. Seven-foot muggers held no terrors for her, but she was afraid of spiders.

That he could understand.

The spider and the fly had been one of his father's greatest triumphs, and Duncan could comprehend her fear because he had experienced it himself, made to watch it by the great man.

A simple enough, everyday scene. Nothing exotic, or something you couldn't see any day in the country. But the way his father had shot it made it seem like something out of a horror film. You actually identified with the fly, a rather charming innocent, bumbling sort of creature. Bumbling about, it had caught its leg in a web as a man might become entangled in a bramble.

At first it seemed not too worried. It lifted itself round and had a good look. It prised at itself quite casually with another leg. It flapped a little in an experimental sort of way. Puzzlement seemed to give way to irritation. It whirred and leg-lifted some more. It tugged and heaved, becoming a little more entwined. A measure of desperation at last seemed to set in, as though it sensed an impending danger.

Then, abruptly, heart-stoppingly, the spider appeared at the top of the frame; huge, evil, ugly, implacable. It stood poised for a long moment and then it dropped with ghastly speed towards its victim. And now the fly really began to panic. The spider paused again, just out of reach of the flailing wings, waiting for the fly to exhaust itself, to come to terms with its fate, to acquiesce. And, sure enough, the moment came. The fly's wings stopped beating, its whole body seemed to bow submissively before its fate, and the spider pounced with a terrible numbing bite. The fly stirred a little, twitched and fell still.

You felt completely drained when you watched it. All life

was there. And Duncan knew, had known when he was seven years old, how it would be when the end came, the awful inertia, the terrible submission.

'You ought to be glad,' Jo said again, bringing him back with a little tap on the shoulder.

'I *am* glad,' he said.

He was. He wanted her on his side, but he wanted her more on his front, riding him like the Charge at Omdurman, so he could forget these memories of fear that suddenly welled up when he thought he'd forgotten them for good.

'And now I think it's time we went down to Level 10 again,' she said. 'There's tension in you. You'll pull a tendon next. You see, Duncan, I always know. There's no corner of your mind I can't see into.'

Twenty-Eight

So the summer passed. Lessons, Level 10, the fine-tuning of the film company (summer perhaps was not a good time to start and so the launch was postponed), sporadic research on advertising agencies which Jo herself would never go into – she called them satanic mills – meals out, meals in; a closed, over-close, unjoined association in which, it seemed to him, desire was turned to some darker substance that accumulated, throbbed and mounted like a whitlow. All this was soon to end.

One evening, uncharacteristically late, walking through Notting Hill to the bus stop after seeing a film called *Bad Risk* she had particularly wanted to go to – it featured self-defence techniques – walking on the outside of the pavement on a September night of curious heat, after an Italian meal and two glasses of Est! Est! Est!, it happened.

'Yellow,' she said suddenly.

She had taught him the Colour Code a couple of weeks earlier.

'This is a system,' she had said, as he yearned for her in her blue trainer-trousers and her loose-fitting jacket above the light-grey sweater (convex when she wasn't wearing it through the constant pressure of her breasts), 'this is a system to mentally gauge your situation and to cut down wastage of valuable seconds in response.'

'Right,' he said. 'Is this the SAS system?'

152

'This is the SAS system simplified for the layman.'

Lay man, he thought. Ah me!

'This is the SAS Colour Coding,' she said.

He had to admit that, whatever new subject she introduced, she knew her stuff. Whoever had taught her, Eddie or Smail or a whole army of mercenaries, had taught her well. Her theory was excellent, her practice beyond reproach, and she kept studying. She had a whole pile of books in her room – he had at last managed to peep in – and video cassettes which she played on the recorder he had bought her.

'White,' she told him, 'is unprepared. You're watching TV, reading a book, eating your dinner. You've switched off. You will take at least three seconds, probably more, to react. You are, in a word, unready.'

'Like Ethelred,' said Duncan.

'Please don't interrupt, Duncan,' she was like a priestess when she instructed. 'The next stage, what we call the minimum condition, is Yellow. In Yellow, we are alert, Duncan, prepared for the possibility of attack, and prepared to do something about it. What do we do, Duncan? Responses.'

'We keep our eyes peeled.'

'And . . .'

'We keep eyes in the backs of our heads.'

'Correct. We maintain a constant 360-degree watchfulness, taking in strangers, anyone who's getting too close, strange cars and the people inside them. We maintain a dominant position. We swing wide around corners. And . . .'

'We keep on the outside of the pavement.'

'Right. We can maintain a state of Yellow constantly. If we are attacked while in Yellow, it takes only 1.5 seconds to react. But now, Duncan, we have a specific threat and we move into Orange. We are expecting attack now. A car is following us with intent. Two muggers block our path. We must concentrate, *concentrate*, Duncan, are you concentrating?'

'Yes, Jo.'

He was concentrating on her bottom as she leaned forward.

It was the most glorious work of the Creator, surpassing, he thought, the beauty of the flower or the majesty of the redwood tree. You could worship a bottom like that. It should be placed in a shrine. Haydn should have written an oratorio to it.

'Good. We must concentrate until the matter is resolved. We must be aware of everything around us and avoid what we call the tunnel effect. We must display confidence but avoid conversation with our potential assailants.'

'Why?'

'It lets them get too close. It slows us down. There are, of course, exceptions to the rule but on the whole, like the old slogan, talk costs lives.'

'But jaw-jaw is better than war-war, surely?'

'Are you taking this lesson or am I, Duncan?'

'You are, Jo.'

'Then kindly don't interrupt. I'd like to see you jaw-jawing with a drug-crazed junkie with a knife in his hand. Where were we?'

'Orange.'

'Right. We can only keep in Orange for a limited time. It is high tension stuff, Duncan. Fighter pilots who have to fire in a split-second are trained to stay in Orange for minutes on end, but even they cannot do it indefinitely. They would burn up.'

'So we can either go back to Yellow if things sort themselves out. Or what?'

'Red, Duncan. Things are clearly getting ugly. This is no time to stand and stare. Now's the time to rend and tear. Act positively and *immediately* now, Duncan. Once you're in Red, you must pull the mental trigger. Rip testicles, gouge eyes, if you must. This is them-or-you time. We will practise interaction and I will be creating scenarios of violence which together and/or singly will be overcome.'

How he wished now that he had spent less time thinking of what are, after all, only fatty deposits and musculature and more time practising his lightning responses, for there on the Notting Hill pavement in front of them loomed two large black men who showed no signs of moving over to let them pass.

'Orange,' she said, and swung out beyond him into the narrow street they had used as a short cut.

Two figures moved out of the shadows onto the pavement in front of them. He hadn't even noticed they were there, but she must have sensed them seconds ago.

He looked around – mustn't have tunnel vision. There were few lights on. The little street was more like a mews, really. It seemed full of dark lock-ups and hopeless little specialist garages. What were they doing walking in such a place at such an hour? What did she in the woods so late a furlong from the castle gate? It was uncharacteristic of her; but it was too late to question or debate.

They *were* black men. He could already tell from that distance; the blacker darkness under the shadows; the impression of two burly tracksuits, tipped with trainers, with a swaggering, menacing life of their own.

The bigger of the two men advanced swiftly towards Duncan, as the other made for Jo.

She had just time to hiss 'Knees' at him before the men were at their muggers' business of blocking their way. Even out of the corner of his eye, he could sense that Jo had somehow managed to distance herself from her man, but there was no possibility of him evading the bulk that loomed ahead of him. Events, as Jo had often warned him, had simply moved too quickly.

'Hand over your wallet, fucker,' said the black man, 'or you're dead meat.'

Even in the adrenalin rush, Duncan was surprised at the tiredness of the formula. However, he supposed it must work. At last, his training began to creak into action. He retreated at an angle of 45 degrees from his assailant and started to glide backwards again, getting off the line.

'Stay where you are, dickhead,' said the black man, making a grab at him which Duncan evaded.

The black man produced something that glittered in the darkness. It made Duncan horribly afraid, but he simply could not give in with Jo at his side. The small amount of trouble he was causing, however, was enough to deflect the attention of Jo's adversary. He had half-turned his face to look at what was going on, and that was enough for Jo. She sent her palm crashing against the man's nose, causing it to make a noise like a broken pencil, then she sent her right foot, with toe upturned in the recommended manner, smashing into the thug's left kneecap.

'Aaaargh,' yelled the thug, and went down, clutching his face and leg.

It was Duncan's man's turn to look aside, and Duncan, taking his cue, sent his own shoe into the man's knee. Not quite high enough to incapacitate him, but sufficient to give Duncan a nasty jar to his toes. It also made the fellow absolutely furious.

'Oh you would, would you, fucker,' he said. 'Well, now I'm going to let the shit out of you.'

It was not a pleasant image, and Duncan was hard put to know what to do. There was a wall on one side of him and the man on the other. All the gliding in the world wasn't going to get him out of this one. The man, however, made the mistake of playing with him, feinting at him with the knife, making a mock lunge or two. Then suddenly, his face contorted and he too sank to the ground as a tremendous blow caught him on the seventh vertebra.

Duncan was just wondering whether to stifle his squeamishness and kick the man hard in the balls when he felt Jo's hand upon his shoulder.

'Run,' she said. 'Now.'

But it was too late. The man who had originally made for her, getting to his feet with astonishing speed, caught her a fearful blow across the small of the back which spun her round, causing her to fall heavily against the wall. Duncan could see that she was hurt even though she made no sound.

Everything seemed to happen very quickly after that. The other, taller man was up again. How he had survived Jo's attack was a mystery to Duncan. Perhaps the sheer bulk of the man had helped protect him. Perhaps he was high and felt no pain. Anyone of lesser stature would surely have given up the ghost. The two of them, horribly alive, now closed in on Duncan.

While one caught him a tremendous crack on the head, the other struck him very hard in the stomach, and he keeled over, retching on the pavement, passing in and out of consciousness.

The smaller of the two black men wanted to kick his face in with his good leg there and then, but the bigger fellow had other plans.

'Forget 'im,' he said. 'We'll do 'im later. Get the girl. We'll 'ave some fun.'

They seized Jo where she half-stood, half-sat, slumped against the wall, and pulled her into a little side alley where there were no houses, only garage doors and workshops. She tried to struggle but she was too weakened by the attack. Duncan watched through a veil of pain and shame, the comings and goings of an uncertain consciousness doing nothing to ease the knowledge that, had it not been for him, she would have made an easy escape.

They tore off Jo's skirt – she had dressed for an evening out, and Duncan had said he liked her like that sometimes, it made him feel she was more than simply his instructor – though he cursed himself now for the fuel it gave to their assailants.

Even in her pain and weakness she fought tigerishly, lacerating the face of the big man, who seemed impervious to trauma.

Then they pulled off her shirt and while the big man held her, the smaller fellow started squeezing her breasts, those that had been so buoyant under the tracksuit, once so proud, now so vulnerable – while the big man ripped off her tights and started unbuttoning his trousers.

Jo screamed now. It was not a professional scream. It was the scream of a little girl who has been assaulted by her uncle but was never allowed to make a sound. The noise, though substantial and piercing, seemed curiously deadened by the surrounding wood and was soon stifled by the black men who bound her shirt across her mouth.

She was now virtually naked, and was clearly in shock. Her body thrashed palely around in the darkness, flapping like a landed shark.

Duncan realized that his bouts of consciousness were becoming longer, that, yes, he ached and he hurt, but he was again in control of himself. He had to do something now, instantly, or it would be too late. There was something he saw in the shadows by the wall. He reached out and found himself clutching a length of exhaust pipe, no doubt idly left out by one of the mews garages. It might be rusty, it might shatter in pieces, but it was all he had.

The two men were concentrating totally upon the girl. The bigger one was even now about to penetrate her, so they did not see Duncan rise up like an avenging crusader and smite the mugger with all his might on the back of his head. The black man fell back with a strange, bubbling gasp. The other mugger took one look at his friend, another at Duncan's length of iron, and decided to run for it. The first man, incredibly, managed to pull himself up; and, after a minute or two, he dragged himself away.

Jo lay there with tears streaking her beautiful face and an unforgettable look in her eyes.

'You saved me,' she said. 'I love you, Duncan.'

'It was my fault,' he said. 'You would've escaped without me. You saved *me*.'

'We saved each other,' she said.

He swayed as a remnant of his faintness overcame him.

'You're hurt,' she said.

'It's not too bad. And you?'

'I hit my head,' she said. 'That was the trouble. I half passed out.'

'Me too.'

'Take me, Duncan.'

'Home? Of course.'

'No, no. Now. I want you. Now.'

'Now? Here?'

'I want to feel you inside me. Not my uncle, not those animals, but oh it's so wonderful, Duncan . . . just you.'

He made love to her painfully in the breathing darkness while the police cars and the fire engines and the ambulances wailed up and down, to and fro, in the forests of the Notting Hill night. It was an act of sweetness set off by pain, an oriental supper of the senses. The moon rose and threw pearls and diamonds about them.

Presently they rose up and, arm in arm, limped back towards South Ken.

Twenty-Nine

Lessons and lovemaking with reiterated visits to Level 10 were again the order of the autumn, though there was even less emphasis on the film business at this stage. It came a very poor third, postponed again. Even Reinacker, it seemed, had given up.

Every day Duncan would make breakfast and take it up to Jo in bed; fresh orange juice, muesli and brown wholemeal toast. She rarely touched coffee except at Luigi's where she would only have the weakest of cappuccinos; and in the morning it had to be Harrogate tea because they don't know how to make tea in the south.

'You spoil me,' she would say, smiling her panther's smile, and indeed he did.

There was nothing he would not do to keep her indulged. It was an art of its own, Jo-indulging; for there was no knowing when she would slip from the pinnacle of appeasement and come hurtling down, all tiles and temper.

'Bed-crumbs,' she would say, he could imagine her saying, crossly, 'I hate bed-crumbs.'

And he would know that it was his fault for bringing trays of food into the bedroom even though she had said the evening before that she loved it. Far from being infuriating, however, it merely served to sustain and even heighten his interest in the pursuit. Had it been a low art, unattended by despair and punishment, there would have been no sense of struggle, no triumph at the very top.

During all this time, though, she was benign and Duncan was almost drunk with happiness. His face found expressions of pleasure it never knew it had.

This was love indeed, a hard drug; but it was not after all the perfect love that casteth out fear, because he felt fear again now, a concentrated kind, not vague at all, really. It was the fear of loss and it was the greatest fear of all. Was fear, then, also an addiction, he wondered sometimes, was that why just when I think I've got rid of it, it returns with its surge of adrenalin? Is that my craving?

He tried to put it to the back of his mind, however, and Jo had pastimes to help him do it, sometimes varying the lessons with her version of hide and seek.

It had been a game that had given him the most terrible nightmares as a child, but now it was magically transformed into a game of love. That was the clever thing about Jo; on the upside, she could do these things.

'Shall we play the game?' she would say, eyes sparkling, her lips slightly puckered forward in a purse that seemed to beg a kiss.

It was her energy and enthusiasms that carried him along; he couldn't resist it. It made anything else seem milk and watery.

'Shall we play the game?'

To begin with, it would be through the house or garden. He would give her a count of forty, and then call the old formula: 'Ready or not, here I come!' Then he would start the hunt, the old excitement singing in his blood.

It wasn't a large house, but she contrived to make it seem so. Sometimes she was impossible to find. And if he did locate her, ah then!, she would reward him by letting him make love to her where she lay or crouched or stood. She did not move from the position he found her in. It was her pleasure not to.

Then it was his turn to hide. She would give him a full minute, sometimes longer, and he would contrive the most ingenious concealments. He would wait there, heart

161

pounding, the old atavistic dread of being caught mingling with his childhood memories of panic, recalling how as a young boy he would close his eyes and wait in the open, reasoning that if he could not see, it followed that he could not be seen. And then the frightening hands would come, squeezing round his throat . . .

'It's unfair,' he would protest. 'You were watching.'

But she would only shake her head and laugh. If she found him, it was up to her to decide on reward for effort, or forfeit. Later, as they exhausted the possibilities of the house, the game took them out of doors. At first, these were neighbourhood games – using the locality as a larger version of their old arena. The rules were strictly defined. You couldn't cross the road or go into strangers' houses, though shops were fair game. The area covered was no more than a block.

She still managed to hide in such a way that he could claim his reward on finding her. It added a particular relish to the game to know he would enjoy her in the corner of a deserted basement or in the gardener's hut of the communal gardens. At the same time, it seemed to increase the wildness of the game, to heighten the tension of waiting to be found, and the shock of the encircling hands . . .

But once again, they ran out of places to hide, even on this larger scale, and the rules of the game changed once more.

'I'll count up to a hundred,' she told him. 'And then I'll come and find you.'

'Find me? But where?'

'Anywhere you like.'

'But . . .'

He flapped his hands vaguely. You couldn't have a game like that. The board was too large. He told her so.

'That's what you think,' she said. 'Don't you think I'll find you?'

'How can you?' he asked. 'I might go anywhere.'

'Do that,' she told him. 'If I haven't found you by six o'clock, you get the prize.'

'Anywhere?' he asked her again. 'Anywhere in town?'

'Or out of it. But let's say, if you're nervous . . .'

'I'm not nervous,' he interrupted. 'I just don't want to make it impossible for you.'

'That's my problem. I know you, Duncan, remember. I should think I know you better than you know yourself.'

'Well, all right. If you're sure . . . It just seems a bit one-sided.'

'Don't you want the prize, then, Duncan?' she asked.

Of course he wanted the prize. He wanted it more than anything in the world, more than the respect of his peers or the dignity and peace that are the ripe fruits of patient avarice.

'Very well,' she told him. 'I shall count up to one hundred and then I shall come after you.'

She turned her back on him and started counting. He had learned enough from her instruction to know that there wasn't a second to lose. Without further ado he seized an umbrella – there seemed to be rain in the offing – and hurried down the front steps. He had no idea where he was going to go, but his first instinct was to head for the underground station.

As he walked up towards Gloucester Road, the first drops of rain began to fall. A minute must have passed. She would see him as soon as she came out – the road was long and straight. He started to run; and then he heard the familiar diesel warble of a taxi.

Miraculously it had its FOR HIRE light on and he waved frantically.

'Where to, guv?'

Duncan gestured expansively.

'Anywhere.'

He got in and the driver slid the glass partition. Duncan looked behind him. Far down the road a figure was rounding a corner, was even now breaking into a run. He was seized with panic.

'Drive on,' he said. 'Quick.'

'Yes, guv. But where?'

'Anywhere. I told you.'

'Can't do that.'

The man was old, even by the standard of London taxi drivers. Indeed, he seemed to be almost senile. His little wizened face had something of the lemur about it, though showing none of the intelligence and tristesse of the creature. Dribble played marshily around the corner of his mouth.

'For goodness sake . . . Kensal Green Cemetery, then.'

Duncan had no idea why he chose that particular destination. Perhaps it smacked of open places and strange sheltered niches where one might hide. Perhaps he was intrigued by the notion of making love to Jo surrounded by the reminders of mortality. He had never been to Kensal Green Cemetery as far as he knew.

'You're not one of them weirdos, are you?' asked the driver.

'No I am not a weirdo,' snapped Duncan. 'I am going to visit the grave of a relative.'

He could almost hear Jo's running footsteps now. He ducked down below the window.

'DRIVE ON!' he shouted.

'All right, all right, keep your hair on,' said the driver.

Very slowly and with a dreadful transmission whine, the taxi crept forward. It was almost as old as the driver himself and no match, in terms of 0–20 mph acceleration, for Jo. She almost drew level in Onslow Gardens but mercifully the lights at Stanhope Gardens turned green, and the ancient diesel, nearly tearing itself out of the coachwork, propelled them up towards South Kensington station, leaving the pursuer standing vexedly outside the Sala Romana restaurant, and consulting what looked like a map.

Thank God there had been no other taxi around. It would have been no contest if she had hailed one. Duncan settled himself back into the shiny upholstery, scarred by the regulation Stanley-knife seat slasher, and told himself not for the first time that he must be mad. Give up a comfortable if solitary existence? Leave respectability behind? A song his mother used to sing when he was small came into his memory.

> 'Last night you slept in a goose feather bed
> With the sheets turned down so bravely-o,
> And tonight you'll sleep in a cold open field
> Along with the raggle-taggle gypsies-o!'

Yes, there was something wild in Jo. She sang so high, she sang so low. Her call to him was irresistible. So here he was in a decrepit taxi, playing a children's game, albeit with adult cadences, journeying to a cemetery he did not know, on what had to be a wild-goose chase, for it was certain that she would never find him.

The taxi trundled on up Exhibition Road, through the park, and on past the Middle East of the Edgware Road. There was dust here, Duncan reflected, but very little heat. What did these people find here to like?

'I fought in the War,' said the driver, suddenly sliding the glass partition back. 'If I'd known I was fighting for this I'd have fucking deserted.'

Duncan felt sorry for all of them. He felt sorry for himself. The one person he did not feel sorry for was Jo. He felt envy for her, for being Jo. What must it be like to be mistress of that privileged domain?

On into North London hobbled the taxi, lumbering under blackened girders, overtaken even on the straight by boys on bicycles. It was early summer again, but the new leaves on the avenue trees were already coated, like the children's lungs, with layers of fine diesel particles – layers that no amount of London rain could ever wash off. The taxi's wheezing progress made it seem as if its own exhalation, its very existence, was poisoning itself – perhaps a metaphor for the human condition.

What was Jo doing now, Duncan wondered. How could she possibly know where he was going? His very choice of destination had been a spur-of-the-moment affair. There was no way, as Delice would have said – she liked to use the streetwise terms of yesteryear – there was no way Jo could follow him.

Suddenly, on another whim, it was almost like a voice in his head, he decided to change cemeteries. What was the point of coming to North London – a place where he had always felt a sense of loss – when there was a perfectly good cemetery nearer home.

He leant forward and tapped on the window.

'Yer?'

The driver cocked a bushy grey ear.

'I don't want to go to Kensal Green Cemetery.'

The driver put on his brakes very hard, so that Duncan fell off the seat and landed in a heap on the floor.

'Where jer wanter go, then?'

'The Brompton Cemetery,' said Duncan, picking himself up and rubbing his elbow.

'But that's back where we started.'

'Sorry. Changed my mind.'

The driver made the simple turnaround seem like a labour of Hercules, but it was finally achieved, and back they trundled towards Kensington. If by any chance Jo had been following him north, Duncan felt she would now be totally off the scent. Even so, as the taxi finally pulled up outside the imposing gates in the Old Brompton Road, he could not stop himself from casting a fugitive glance up and down the street. Of course there was nothing. He gave the taxi driver a £20 note, and waited impatiently as the fingers fumbled with the change. Yes, he had to admit it, he was nervous. Hide and seek always used to affect him like this. There was always this panic that he wouldn't be able to hide in time.

'Hold on a mo', guv.'

Coins spilt out of an evil-looking leather pouch and tumbled about on the taxi floor. The old man dived after them like a performing sea lion. Duncan almost danced with exasperation.

Another cab was approaching, a red one. It couldn't be, it might be her . . .

'Oh, keep the change,' he shouted at the driver, and ran off through the wrought-iron gates, leaving the man gaping at him as if he were witnessing an indescribable obscenity.

Once inside the cemetery, Duncan felt better. Tombs and tombstones, almost as various as the people who lay within them, stretched in all directions, intersected principally by a gravel lane, and on either side by pathways. In the distance a colonnaded mausoleum loomed. To left and right, graves and memorials marched away into a wilderness of groves and thickets.

This was better. He turned to look back at the gates, and saw the taxi driver having an animated conversation with what could have been a member of the staff. The old boy could evidently move faster than his cab. As Duncan turned, they saw him.

'There he is!' the old man cried.

Duncan didn't wait for the attendant's reply. He made off like the wind, indeed rather faster than the listless thing which was passing itself off as wind today, towards the nearest cover, a patch of brambles over to the left. This led, as luck would have it, to a series of further patches which would confuse any pursuit. At length he found the hiding place he was looking for. Here a thick grove of elders and brambles had established itself around the rusted railing of a nabob's tomb, an edifice rather like a miniature Gothic church which seemed to offer the promise of shelter both from the rain – it had started once more – and from the beady eyes of Jo and anyone else who chose to follow him.

His eyes took in the inscription on the monument as he climbed over the chain. 'Sir Josiah Whitmore, late of the East India Company, beloved husband of Clarissa and father of Edward and Georgina, born 4th February 1787, departed this life 5th April 1857. "Well done, thou good and faithful servant".'

He had doubtless been a proud man in his lifetime, and might well have disapproved of having his last resting place used as a hide; but he would most certainly have blenched at what was going on in there already. A rug was spread across the tomb, and upon it a youngish man was ravishing someone whose face Duncan could not see, but by whose buttocks he took to be another youngish man.

'Ah,' Duncan said. 'Sorry.'

'Bugger off,' said one of the youngish men, but it wasn't.

Now Duncan realized why the taxi driver had asked him if he were a weirdo. Cemeteries, it appeared these days, doubled as rendezvous for the quick as well as the dead. Wherever he went now, tomb or thicket, he kept stumbling upon scenes that would have raised eyebrows in the Cities of the Plain.

'Looking for someone, sweetie?' said a black leather clad man, smoking a joint, lurking behind a sarcophagus.

The game was no longer amusing; the day suddenly seemed darker; the garden sinister, dangerous.

There was a scampering of feet behind him where bones lay gathered under a tree, strange voices floated past, hands clutched from grilles and pillars, wet lips mouthed from arching windows, shadows flew across the grass, flesh moved with painful coquettishness to hidden music, and sounds of hollow places filled the evening.

Duncan began to run. A sensation of being enfolded oppressed him. There seemed nowhere in this garden of death and love for a self-defensive man to hide.

Eventually, however, he found shelter. Someone had forced the door of one of the mausoleums that had been built against the wall of the railway line. Here in the musky twilight, coffins lay on shelves, some spilling out their bones, while around them strange fungi reared from the rotten wood, pale and ossiform.

It was here that Jo found him, sitting disconsolately on the ground amongst the odours of mould and grass clippings, looking out at the rain that had started to fall once more, lost in reverie.

She approached softly, suddenly putting her hands round the back of his neck and squeezing so hard that he gasped and struggled frantically. He knew there had been a murder in the cemetery not so very long ago.

'Wha ... aaargh ...' he cried.

'Not clever,' she rebuked him, letting him go. 'What do we say? Eyes in the back of your head.'

'Yes but ...'

How could she possibly have found him? It was beyond nature.

'You're so obvious, Duncan,' she told him. 'A child could have picked up the trail.'

He didn't agree with her, but the familiar sweet acquiescence overcame him. They made love on the floor of the mausoleum among the bones and coffin dust. If he had believed in such things he would have thought she was possessed.

Thirty

But there were other days as winter progressed when her mood would suddenly swing – a complete change like a geological fault – and he would remember how he had felt as a very small child, trussed up in his bed unable to escape.

This life with Jo, he would realize after these scenes, was his bed. He had made it and he had to lie in it. Whichever way he turned, however hard he twisted or struggled, there was no way out.

The last time he had tried to run away, after a particularly irrational, yes, almost mad contention, she had given him a beating; oh, she was sorry afterwards in the car, but what was the use of that?

'I don't know what come over me,' she said. 'I'm ever so sorry.'

He looked at her without speaking. Even looking wasn't easy. One of his eyes had almost closed up.

'Say something,' she told him, 'even if it's just to say "I hate you".'

'What is there to say?' he asked her. 'I don't hate you.'

But that set her off.

'Oh well,' she said, 'that's very nice. He doesn't hate me. We're supposed to be lovers but he doesn't hate me. I'm sure we can use that to build a relationship.'

She had caught up with him in the Seven Sisters Road, a depressing street flanked on the south side by more hotels than you would think the neighbourhood could conveniently sustain. Opposite them, a lugubrious-looking park, dotted with blighted larches, stretched away towards a sad canal. It was in one of these places that he had taken refuge, entering his name as Mr Blake in a visitor's book.

The woman at the desk, a large Spanish-looking person with flashing eyes, noting his lack of luggage demanded an excessive amount of money, and he had just handed it over when Jo burst in.

'What's this?' she had demanded, knowing perfectly well what it was.

'This is hotel,' said the large Spanish-looking person. 'We no want trouble.'

'I'm staying here,' Duncan said. 'I just want to sort myself out.'

'Sort yourself out,' snorted Jo. 'You come with me and I'll sort you out.'

'I no want trouble,' said the Spanish lady.

'I'm staying,' repeated Duncan. 'I must, don't you see?'

But Jo had picked up a chair and was holding it outstretched with one hand.

'Out,' said the Spanish person, hanging on to the money. 'Both of you.'

Jo dropped the chair and snatched the cash from her with a peremptory flourish.

'Mine, I believe,' she said.

She marched Duncan out as the Spaniard launched into her repertoire of insults, taking care to stand well back inside the door as she watched them go. For a moment, Duncan had thought that Jo would opt for home, but instead she suggested a little walk to clear the air, she said. They strolled across the grass towards the railway line and, when she had ascertained there was no one else around, she had suddenly laid into him.

There wasn't time to take defensive action. The attack was entirely unexpected – suddenly a blow to the side of the head that made his brain spin, followed by a numbing wallop to the nerve centre on the back of the shoulder, and a crack across the shin with the heel of her shoes that made him cry out with pain and indignation. As he bent to hold the injured leg, she kicked him hard on the buttocks so that he sprawled in the grass.

'Run out on me, would you?' she said. 'Get up.'

He didn't react quickly enough so she kicked him again, fairly lightly, in the back, not quite on the kidneys but near enough to send a tremor of nausea through him. He heaved himself up with dog-turd hands.

'Look at you,' she said. 'You're filth, d'you know that? No wonder no one would have you. Now . . . move.'

She pursued him across the park, kicking quietly but accurately at him so that he fell again, and again had to scramble up to avoid the heel and toe. He could, he should have run, but she had his cash, she had his house; and he still loved her, or – what was it he felt? She had this extraordinary hold over him.

Not that he was normally so weak. He had been perhaps an emotional recluse, but that didn't argue wimpishness, quite the contrary. Many would have run for company, not held aloof; it takes courage to persist in solitude. But there was something about Jo that he had never met before; she seemed to have got into his mind like, what was it?, some sort of computer virus. That was her strength; her physical prowess was the weaker force. He was nearly as good as she was now, but what was the use? Something in the mind gave her the edge. So as she kicked and dragged him across the drab park, with the clouds pouring like folds of gruel overhead, and the east wind shaking the young trees free of their stanchions, he knew that he wasn't going to escape again. He was going to go home with her and face whatever music she intended to dole because he simply couldn't contemplate any alternative. She was his stanchion. How could he have thought that he could endure to spend an hour, let alone a week in that hotel?

172

How stupid of him! He tried to tell her, but his mouth was swollen where she had struck him with a palm.

'I was wong,' he said as she kicked him into the car. 'I see id dow.'

'Don't!' she cried, striking him again. 'Don't try and ingratiate yourself with me.'

Men in shirt-sleeves, he noticed, were watching from a dozen partially drawn net-curtained windows, men to whom these hotels were home. He could have been one of them. They were the hollow men, travellers, men who had travelled as far as they were going to go.

A man shouted from a window: 'You all right, luv?'

The irony was, it was addressed to her and not to him. He knew, suddenly, that if he did not get away – right away, not just physically but emotionally – something dreadful might happen and, worse, he might be the one who did the dreadful thing.

'I don't know what come over me,' she said. 'I'm ever so sorry.'

Thirty-One

And then, just as suddenly, it would all switch back again and it would be as if they were making up for a lifetime of lovelessness in the narrow mouth of a month or so.

She seemed to have developed as a person so that she was no longer the quasiformal instructress with her guard up, permitting only intermittent glimpses of the woman; now she was herself. They stopped training for a while, and days passed when they seemed to do little but make love, eat, drink and sleep. And of course, there were the hypnotherapy relaxation sessions which Jo never allowed him to miss.

'Essential before physical exercise,' she would say with a shy laugh, taking him down to levels that he had never known, so that he could not, did not know whether he dreamt or woke.

One day just after Christmas, Booth called to say he was in Pembrokeshire again – he had rented a cottage on Selsey – but it meant little to Duncan. He was filming the birds, the seals, the roving seal which mobbed boats and caught crayfish. She's mobbing the males, he said, she won't be caught, not she!

'Fine, fine,' Duncan said vaguely.

Mackworth Scientific Films was sadly neglected – which was a mistake since it was still early days for the enterprise. They had decided against an official launch. Why not just start it and see what happens? The answer was, very little.

The telephone rang increasingly rarely. But they didn't care. There was a self-devouring voraciousness about them which was as satisfying as it was reckless, perhaps even satisfying because it was reckless.

'We can't go on like this,' he would sometimes say, smiling because he didn't mean it.

'Why ever not?' she would reply.

She really didn't want anything else – ever. So they fell to their lovemaking and their sleep, punctuated by refreshment, mainly from cans, until the cans ran out. Then they would stagger out together for more supplies.

He caught sight of himself one day in a supermarket mirror. Could that long-haired, white-faced, red-eyed creature really be him? He looked – what was the word they used to have at school? He looked really shagged out.

'I look really shagged out,' he told her.

A ghost of a frown crossed her handsome face – if anything, love was making her more beautiful than ever.

'Shagged out?' she asked. 'What sort of talk is that?'

'Shagged out was what we used to say at school of a master if he was married to a pretty wife and came into a classroom yawning,' he told her.

'I don't think I like shagged out,' she told him. 'And what was that about pretty?'

'Some of the masters used to marry. Sometimes they had quite attractive wives.'

'So you think other women are attractive, do you?'

A strange look had come across her face, as if there were wires latticing the inside of her forehead. He had forgotten the possibilities of danger in the garden of love.

'No, of course not, now,' he said. 'There's only one now. But that was then.'

He could sense that the wires were still there, but they were fading. It had been touch and go.

Once when he was out collecting stores – Jo had stayed in because it was her time of the month – he met Gerald, his

175

accountant, clutching a folder. He had the feeling that their meeting was not coincidental.

'Hullo, Duncan.'

'Hullo, Gerald.'

'Where . . . been? Must . . . talk . . . accounts . . . pension . . . Tax return . . .'

He found he could not hear – or was it follow? – what Gerald was saying. It was like a parallel universe from which ghosts came. He shook his head slowly from side to side.

'Sorry, Gerald,' he said.

It was strange how, at home now, he was starting to experience more of the dislocated sensations he had felt on meeting Gerald – and not simply in terms of space but time as well, which seemed to be running on a loop, so that things he felt had already happened kept happening again.

Conversations would begin in exactly the same place, follow the same course, pause for the same amorous punctuations.

'We can't go on like this.'

'Why ever not? I don't want anything else than this. Do you?'

'No.'

'We'll sleep and eat and drink and make love for ever.'

It was difficult even to know which one was speaking. They had entered each other and lodged there.

'We can't eat and drink for ever.'

'Why not?'

Hands would be inside shirts, fingers nibbling; sighs, involuntary starts, moistness, fragrance, painful sweetness, shudderings and sighs followed in circling order.

'We've run out of food.'

'I'll go.'

'I'll go.'

'I can't let you out of my sight.'

He saw himself one day in a shop window. Could that white ratty creature really be him? They'd had a word for it at school: shagged out. That was what he was. How was it Jo managed to stay looking so healthy?

'I look utterly shagged out,' he told her. 'You look better than ever.'

'You're feeding me,' she said. 'But shagged out? What sort of talk is that?'

'I told you.'

'You never told me.'

'It's what we used to call masters who looked peaky in the morning, especially if they had a pretty wife.'

'So you find other women attractive?'

A strange look had come over her face as though there were filaments burning behind the eyes. It had happened so often that the flip from safe to hazard shouldn't come as a shock, but still it did.

'No, of course not. How many times do I have to say it? There's only one now. One, one, one. You are the one.'

'The one,' she repeated, appeased.

The filaments slowly faded.

Once when he was out collecting stores – Jo had stayed in because it was her time of the month – he met Delice. He had the feeling that their meeting was not coincidental.

Delice's universe seemed nearer than Gerald's. Even so, he had to force himself into contact.

'Delice,' he cried. 'Fancy meeting you in this neck of the woods!'

'Oh Duncan,' she said. 'What is she doing to you?'

'Doing to me? What do you mean?'

'Look at yourself, Duncan.'

'I have looked at myself,' he said. 'I look shagged out.'

'That's putting it mildly,' she told him.

He began to get annoyed. Really, Delice was the last person he wanted to see. Who was she? Was she Delice at all? And if she weren't, did it make any difference?

'You look like a white rat someone's been experimenting on,' Delice continued, warming to her theme.

'"A truth that's told with bad intent, beats all the lies you can invent",' he quoted.

'But it's not with bad intent,' she replied. 'It's with good intent because I care about you.'

'I don't want to be cared about. I want to be ignored. I want to be put out with the rubbish,' he said. 'I want to be as though the wind had passed over me and I was gone.'

He hadn't thought of it like that before, but in terms of his past life that was exactly what he wanted. Suddenly she burst into tears. She had been saving them up for some time.

'There are letters for you to sign,' she said. 'See.'

She had them with her.

'It's no good,' he told her. 'I am not myself.'

He hurried away, for he thought she would drive him mad. When he reached home, Jo knew.

'She's been after you, hasn't she?'

'Who?'

'Don't fucking play around with me.'

'What?'

'You know what. Play around.'

'Around?'

'You've been seeing other women.'

'I have not.'

'Yes you have.'

'Oh you mean Delice?'

'Yes, I mean Delice.'

She mimicked him savagely.

'But that's absurd. I didn't know I was going to see her. She lay in wait for me. I told her I'm not me. I'm half you now.'

She ignored the olive branch.

'A likely story. You sneaked out – you knew I wasn't well today – you sneaked out for an assignation.'

'But that's ridiculous.'

He looked at her. There it was again, that redness behind the eyes. It seemed to come particularly when she was having her periods. Could there be some outlandish seepage upwards from the womb to the optic nerve? It was well known at school that sex could make you blind. If that were so, periods could make a girl see red. It could be so. Why did he have to desire her so much? Why could he not have been content with a wife and babies? And where indeed would they be if he had had them and then met Jo? These thoughts, occupying his mind, muddied his awareness and made him forget the disciplines of precautionary footwork.

He was suddenly struck a sharp and painful blow to the shoulder which also caught him on the chin.

'What?' he cried. 'Ouch.'

But he slipped into a defensive mode, for he had become used to these sudden bouts of violent sparring in the home when the mood took her. This time, however, it was different. There was real force and drive in her movements. She caught him again round the side of the head with a flat palm as she had done in the park, making his brain spin.

He got off the line and threw a cushion at her, which she sidestepped and kicked him hard in the balls, which she hadn't done before. He doubled up and clutched at himself, moaning.

She stopped then and stood over him.

'Let that be a lesson to you,' she said.

He could manage nothing by way of reply.

She appeared to relent slightly and watched him with some concern. Had she killed the thing she loved?

'You shouldn't wind me up,' she said.

Even in his pain, he couldn't help admiring her as she stood over him, crossly uneasy. He struggled up and sat on a chair.

'Don't ever make me jealous,' she told him.

'But . . . but I didn't . . .' he was at last able to speak again. 'She means nothing to me. How could you think so?'

'There's no smoke without fire,' she said, obscurely.

'But there was no smoke.'

She passed a hand down her face, pulling it down across

179

her chin as if it were a curtain, or a palimpsest, wiping out the expressions it had worn.

'No smoke?'

She was smiling now.

'None that I could see.'

'No smoke without fire? But there wasn't any smoke?'

'That's right.'

She chuckled like an espresso machine. For the rest of the day she was especially nice to him, and in the evening embrocated his bruised person as only she knew how.

That night, he woke to hear her laughing. It was strange, he thought, how her sudden squalls made her sunshine so extraordinarily sweet.

By dint of an exceptional, against-the-run-of-play burst of application, Duncan had managed to send out a sheaf of Mackworth Scientific circulars the week before, more in desperation than conviction – and more surprisingly still, the phone rang one day and a voice he recognized spoke to him.

'Hi, Duncan. It's me.'

'Ah.'

'Tony. You know from Bowdler and Vipan, the advertising agency. You came to see us last year.'

'Ah yes.'

'Tom had to go back to the States, but he asked me to say Hi. He doesn't work with us anymore.'

'Oh. Thank him for me. Say Hi back if you speak to him again.'

'The thing is, there's the possibility of a job. Could you come in?'

'Come in?'

'Yes.'

'All right, I expect so.'

'You scientific film people are very laid-back,' said Tony. 'Ordinary commercial film companies say: great, when?'

'Consider it said,' said Duncan. He was feeling tired just thinking about it. 'Tomorrow?'

'Tomorrow's fine. Three o'clock?'

He would have to talk to Jo about it. There might be trouble.

'Three o'clock's fine,' he said. 'Oh, and thank you for thinking of us.'

'See you tomorrow.'

He broached the subject that evening, seeing Jo was in a good mood, or seemed to be in a good mood – you could never quite tell these days.

'You won't mind if I leave you . . .' he started.

'Very much,' she told him. 'I'd probably kill you.'

'I mean, just for the day.'

'Just for the day . . .' she pretended to ponder. 'Well . . . let me see. You'll have to make it up to me.'

'Oh . . . I will . . .' he said, and he would.

'In that case,' she said, 'I think I could just about manage to spare you. In fact, it's about time I did a bit of training with the boys.'

'The boys?'

It was his turn to feel jealous.

'That's right. And I thought we could get Eddie to sort out your cellar.'

They had discussed turning it into a shelter. She had said survival might depend upon it after the nuclear war. He had pointed out mildly that even the government seemed to be decommissioning theirs, but she told him Captain Smail reckoned that with nuclear proliferation you couldn't count on anything.

'Eddie?' he asked.

'He's the shelter man.'

'Do we really need one?'

'Forewarned is forearmed.'

'But we haven't been warned.'

She didn't think this was as funny as the smoke joke. In fact she didn't think it was funny at all.

181

'I wouldn't feel secure if we didn't have a shelter,' she told him. 'It doesn't seem much to ask.'

'Oh, all right. But I don't want to see him. I don't like him. I don't want him all over the house drinking cups of tea.'

Or doing anything else I wouldn't like, he thought, fingering furniture or taking impressions of my keyholes.

'You're just jealous,' she said. 'Go on, go and sell your what d'you call it, your footage. Sell your footage to the man.'

Thirty-Two

He had thought, when things went smoothly with Jo, that it was as well that he had given up the law. It had made it so much easier to put his past behind him. He had never really liked his past, which made his rejection of it easier still. It had been a cloudy land, his past.

And yet, coming into offices again, this office in particular – it didn't seem so strange this time – with spring in the air, memories of the past, those pretty girls, the prematurely balding men making the earnest conversations about matters of no consequence, counterbalanced by the flippancies that accompanied any subject of merit, all reminded him of the world he had left, and the utter unfathomability of his chosen course.

He had no life. His life was a strange woman. He could have managed to extricate himself from her, the strange woman, he thought as he listened to a curly-haired girl talk about rights, but whenever he got near to it, a kind of lethargy possessed him, a strange fatigue of spirit; he could not, would not do it.

'So you have the rights to this, Duncan?' the girl was saying.

I have the rights, curly hair, and yet I seem to have no rights. I have lost my rights.

They looked at him curiously. Perhaps he smelt. What was the hateful phrase? Reeked of sex. Perhaps he did reek of sex. And yet, Jo would have told him, wouldn't she? Of course she would – unless she reeked of sex, too.

He shifted away from the curly-haired girl, afraid of his haddock.

'The rights?'

She was craning over towards him; she had no fear of fish.

'Of course. So sorry.'

'Yes, but do you have them?'

'Them?'

'The rights.'

People kept opening their mouths. Sounds came out but they did not always convey meaning. The development of speech provided the great leap forward, 70,000 years ago, from *Homo erectus* to *Homo sapiens*. He did not want to raise the subject now for it would have been belittled.

'Ah. Right.'

'That's good. We have to ask. It all has to be cleared.'

'Of course.'

The piece they wanted showed bees fanning the hive to maintain a steady temperature (the commercial was for a small portable air-conditioner). It was a famous sequence his father had shot in Bolivia. The original, which he kept at home, must be worth a fair bit now. The fee, just for use, ran into hundreds. Was he adequately insured? It hardly seemed to matter any more.

When they had finished talking about the rights, they took him to lunch. There was wine before the meal and wine with the meal. And during the meal he thought: perhaps I have misjudged these people. They seem to be particularly amusing and intelligent. As for the girl with the curly hair, he could not believe that her twinkly blue eyes and general good humour could ever be thrown off course by the kind of trifles that upset Jo. She was particularly attentive, and hoped she would see him again, kissing him on both cheeks when they parted.

He walked home down Piccadilly, through Knightsbridge and on into South Kensington in great good humour. Perhaps this Jo thing was a mistake. Perhaps he could come back to the mainland after all. Perhaps at last the dream was over.

It is strange how a kind of disgust can rear its head, even amid the feast of love, or should one call it addiction, in which case it is not strange, he thought.

It is not strange that a domesticated creature like me could grow tired of the uncertainties – fascinating though they might be at times, terrifying at others – of the wild. I could flip like the Gulf Stream, no longer directed towards north-western Europe, precipitating an Ice Age. (It had been a global fear.) There are laws that govern such random-seeming events, he thought. I could switch on the big frost at number 74, Enderby Gardens, corner of Old Brompton Road.

As he drew nearer Enderby Gardens, he remembered having a debate with a client once, a schoolmaster – a philosopher of sorts – who wanted a will drawn up. The philosopher had complained humorously of his lack of financial success in the world. But, said he, I have an interesting life – better an interesting life than a comfortable one. Duncan had disagreed. Comfort is the way of the law, he said; interest is the way of the outlaw. The philosopher had laughed.

'Comfort is the way of the in-laws,' he said.

Be that as it may, thought Duncan, fortified by the good wine of the advertising agency and the kind eyes of curly-hair, comfort may be the way of the Mackworth.

He had some trouble fitting the key into the lock – there had been a spate of chewing gum vandals again in the area, and Duncan was heartily cursing the waywardness of things – when the key slid in smooth as an uncontested writ, and he stepped into the dark cave of the hall.

There was no sign of Jo, which in a way was a relief. She had a knack of knowing when he had what she would call bad thoughts. In spite of the wine and the firm intentions, he rather dreaded a scene.

His first call was a visit to the cellar; he wanted to assure himself that Eddie had gone. There were signs of activity, but still no Jo. He climbed back upstairs, went through to the kitchen and found a note. 'Gone out training, back after supper.' He could tell it had been written off-handedly. It had fallen off the table onto a chair. She hadn't even bothered to stick it on the table.

Back after supper? Since when did she go out in the evening? Had she gone with Eddie? It worried him. It gave him suet in the stomach. His new-found sense of independence vanished, and all he wanted was for Jo to come back.

He helped himself to a glass of Australian Chardonnay from a box in the fridge and turned on the television. There had been a murder in North London but the police were hopeful. He switched to another channel and watched a show called 'Half a Knicker'. Gales of laughter; more Chardonnay. Jo didn't come back till half-past ten and by then he was slightly drunk.

'Hallo, you,' she said. 'Nice day?'

'Fine,' he told her.

He wanted to ask her where she'd been, but didn't like to seem jealous.

'I've been working out,' she said. 'I was getting soft.'

He liked her soft.

'What about you?' she asked.

'I went to the ad agency,' he said. 'I think they want my bees.'

'I bet you went out to lunch with them,' she said. 'I bet you wanted to screw some nice little PA.'

She was uncomfortably near the truth as usual.

'Of course not,' he said. 'You know me.'

'I know you, Duncan,' she said. 'You're like a pit pony that never saw the light of day. I showed you the light of day and now you can't get enough of it.'

'Can't get enough of it?'

'The light of day, silly.'

'Do you mind?'

'If you want the light of day, Duncan, who am I to mind?

186

I showed it to you, didn't I? Go ahead and enjoy it, and the light of night too for that matter.'

'You mean . . . you want me to go out?'

'Why not? If that's what you want.'

'But . . . what about us?'

'What we've got, Duncan, what we've got is too strong for pettiness. We've both got our lives to lead. We can't be self-absorbed the way we were.'

'You didn't like that?'

'I liked it, Duncan, but it was unhealthy.'

He couldn't tell whether she really meant it or not. Sometimes she would do this, lead him on, encourage him to say or do something, and then she would fly into a rage the first time he did or said it.

'Do you really mean it?' he asked.

'Duncan . . . do I look as if I'm joking?'

There was no doubting the air of candour. Her eyes were lustrous with it. He felt ashamed of his excitement at the prospect of taking curly-hair out – which was what he knew the old pony was going to do.

Thirty-Three

April graduated greenly into May. The curly-haired girl, her name was Kate, rang Duncan up a couple of days later.

'We've cleared the script with the Copy Committee,' she told him, whatever that meant. 'There was a hiccup about the use of the word "natural".'

'Oh. I'm glad.'

He didn't mind about the word 'natural', but he did care about the money. It meant an extra £1,000 into his sadly depleted bank account. There was a slight click at the other end of the line. He wondered for an instant if Jo were listening, but he knew she was doing her exercises. She never stopped her exercises for anything.

There was a pause.

'Are you there?'

'Yes.'

'Only we've been having this trouble with our switchboard.'

'No, I'm here all right.'

'I wondered if you'd like to come to this new Dolphin film.'

'Ah.'

He had to think quickly. Now that the moment had come, he was uncertain. Did he really want to go out with someone else? At the same time, if he didn't show his independence soon, he'd never do it. Jo would respect him more if he did. She had surely almost said as much. Perhaps things had been getting too introverted. Perhaps she didn't want to take him for granted. There are always such considerations in love, he understood. So he made up his mind.

'All right,' he said. 'That would be very nice.'

'What about Thursday?'

'Thursday's fine.'

They arranged where to meet, and the conversation ended. The decision being made, Duncan spent the rest of the day in high humour. Somehow the prospect of breaking out of the pattern he and Jo had established filled him with hope. Things seemed to have been weighing on her recently. The old balls-of-the-feet energy and bounce had turned to something he would almost describe as sullen.

'I'll be going to a meeting at the advertising agency on Thursday,' he told her. 'They may want me to go out with them afterwards.'

It wasn't that he didn't love her still (more if anything) but there was a need for – what was it they called it? – space. He needed space.

'I thought you hated the advertising set,' she said.

'We need the money.'

'That's not why you're going.'

'I thought you didn't mind. You said you didn't mind.'

'I don't mind. Just don't tell me lies, that's all.'

She was perfectly pleasant for the rest of the day. They even had a work-out together, and she gave him knife training.

'Never stab. Slash at the bigger target – upper arms, chest and stomach, with alternating forty-five degree passes.'

And first, of course, as ever, she took him down to Level 10, where she kept him longer than usual. Increasingly these days he had the feeling that more went on there than he knew. Increasingly these days he had the feeling that more went on there than he needed. At the same time, he could not say he wanted it to stop. He did not know what he would do without Level 10.

The weekend passed uneventfully, though Duncan noticed a certain unforthcomingness about Jo. It was as though she were holding something back. Monday brought a letter from Alec Booth. The rogue female was biting the young bull seals' penises. It was a practice, said Alec, usually adopted by the senior male – the wound, as it healed, warped the genital, making penetration impossible. Unheard of in a female, eh? Something to do with overcrowding, he thought. What a scoop!

Duncan wondered if Booth were going slightly mad, a late menopause.

Tuesday brought a contretemps when Jo accused Duncan of being unfaithful. It sounded like pure fabrication.

'I know you want to get inside her knickers,' she told him.

'That's not being unfaithful,' he retorted. 'That's wishful thinking.'

'The wish is father to the deed,' she replied. 'So you admit it, then?'

'She's a client, for heaven's sake.'

'Go where you like. Do what you want,' she said. 'I'll get Eddie to give me dinner somewhere, take me to a show.'

'You don't have to do that. I'll take you out any time you like.'

'I'll get Eddie to take me.'

'Look,' Duncan said, flapping his hands, 'can't we put this in perspective? You said you didn't mind my going out, and you were pleased we were making some money.'

'It's the way you're doing it, I don't like, Duncan,' she said. 'It's the nasty little grin you've got tucked into your mouth.'

But when the day came, she made no complaints. Rather, she seemed to encourage him, entering into the spirit of his evening out. She chose a tie for him, advised on which jacket to wear, gave him an affectionate kiss when he left and even told him not to worry about being out late.

This acquiescence on her part, almost connivance you might have called it, helped evoke in him a strange recklessness. If she wanted him to go out with other women, he would

190

try to oblige her. God knows, he had left it late enough in his life.

He met Curly-hair at the agency after work and they went round to a wine bar for a drink before the film.

'I was so glad you could come,' Kate said. 'I thought it would be right up your . . . well, street seems the wrong word for your kind of work . . . green lane or coast path might be better.'

It was the sort of remark that Jo would never have made. She didn't think round the corner of phrases. He smiled. He was going to enjoy the evening in spite – or because of – the guilt he felt.

'I'm not really the film-maker,' he told her. 'That's my father's assistant, a man called Booth. He's the real expert. In fact, I've only started to do this as a business over the last year. I was a lawyer before.'

'Oh but this is much more important than the law,' she told him.

Her eyes were bluebell blue, very bright and deep and spark-ling, bluebells washed with rain, he thought.

'I suppose you were born in May,' he told her.

'How did you know?'

She was astonished.

'The eyes.'

'This is a very good start to the evening,' she said.

He felt no fear, no diffidence, simply contentment as he sat beside her drinking the straw-coloured white Rioja. Presently they left and walked down Piccadilly to the Film Institute cinema, arm in arm. He felt he had known her for years, and she too remarked upon it. It was strange to be walking with someone so much smaller than Jo, more fragile, more pro-tectable in spite of her (what was the word?) street cred.

The film was both interesting and moving, a lyrical piece exploring the dolphins' relationship with humanity, the legends, the myths, the brutal present. Afterwards, they walked back to an Italian restaurant in Soho and had dinner.

'You know, Duncan,' she told him, 'you're something of a mystery.'

'Why's that?'

She sipped her Campo Fiorin, raising the glass so that her eyes turned red in the wine's shadow. He was reminded suddenly of Jo, shocked and relieved to realize that he hadn't thought of her for two hours.

'You won't mind if I say something strange? I only mean it in the best way.'

'I won't mind anything you say,' he told her.

'There's something of the innocent about you,' she said, 'as if you've never been part of the real world, well, not the world I live in.'

'You mean, I'm a sort of noble savage?' he smiled. 'Not sure about the noble.'

'No, I mean it. Perhaps it was the law – that's a sort of land that time forgot. Coming out of it, mixing with the real world, perhaps that's what I mean. But there's something else. You're not really out of the wood yet, are you?'

He had to agree.

'Maybe I'm not. Maybe it's better not to be entirely what you say, of the world, contemporary, up to date.'

'Oh, I agree with that. But you don't want to live in a prison, do you?'

'We all live in prisons of a kind,' he said. 'We just don't call them prisons. We call them disciplines or necessities, like going to work, earning a living, looking after dependents, paying taxes, stopping at red lights . . . Total freedom would make us mad. You can't play tennis without lines and a net. Freedom is as much prison as you can enjoy.'

She laughed and looked at him with May-morning eyes, putting out her hand to touch his.

'I hadn't thought of it like that.'

Later she took him back to her flat and made him coffee. How different it was from the nightmarish evening in Battersea. Kate was such a bright and sensitive creature; and her flat wasn't in Battersea but in leafy Chelsea. The place smelt not of gas or monkfish but of lavender, coffee and Kate's eau de toilette which had a poignancy that seemed to reach straight to the heart.

It was a ground-floor flat in a mansion block, the entrance all polished wood and respectable marble. Inside, low lights and deep chairs reaffirmed the sense of commodious living; a high ceiling and tall windows gave an air of lofty grace. The curtains, drawn now, swayed in the warm May evening breeze, moving in and out with a measured voluptuous sweep as if they were playing at Bellini courtesans.

She had directed him to a sofa and now she put the coffee cup on a small table beside him.

'It's very grand,' he said. 'Do you live here by yourself?'

'It belongs to a girlfriend, really. I pay her rent and look after it for her. She lives in the States most of the time. Just as well. She always borrows my clothes when she's here.'

He was silent for a few moments as his eyes continued their tour of the room. There were pictures of Old Chelsea by Walter Greaves which he recognized.

'It's good to live near the river,' he said. 'I go and look at it a lot. It's good for the mind, the ebb and flow.'

She stood and looked at him affectionately, as though she had known him a long time.

'Would you like anything with the coffee?' she asked. 'A whisky? I have some Macallan.'

His father's grandparents had come from Ayr. The family had intermingled with Southerners since then, but Duncan's heart lifted ritually at the mention of the malt.

What an intelligent and perceptive girl she was. He couldn't help thinking again how different she was from Jo, who thought a malt was a milk drink. It was disloyal of him, he knew. If it hadn't been for Jo and what she'd done for him he wouldn't be sitting here now, daring to fall in love with this girl. This girl . . . he found himself now telling her about

193

himself; his family; his father; his early life; and finally . . . his fear.

'You mean . . . a phobia?' she asked.

'No, no. That's too specific. It could include specific things, but on the whole it was a general sense of dread, as though at any moment something fearful would happen.'

'We all have a bit of that,' she said.

'But not the way I had it, or everybody would be like me.'

'I wish they were,' she said, taking his hand again.

It was odd that his sense of disconnection, so pronounced when he met Gerald, and again in his conversation with Delice, should so completely have left him. He couldn't believe his good fortune at the turn events were taking. They were sitting on the sofa now, well back, deep in cushions. Every now and then he would stretch up, as from a boat, and take his whisky from the table that stood beside him like a polished island.

At length, when he stretched forward, she rose up to meet him, and they kissed. It was not a passionate kiss nor yet a timid one. It was a kiss of discovery. Buoyed by happiness, he felt able to tell her the bad news.

'I have a girlfriend,' he said.

'That's not so terrible. Why do you say it as if an asteroid's approaching?'

'Well . . . in a way it is.'

He told her about Jo, or as much as he could tell her about Jo, because there seemed to be some kind of censorship in his mind that only allowed him to say so much. He told her about the self-defence lessons, the vulnerable parts of the body, the seventh vertebra, the hide and seek.

He didn't tell her about the violence, the swings of mood, the days of devouring love. Even so, Kate looked concerned.

'She sounds rather formidable,' she said.

'I've never met anyone like her,' Duncan told her. 'I think her childhood wasn't at all easy. How was yours?'

'Amazingly ordinary,' she said.

'An oxymoron of a childhood,' Duncan laughed.

'Not a little dull,' she said. 'Litotes.'

They smiled at each other.

'I used to think it was good to have some hardship as a child,' he continued. 'Like a sort of carboniferous deposit, blackness you could dig up and use as fuel later. But after meeting Jo I'm not so sure. I wish I'd met you first.'

'It's not too late,' she said.

She suddenly leant over and kissed him. He put his arms round her and kissed her in return. He could feel her breast brushing his wrist as he held her, and the india-rubbery swelling of her nipple. Her thighs made little silky whispering noises as they moved.

He desired her so much it made him panicky.

'I'd better go,' he told her.

She shook her head.

'Come upstairs.'

'I'd . . . better not.'

Why was he saying this?

'You're right,' she said. 'First date and all that.'

'Next time.'

'My girlfriend's coming back for a day or two from New York. She'll be here tomorrow,' she told him. 'But, sure, yes, next time.'

'I'd better go then,' he said again, getting up.

There was a little awkwardness between them.

'I'm sorry,' he said. 'It's not that I don't want to, it's just . . .'

'I know,' she told him, kissing his cheek lightly. 'I want to too. But there's Jo to think about.'

'It's not that,' he said. 'I can't explain.'

Something told him he would fail if he tried to do it with anyone other than Jo. It was ridiculous, of course. He cursed Jo now; he hated her.

'May I see you tomorrow?' he asked.

Kate shook her head.

'I'll be looking after Mel. I only see her twice a year. Next Tuesday she'll be gone.'

'Tuesday, then,' he said.

They held each other for a moment. The awkwardness had passed. She held the door for him and he walked out into the night.

It was strange, he reflected as he walked down the steps, that the laurel bushes swayed like that when there was so little wind; but London was full of turbulence.

When he arrived home, there was no sign of Jo. She had said she would go out, so he wasn't unduly alarmed. In fact, he noted in himself just the faintest wormcast of relief. Even so, he looked round the house attentively, and finally went down to the cellar to see whether she were there, inspecting the progress. He noted a new door: nothing he would have described as nuclear-proof, but sturdy enough in its way.

He went inside to see whether there were any other works going on, saw nothing, turned, and just as he was turning he noticed the door closing behind him. It was only when it clicked that he realized there was no handle on the inside.

'Eddie!' he called.

No response.

Had the wretched thing swung to in the draught? Or was it pushed? Damn the thing – he had never wanted it in the first place. Trust Eddie to make a door with no handle.

He wondered what time Jo would come home.

Thirty-Four

There was not a great deal of room in the cellar. Nor, for that matter, was there any wine. It had been drunk in the days of roses. Apart from the racks, and an old bin that his mother had used for chicken meal, and a broken chair, the furniture of the place was on the skimpy side. You would not have expected a bed, but there was no covering of any kind. No cushion, no palliasse, no cobwebby old mackintosh. Had it been cold weather, he would have been in trouble. Happily, if that was the word, it had been a week of muggy heat. Air, at the moment, seemed in reasonable supply. It seemed to come from a grille in the far wall. There was no other access to the outside world.

Duncan had ample opportunity to take all this in. He was not too worried at this point.

He tried standing on the chair and beating at the roof near where he guessed the pavement would be, but he left off after half an hour when the chair broke. As the hours passed, he became at first hungry, then thirsty. All there was to drink was a bottle of rectified spirit from Poland which Duncan had not attempted before, fearing it might make him blind. He tried it now and it merely increased his thirst.

Midnight came and went, and there was still no Jo. He began to think that she might have had an accident, or developed amnesia. And then: what if there were a fire and he were trapped here? Was it a premonitory fear of this place that had stalked him all his life?

He lay down on the floor, huddling into a foetal position, and slept fitfully, pursued by vague dreams of violence.

He woke parched and hungrier than he'd ever been in his life. What on earth was he going to do? He wondered how long you could last without food and water. Food, he knew, was not so important, but lack of water could kill in a very few days. He hoped it would be quick and not too painful, though he held out no great hopes on the subject.

Meanwhile, he had to have a crap. He hated to do it, because he knew Jo was fastidious about such matters, but what else was there? He crouched in the corner and tried to cover the result with dust.

The morning wore on. He decided he would try and break the door down, but Eddie had made it of stout oak, and there was nothing inside that really doubled as a battering ram. He tried using the wine racks but they snapped like twiglets.

'Hallooo-oo,' he shouted. 'HALLLOOO-OOOO . . .'

The long day waned. He was becoming light-headed. At one point it seemed that Delice came in and talked to him, though he was unable to answer.

'You poor fish,' she said, sadly.

But there was nothing she could do.

It came into his mind, too, that his nurse – the one who had bound him so tightly in his bed – had turned up and was punishing him for some unspecified misdemeanour.

'And don't you tell your mother,' she said, 'or you'll be in even worse trouble.'

'HELP!'

'Hollering won't do any good. You can holler all you like and all you'll get is hard commons. And just for that, I'm going to tie you up again. Truss you up like a chicken, my boy. Go on. Lie like a chicken.'

'No, Nanny, please . . .'

But she was adamant. And, strangely, she had turned into Jo.

'NO,' he shouted. 'NO, NO, NO!'

'Your fate is sealed,' she said. 'Sealed. Remember that.'

And then he woke and beat vainly on the door again, charged to the other end of the cellar and shouted 'HELP, HELP, HELP,' up the airhole until he was hoarse.

At last he stopped and slumped once more to the ground, listless with terror. This was the worst thing that had ever happened to him.

Hours later, he roused himself and sat, trying to think rationally of solutions. After all, he had been trained to cope with emergency.

He was a prisoner, that was obvious. But of whom? Eddie? Jo? It could only be one of them. He had never trusted Eddie. The man was clearly vicious, besotted with Jo. He would do anything to keep her, Jo had said that. But if he were responsible for this kidnap, what had he done with Jo? Persuaded, or more likely forced her to come away with him, no doubt. Perhaps Jo herself was languishing in another of Eddie's little hideaways. What on earth was he going to do? Surely Eddie didn't intend to kill him? Therefore he must be planning to come back, mustn't he? Or must he?

Duncan waited in hope, in anger and frustration and, finally, once again in exhaustion and despair. The fund of reason he had found earlier had quite eaten up his reserves of energy. Hours passed, perhaps another day, it was impossible to tell, and since he did not care, the measuring of time had no meaning for him. At some point he had forgotten to wind his watch and it had stopped.

He dipped in and out of awareness, waking to misery and descending to levels far removed from those he had known under the guidance of Jo; sad and hellish places he visited, full of sighs and pain, regrets and betrayal.

When he woke up, Jo was dribbling water into his mouth and feeding him salt and glucose.

'There you are at last,' she smiled. 'You poor thing. You must have been in here three days at least.'

'What day is it?' he croaked.

'It's Tuesday now.'

'Four days,' he said.

'We'll have you well in no time,' she told him.

'What happened to you?' he asked. 'Why didn't you come back earlier?'

'I thought you needed a break,' she told him. 'I went back up to Durham. Lucky I came back when I did. I nearly stayed another night. That bloody fool Eddie. He could have killed you. Fancy not putting a handle on the door!'

'Fancy!' echoed Duncan.

He felt too weak to speculate on the meaning of all this. Even in his feebleness, he knew that all would not necessarily be what it seemed. It never was where Jo was concerned. She continued to kneel there, stroking his head with cool hands, giving him water.

'We'd better get you upstairs,' she said.

A bell rang in his memory. Tuesday? That was the evening he was meant to be seeing Kate again. What on earth would she think of him, standing her up like that?

He tried to get to his feet but his knees buckled under him.

'Come along, old boy,' said Jo, supporting him. 'Let's take you up and sit you down. Then I'll bring you something to eat. What would you like? You'll feel better in no time.'

She was being overwhelmingly pleasant.

'Baked beans on toast,' he said, even in his weakness knowing the limitations of her cooking. 'And about a gallon of tea.'

He doddered out into the passage with her, and by dint of pushing and half-carrying she got him up to the ground floor and into the drawing room. How strong she was! It had its advantages at moments like this. It was remarkable how much better he was feeling already. Perhaps it had been the bad air in the cellar, or maybe it was just the psychological effect of being free again.

'There you are,' she said, bringing him a tray. 'When you've got that down you, and had a bath and a sleep, you'll feel quite your old self again.'

When he had eaten, he looked at his watch. Perhaps he could slip out, make a phone call and explain himself to Kate. But Jo, as though reading his thoughts shook her head.

'You don't have to go anywhere,' she told him. 'Relax . . . you're very tired.'

It was true. He felt suddenly filleted.

'One or two things to do,' he said, weakly.

'Things to do? You don't want to worry about all that. I've taken care of everything.'

'Everything?'

What could she mean?

'Everything. Cake?'

He ate the cake, and some bananas and ice cream, washing it down with fresh orange juice which she said was better than tea.

'You look tired,' she said. 'I bet you feel even tireder now. I can just feel how tired you are. Come on, I'll take you up to bed. You can have a bath later.'

She held his arm as if he were an old man while he made his way to the stairs. A thought struck him and he stopped, agitated and old-mannish.

'The cellar,' he said. 'It's a terrible mess.'

He didn't like to think of the filth he'd left in there.

'Don't worry,' she said. 'I'll see to all that.'

She tucked him up, rather professionally, he thought.

'Yes,' she smiled. 'I trained as a nurse for a while. You didn't know that, did you?'

He could feel sleep covering him like sea across the sand.

'Didn't . . . know . . .' he mumbled.

'No, you didn't, did you? You didn't know anything . . .' he heard her say, and then the tide was over him.

Thirty-Five

He was having a nightmare, one of his childhood ones which recurred from time to time. He had been put in a coffin and someone who didn't realize he wasn't dead – or did he? – was banging the nails in. His mother said he got it from reading *Great Tales of Mystery and Imagination*, but he thought it came from Cousin Ian who had the family trait of taking his own fears out on other people. Cousin Ian knew Duncan's fear of lying like a chicken. In fact, Duncan wasn't sure that it might not be Cousin Ian (a pasty-faced relative two years older than Duncan) who was banging the nails in himself.

Bang, bang, bang.

'No, I'm alive!' Duncan called, struggling in his winding sheet. 'I'M ALIVE. HELP!'

But it was no good. The hammer went on, implacably going about its business. He wondered how long he could live with the small amount of air that was left in the coffin, and what it would feel like when it was used up. Already he could feel the tightness in his chest, the rasp in his throat . . .

'HELP! HELP!'

He woke to find himself struggling in bed with the sheets tightly wrapped around his face and body. Downstairs, some-one was beating on the front door. Why did people keep doing that to him?

'Jo?'

Duncan tried to feel beside him. She wasn't there. Perhaps

she was in the spare room so that he would sleep better.

'Jo,' he called louder.

Still no response. He turned on the light and disentangled himself from the sheet. At least he was feeling better now; the sleep, in spite of the nightmare, had done him good. He looked at the clock; half-past nine. He had slept for ten hours.

'Jo?'

The unease engendered by the nightmare was still with him, and starting to turn back into fear again. There was no one in the spare room, indeed no sign of her in the house. Meanwhile there was the front door to attend to. Mindful as ever of security, he squinted through the spyhole, but in the darkness it revealed nothing. Putting the chain peg in its hole, he opened the door and stood well back.

'Open up,' said an authoritative voice tinged with ill temper. 'Police.'

'Police?' said Duncan, still slightly stupid with sleep.

Were they real police or Captain Smail and Eddie? He would have a thing or two to say to Eddie.

'Police. You must have heard of us,' said the voice. 'Undo the chain, please.'

'Blue uniform, tall helmet,' said another voice, helpfully.

'I should like to see your identification,' said Duncan.

After all, he had been schooled in this sort of thing; it would have been madness to go against months of training, but it put the voice into an even worse temper.

'Open the door or I shall ask this officer to break it down.'

The voice was now revealed as a tall, thin man with a face etched by alcohol and acid indigestion, and a mouth curved into a permanently unamused smile. Duncan unhooked the chain and let him in. This was demonstrably a policeman. He was accompanied by a younger companion who reminded Duncan fleetingly of the fish footman in Alice.

'What can I do for you?' he asked.

'Duncan Mackworth?' asked the unamused Inspector, extending an identification card.

'Yes.'

'I'm Detective Inspector Liphook, CID. I'm investigating the murder of Melanie Ashburton on the night of the 12th of May.'

Duncan stared at the man blankly. He had never heard of the woman.

'We'd like to ask you a few questions,' continued the policeman.

'Wha . . . wha . . .'

Duncan opened his mouth several times but only that one inconclusive syllable emerged.

'Would you like to sit down?' asked the fish-footman-faced constable who had come in with his superior. 'I think he would answer better if he sat down. Tea? I think he might answer better if he had some tea.'

There was indeed something strangely Alice-like about the scene. Duncan led them into the drawing room and they all sat down. No one made any effort to make tea.

'Well?' asked the Inspector.

'Who is Melanie Ashburton?'

'Who *was* Melanie Ashburton?'

'All right. Who was she? I've never met her in my life.'

'Denies all knowledge,' said the constable, scribbling busily.

'Not so fast,' said the Inspector. 'He denies knowing her name, but he could still have met her.'

'Touché,' said the constable.

'I never met her and I didn't know her,' said Duncan.

'Denies all knowledge,' said the constable.

'How come, then,' asked the Inspector, 'that your business card was found on the body?'

Once again, Duncan was struck dumb.

'My business card?'

'That's what I said.'

'But it can't have been.'

The Inspector consulted his notebook.

'Mackworth Scientific films. That's you, isn't it?'

'It is . . . But I don't understand. You're not from Captain Smail, are you?'

'Never heard of him. Who's he?'

'Oh nothing. It doesn't matter. Look here. You don't suspect me, do you? I couldn't have killed this Melanie . . .'

'Melanie Ashburton,' said the fish-constable. 'Five foot seven, curly brown hair, Caucasian, mole on left buttock . . .'

'I couldn't have killed her. Apart from the fact that I never met her, I was locked up here.'

'Locked up?' repeated the Inspector. 'Are you normally locked up?'

'Are you obsessionally handicapped in some way?' asked the constable.

'I was locked up because we were having a shelter built in my cellar. When I came home on Thursday night, I went down to see how it was getting on and locked myself in by mistake. The builder had left no handle on the inside.'

'Check the cellar, Mulgrave,' said the Inspector.

The constable left the room.

'Look here,' said Duncan. 'There's been some terrible mistake. I'm a solicitor you know.'

'A solicitor, sir? I thought you said you were in scientific films.'

'I was a solicitor. Then I switched to scientific films. I found them more interesting than the law.'

'You feel above the law, sir?'

'Not at all. I didn't say that.'

'Can anyone confirm your whereabouts on Saturday, sir?'

Duncan paused. For some reason he didn't want to bring Jo into all this, yet it seemed he would have to, sooner or later.

'My er friend,' he said.

'Ah, your friend, sir. Name?'

'Jo.'

'Jo what, sir?'

'Jo Lindup.'

205

'Sex?'

Duncan didn't see what business it was of the police, but it was easier to reply.

'Yes, of course. Sometimes.'

The policeman sighed. This one was a joker.

'We're not interested in your carnal relations, sir. I meant what sex is Jo Lindup? Male or female? The name is androgynous.'

'I said she was my friend,' retorted Duncan.

'Friend covers both genders these days.'

'For heaven's sake . . . female,' said Duncan.

'Thank you, sir. So . . . this female friend Jo can vouch for your presence here, locked in the cellar, over Saturday?'

'Yes,' said Duncan.

'Funny things people get up to,' said the Inspector, sighing again. 'Yes?'

The fish-constable had come back. He was breathing rather hard through his mouth.

'Nothing in the cellar, sir. The door's a thin pine affair with no lock and George Fredericks both sides.'

'Speak English, Mulgrave. And if you're going to attempt rhyming slang, get it right.'

'Sorry, sir. Handles, sir.'

'Ah. And what do you have to say to that, Mr Mackworth?'

'There must be some mistake.'

'Come and see if you like.'

So they trooped off down to the cellar, and it was as the constable had reported. An ordinary pine door which he could have kicked down any day stood where the solid oak had been. Its somewhat battered brass knobs, protruding from each piney face, glinted in the naked bulblight. Someone had put the old door back in position.

'That's the old door,' said Duncan. 'I don't know how it got back.'

'A likely story, Mr Mackworth. And now . . . where's this female friend of yours?'

206

This time it was the same, only worse. Duncan told them all about Jo, how she had arrived, what she had taught him, how they had lived together; but when it came to looking for any trace of her, they drew a complete blank. The house was devoid of her. A thoroughly professional job had been done – but that, of course, was what he would have expected.

'I can't understand it,' Duncan kept saying. 'I don't know what's happened to her.'

He told them how Jo had disappeared once before, and how the police had come round, but they weren't police.

'You have either been much put upon, Mr Mackworth, or you have a lively sense of fantasy. Either way, it still leaves us with a murdered girl and your business card.'

'Can you tell me anything more about her?'

'She spent most of her time in New York but she had a flat here in . . . let me see . . .'

The Inspector fumbled for his notebook, but Duncan had a terrible feeling he knew where she lived, and an even more terrible feeling that he knew who had killed her, mistaking her for another girl with brown curly hair. Could Jo really have done that? Yes, he had to admit to himself that she could.

'Cheyne Walk,' said Duncan.

'That's right.'

The Inspector looked surprised.

'How did you know?'

Duncan explained how he had spent the evening with Kate.

'So you admit you had a relationship with her flatmate,' said the Inspector.

'Of course. But it wasn't a relationship as such.'

'When is a relationship not a relationship?' asked the fish-constable. 'When it's a ship full of relations.'

'That will do, Mulgrave. Yes, Mr Mackworth?'

'It was early days. It is early days. Presumably Kate, that is Miss Greenwood is all right?'

'She was the one that found the body. Naturally she was very distressed. She told us she'd found your card on Miss Ashburton's body.'

'So you knew all the time I had been out with Miss Greenwood?'

'Just checking, Mr Duncan. Just checking. It seems to me that this bears all the hallmarks of a ménage à trois gone hideously wrong. What do you say to that?'

'I'd say *you* had gone hideously wrong,' said Duncan bravely.

'Well now, let's see.'

The Inspector put his fingertips together and looked judicious.

'On the one hand, we have you and this supposed girlfriend living here. On the other, we have this Miss Greenwood, for whom you have developed an obsession . . .'

'Affection,' Duncan corrected him.

'Obsession. You are a man who is, shall we say, a mono-maniac? You do not wish to share Miss Greenwood who you suspected of having a relationship with Miss Ashburton. And in a towering fit of jealousy, you killed her.'

The thought of such a lesbian relationship dealt Duncan another blow. Could it be true?

'Was she?' he asked.

'That does not matter, Mr Mackworth. What matters is that you thought it might be.'

'But I don't.'

'That's what you say now.'

'And how was this wretched girl killed?' Duncan asked.

'Are you sure you don't know, Mr Mackworth?'

'Guess,' said the fish-constable. 'Pint of Export on the way to the nick if you get it right.'

'You must excuse DC Mulgrave, Mr Mackworth. He's one of the new breed of graduate officers. If we give 'em enough rope they hang themselves. You were saying?'

'A blow to the seventh vertebra, I should think,' he told him.

'There you are,' said the constable triumphantly. 'You're on.'

'I'd like you to accompany us to the station, if you would be so kind, Mr Mackworth. Perhaps you would explain to us there how you came by that information.'

'Are you arresting me?' asked Duncan.

'Working on it, Mr Mackworth, working on it.'

Thirty-Six

They let him go home again after questioning him for several hours, though Inspector Liphook made it quite clear that he was high on the list of suspects.

'You won't be going anywhere, will you, Mr Mackworth?'

'I had no plans to. Not out of London.'

Not anywhere, really, he thought as he let himself into the strangely deserted hall. Not going anywhere.

He sat for a little while on a chair – a rather nice Georgian one which he never sat on; it was in the hall because it filled a corner – he sat and allowed his thoughts to fill the silence. Where was Jo? Why hadn't the police believed him when he had told them she lived here? It was quite evident to him that she must have killed the girl. He had told them about his self-defence lessons with a female instructor, but it merely confirmed their impression that he knew how to kill. The only thing that foxed them was a motive; even Inspector Liphook thought the jealousy angle was weak. Kate certainly wouldn't have told him about a lesbian relationship, even if it had been true; and it wasn't. Was it? Of course not.

Finally he stirred himself, walked over to the telephone and dialled her number.

'Kate?'

'Duncan.'

Her voice sounded coldy and subdued.

'Are you all right?' he asked.

'Not really.'

There was no point in asking her what was wrong.

'I wish I'd never met you,' she said. 'If I'd never met you Mel wouldn't be dead.'

'I didn't kill her.'

'Yes you did.'

He knew she was right in a way.

'She was wearing my dress. The green one I wore when we went out. That's why she was killed. She was meant to be me.'

'I'm sorry,' he said. 'I'm terribly sorry.'

'It's too late now.'

'Were you ... you know ... what the police said ... ?'

There was silence for a while.

'Hullo,' he said. 'Hullo, Kate, are you there?'

'She was going to be married,' she said. 'You didn't know that, did you? She'd come back to give me the news.'

'I'm so sorry,' he told her.

'I'll come round,' she said. 'I have to get out of here.'

Ten minutes later she arrived. There were bags under her eyes and the curly hair had lost its bounce. He gave her a glass of Gewürztraminer which she drank without tasting. Then she started on another tack.

'I don't think Jo exists,' she said. 'I think you invented her. I told the police that.'

'But why would I invent her?'

'To cover up your ... your inexperience. It was clear you weren't that used to women. You ran a mile when I asked you up to bed. You just didn't want to look silly. So you invented Jo. It was a good story. You made her sound rather attractive. But nobody's like that.'

'Jo's real enough. I'm afraid that's *your* inexperience. She was seduced by her uncle as a child. She's dangerously unstable, I see that now. But she's real enough. Too real.'

'I'd like to meet her.'

'No you wouldn't. She wanted to kill you. If she knew she'd made a mistake she'd want to kill you even more.'

211

'It's the end of everything,' she said.

They sat in silence at the opposite ends of the sofa. A thought struck him.

'Why did you invite me up to bed?' he asked her.

'Because I knew you wouldn't,' she said.

The picture – a rather good unfinished portrait of a pretty girl by Frank Miles – fell with appalling suddenness in the silence that followed her remark. Shattering the glass, it toppled over and dropped to the ground behind them. As they started up, both wine glasses fell over and broke, spilling their contents onto the Persian rug which Duncan's father had brought back from a trip to the Euphrates. Perhaps it was the crack of the wire, but for some reason Duncan thought there had been a shot through the open window.

Kate began to scream, not loud, but long.

Duncan, though shocked, found that his training once again stood him in good stead. He wasn't going to hang around waiting for another shot.

'Get down,' he yelled at her, pulling her behind the Chesterfield.

She stopped screaming and looked at him like a dog waiting for instruction.

'Crawl,' he told her. 'Follow me.'

They padded out, doggily, into the hall and Duncan rang the police.

'We're being shot at,' he said. 'Tell Inspector Liphook. And come quickly.'

Kate sat with her back to the wall, white as mayflower, opening and shutting her mouth from which no sound came. Soon the banshee wail of the police car could be heard, and moments later the place was crawling with constables. Inspector Liphook was not far behind. He examined the wall behind and just above the picture, and discovered a bullet lodged in the wall which the frame had almost concealed.

'You've been shot at right enough,' he said.

'I know,' said Duncan. 'We had that impression.'

'Any idea who did it?'

The time for dissembling was over.

'It's my girlfriend,' said Duncan.

'This young lady? You'd better come with me, miss.'

'No, no,' said Duncan. 'My other girlfriend.'

'Something of a lady's man, are we, sir? Perhaps this will teach you a lesson. What is it with you people? You play with people's emotions and someone gets hurt. Let's see. A revenge shooting? Some relative perhaps who thinks you may have murdered Miss Ashburton?'

'Inspector . . . the person who killed Miss Ashburton and the person who fired that rifle are one and the same.'

'And who would you say that was, sir?'

'Jo Lindup, of course. She's . . . not well.'

'It's an interesting hypothesis, sir. But the trouble is, we have no proof of Miss Lindup's existence.'

Duncan had an idea.

'Ask Luigi.'

'Luigi?'

The Inspector looked at him as though he were completely deranged.

'Loooeeegi?' he repeated. 'Who he?'

'The Italian restaurant round the corner. He saw us together.'

'He may have seen you together, sir, but it doesn't mean he knows who she is. He can't verify her identity. No, no. We need something more to go on. Any other ideas, sir?'

'Well . . . there was Captain Smail, but he never has the same address. And then there's Eddie.'

'Eddie?'

'Eddie was a former boyfriend of hers. But I don't know where he is either.'

'What a tangled web it is.'

Inspector Liphook scratched his head. A ballistics expert came up and said that the rifle had probably been fired from the roof of the flats opposite. The roof had been searched but the perpetrator had probably used the fire escape. A neighbour had seen someone running.

The Detective Constable appeared and threw further obfuscation on the subject.

'This could be terrorist work,' he said.

'Thank you Mulgrave,' said the Inspector. 'That possibility had entirely escaped me. Where do you get these brainwaves? Trinity, Cambridge?'

A sudden sadness for Jo swept over Duncan. What had he done to her? He had had no idea how deeply she felt, how hurt she must have been. And for what? He had given up all their happiness for a one-night stand – no, less than that, an emotional slap and tickle – with someone who perhaps had no real feeling for him at all.

'It strikes me,' said the Inspector, 'you two might be in danger. Let us say you're right. That this elusive girlfriend really is a nutter who's killed one person already. Let us say that. Well, it could be, you're next on her chopping list.'

'No no no no,' groaned Kate. 'No no no no. No.'

'Don't worry, young lady. We'll keep you safe. I'll put a constable on the door.'

Thirty-Seven

'We'd rather not be here tonight,' Duncan told the Inspector. 'I suggest I take Miss Greenwood to a hotel.'

'That's all right, I suppose,' the Inspector said, dubiously. 'Which one? I don't want you going far.'

'In any sense of the word,' said the Detective Constable.

Duncan took Kate back to collect some things, and they booked into the Norfolk at South Kensington.

'A double?' enquired the receptionist.

Duncan looked at Kate. She seemed worn out, vulnerable. She looked back at him, the bluebell eyes rimmed with campion-red. He felt sorry for her now.

'Yes, please,' she said.

At dawn they made love after a night of dreamless sleep. Whatever had held him back before seemed to have gone. It was strange making love to someone new. He had never slept with a woman before Jo, and the pattern with Jo had been unusual. Jo had liked to play the man. Perhaps because of her early experience, she would not submit, she had to dominate. Duncan had been obliged to be more tender, more persuasive, more languorous in return. This tendency seemed to appeal to Kate. She enjoyed the gentle caress, the half reluctance, the shy insistence – which in their turn kindled a kind of reckless fire in her that was perhaps as much a reaction to the drama of the last few days as a tribute to his lovemaking. Whatever the cause, it was almost alarming to see such pleasure in so slender a vessel – it was like watching a dinghy in a hurricane.

'You are a genius at it, Duncan,' she said afterwards; gaspingly, shudderingly spent. 'I never want to do anything but this.'

Was it sex after all that drove the world, he wondered, or was sex just another disguise, another face of the old enemy?

Later, he got out of bed and surveyed the opposite roof before half drawing the curtains. It was odd how Jo's image haunted him still. He would have thought it would be exorcized by what had taken place in the bedroom, but she was still in him. It was she in him who had been making love . . . Where was she now?

'What are we doing today?' Kate asked. 'I take back what I said, you know, about asking you up to bed at my flat. I was wrong about you, wasn't I?'

He leant down and kissed her, and wondered about Jo.

In the morning, the Inspector arrived again and said he wouldn't be surprised if he arrested him for murder. The ballistics expert had changed his mind about the bullet in the wall. It had apparently been carefully rigged, placed (perhaps by Duncan, the Inspector suggested) to look as though someone were after him. The wire had been almost cut through, and a large percussion cap had been concealed inside the frame. A most professional job, he said.

Duncan's initial amazement was tempered by the knowledge that there was no limit to Jo's ingenuity or complexity of purpose.

He complained that he wouldn't have been such a fool as to leave his card beside the corpse if he'd really committed the murder, but the Inspector would have none of it.

'There's arrogance I've seen,' he said, 'beside which that would be discreet.'

'There's arrogance he's seen,' said the Detective Constable, 'beside which that would seem like abject humility.'

216

The Inspector apologized once again, rather charmingly, for the graduate officer.

'We've got to have them,' he said, 'otherwise we fall foul of the Equal Opportunities Commission. Be thankful he's not a graduate woman.'

A mood of fatalism settled over Duncan. He was offered a solicitor but declined, saying he would handle his own affairs.

'I still don't see how you're going to make out a case against me,' he told the Inspector.

'It was the blow to the seventh vertebra,' he said. 'That's another nail in your coffin.'

'It didn't do her much good either,' said Duncan crossly. 'Look . . . I wouldn't have mentioned the vertebra if I'd done it. I'd have guessed . . . I don't know . . . strangling or something.'

'Or flaying, or death by a thousand cuts,' said the DC, helpfully. 'Or a particularly virulent strain of measles injected from the point of a shooting-stick.'

The Inspector gave him a look which would have withered a basilisk.

'Ever heard of bluff, Mr Mackworth?'

After they left, Duncan tried to find reasons for optimism but Kate seemed resigned, lowered by the whole situation.

Next morning, she attended her friend's funeral and had the unenviable job of looking after her parents. The experience subdued her for several days. Duncan did not go with her. As one of the suspects, he felt his presence might be in bad taste.

Meanwhile, he spent his own days in a ferment of anxiety. If the police didn't believe his account of Jo, there was every chance that they might think he really was guilty of the murder.

'The trouble is,' he said to Kate one evening when he called round for a chaste supper, 'because the juries won't convict, the police don't care who they accuse these days. And in my case, because I'm a solicitor they probably *would* convict because they hate lawyers.'

'Don't worry, she'll turn up,' said Kate, who seemed calmer now and inclined to resume carnal relations. 'There has to be something she's forgotten.'

She, at least, had begun to believe in Jo's existence again. Sure enough, two days later Inspector Liphook appeared at Kate's flat.

'We've picked up someone who can corroborate some of your story,' said the Inspector. 'Fellow called Smail. He's been in trouble with us before over firearms.'

Duncan felt a surge of optimism. It was pleasant to be believed.

'How did you find him?'

The Inspector looked slightly sheepish.

'We followed up your suggestion and put an ad in the *Spectator*. Got a reply by return. When we caught up with him he told us there had been a girl who had developed an obsession for one of what he called his team.'

This time Duncan's sensation was almost like a quirk of jealousy. Ridiculous, of course, but perhaps to be noted. Also he felt sorry for Jo being described like that. Surely she deserved better?

'He did recall sending her over to you – to get rid of her, he said.'

Thank you very much, Captain Smail, thought Duncan.

'If it's true, a big if, but if it's true, you both might be in some danger staying here. May I suggest you go away for a week or so while we trace the girl?'

'Can you take time off?' Duncan asked Kate.

She nodded.

'I expect I'll lose my job,' she said. 'But who cares?'

'Better to lose your job than lose your life, eh,' joked the Inspector.

Duncan did not think it was a very good joke. The Inspector did not know what Jo was capable of. They packed up Kate's car, a little Peugeot, and left the same morning.

Thirty-Eight

'Where are we going?' she asked him as she drove off.

'West,' he said. 'Better to go somewhere I know. If Jo follows us I'll have some advantage.'

'But she won't, will she?'

'I very much doubt it. Now she's killed someone she'll be keeping her head down.'

'She didn't just kill someone, she killed Mel. Why on earth did you get involved with her?' she asked, not for the first time.

Duncan really couldn't explain how it had come about. It seemed almost like a bad dream now, but he had been, what was the word?, etiolated like grass under a stone. That weight of fear had blanched him; and he had to thank Jo for taking it away. Oh, sure, she had exchanged it for something else now. But the fact that he was here, with Kate, now, was a kind of tribute to what she had done for him.

'Why does one get involved?' he asked vaguely. 'Actually, my trouble was, I was never involved enough. I was frightened of involvement.'

'And as it turned out you were right.'

'I was right.'

He laughed rather bitterly.

'Poor Duncan.'

She leant across and stroked his hand.

'Still,' she went on, 'there have been some compensations. Where are we going?'

The early cloud had cleared and it was turning out to be a glorious summer day.

'Deddington, I think,' he said. 'There's a hotel there. We'll book in and go and look at some of my old haunts.'

They left the motorway at the edge of the Chilterns as it sinks down towards Oxford, cutting across the ancient Icknield Way, had lunch in a pub near Thame, and wound their way across North Oxfordshire, through Bletchingdon and Kirtlington until they came out near Deddington, a small honey-coloured town with a towered church whose golden pennants coruscated in the sun.

'I don't know about Jo,' Kate said, 'but I couldn't follow where we've been or where we've come from.'

'Here came I often in old days,' he said.

They checked into the Holcombe House and decided to go for a walk. There was absolutely no sign of Jo. Now they were in his home country, it seemed as though it must be closed to her.

'She couldn't be here, could she?' Kate asked.

She was still worried. Not surprising after what she'd been through.

'This is North Oxfordshire,' Duncan said. 'It's a no-Jo area.'

He might joke, but still he felt, yes, a sense of guilt about her, a sort of sharp thin strand of hurt, rather like homesickness, that made its presence known amongst the brightness of the sun and even in the happiness he felt with Kate, though there was a vaporous quality about the happiness which suggested transience.

It seemed Kate was meanwhile experiencing some feelings of guilt herself.

'It seems unfair to be happy,' she said, 'disloyal to Mel, I mean.'

'I think she would rather you were happy, don't you?' said Duncan, not that he knew the girl, but it seemed a reasonable guess.

His reassurance had the right effect and Kate stopped looking troubled.

'Where shall we go?' she asked. 'Somewhere far from roads, please.'

He took her on one of his favourite walks from the old days, where he and his mother used to go, up the disused railway line to the nature reserve by the tunnel at Hook Norton.

Behind them, the grass stretched in a long verdant swerve past may trees and pasture towards a distant perpendicular spire. It was a beautiful summer evening. A skylark sang high above them, all the scents of summer surrounded them, and the sinister rage of the city seemed no more than a dim pattering far behind. Elderflower and dog rose garlanded them overhead; meadowsweet and speedwell, forget-me-not and cowslip fringed them underfoot. Rabbits scampered and scattered before them, and on the little river they passed, a pair of swans floated, motionless as meringues.

They turned and took one more look at the spire.

'Bloxham the long, Adderbury the strong and King's Sutton the beautiful . . .' he told her. 'That's what the locals say.'

'Pity we missed the other two.'

'Maybe tomorrow,' he said.

The shadows were lengthening now, the sky began to take on its marvellous greeny blue and the clouds grew pink and gold and fluffy as a putto's wing. It seemed ridiculous to Duncan that they were meant to be in hiding. And yet, if things had been different, he wouldn't have been here now, looking at this amazing show, feeling so ridiculously fortunate.

It was then that he saw her, just a glimpse, a red-golding of hair at the corner of a trackway into a field. It couldn't be anyone but her. His heart started pounding. Excitement, fear, affection, a strange abyssal sense of helplessness, outrage and fear again swept over him. Something prompted him to say nothing to Kate, who was examining a small red flower and trying to remember its name.

'It begins with a P,' she said, 'I'm sure of it. Par, per, pic . . .'

He looked away for an instant as a trailing bramble brushed his hair, and when he looked back the figure was gone.

'Pimpernel, that's it. Scarlet Pimpernel. They seek him here, they seek him there . . .'

Kate waved the little flower triumphantly at him. He made approving noises and they walked on towards the setting sun. How on earth could Jo have caught up with them? He supposed, hearing him talk about his childhood, she might have deduced that he would come this way. But then again, she seemed in any case to have powers of anticipation that were beyond reason. Even so, it was manifestly implausible that the girl he had seen was Jo.

'You're quiet,' Kate said.

'Sometimes silence is the only thing to say,' he told her, while a blackbird chose very loudly to dispute the point.

They passed near the grey-gold village of Hook Norton with the little brewery that looks like a pagoda. Here we could stop and call the Inspector, he thought. And yet . . . He didn't want to seem panicky or to frighten Kate without good reason. They met one or two other people on the line. Another quarter mile and he thought: no doubt about it, that copper-brown head had been some country girl, gazing at the evening, whistling a dog or calling in a pony.

'Better turn back soon,' he said. 'Last orders at 9.'

Midges skimmed. A late thrush trilled like a Kneller Hall trumpeter. The sun descended, swollen and rubicund as if rehearsing for its red giant phase in three billion years time. The landscape bathed in a delicious freshness, poised between light and twilight. Cattle lay Turnerishly in the faintest vestige of meadow mist. Past Hook Norton, the Cotswolds grow more serious. Hills hump up higher, cuttings are deeper. As they rounded a bend, a little secret valley came into view.

It was a place such as Spenser would have enjoyed, a bower of bliss, a little ordered wilderness, where the birds were so unexpectedly tame it made the humans seem wild. The notice asking you not to pick the flowers or disturb the nesting birds struck the only discordant note. It seemed so totally unnecessary.

'Though I suppose you might need it if you were a goblin or troll,' Kate said.

'Plenty of those around,' said Duncan. 'It's smaller than I remember.'

'I think it's lovely,' she told him and gave him a kiss. 'Thank you for bringing me.'

As he returned the embrace, he looked over her shoulder and saw Jo.

She was gazing at him with an expression of intense hatred in which he saw hurt as well, so that his heart ached for her while his mind registered alarm. She was standing on the village side of the reserve, cutting off their escape both backwards and in the direction of the houses. There was only one other way to go.

'What is it?' asked Kate.

She turned but Jo had gone.

'It's Jo, I'm afraid,' he said.

'Oh my God,' said Kate.

She stood still for a moment, thinking, and then she said: 'She can't do anything here. There are people about.' She corrected herself. 'There *were* people about. But she can't *do* anything.'

'I wouldn't be so sure,' said Duncan. 'I know her. There's nothing she won't do. There was something in her hand. It looked like a gun to me.'

In fact, he was absolutely certain of it.

'What are we going to do? We must tell the police.'

'There's only one way,' he said. 'She can't have a car. I'm not even sure she drives. If we go through the tunnel she'll never catch us. She'd have to go miles round, or come after us. And we've a good quarter mile start. Lucky I brought the torch. I was going to show you a bit of the tunnel anyway.'

He hated tunnels, but he had thought she might have liked a peek inside. It turned out that Kate hated tunnels too.

'Do we have to?' she asked.

'Afraid so,' he said. 'It's not long.'

The elderflower gleamed like streetlamps on either side as they approached the great black O of the cavern.

> *'"Jonathan Joe had a mouth like an O*
> *And a wheelbarrow full of surprises . . ."'*

he said, trying to drum up resolve.

Kate looked as though she wasn't fond of A. A. Milne at the best of times, and certainly wasn't keen to hear it now.

'My mother used to read it to me,' he told her. 'There was a picture of a gaping old gardener and a small boy. I can't remember what the surprises were.'

'Let's hope there aren't any nasty ones in there,' said Kate.

'No surprises, please, tunnel,' said Duncan, looking up.

The tunnel was fringed with fern which gave its mouth an unpleasant whiskery look, and added to the impression of a black, voracious maw with a well-developed case of caries.

'Better hurry.'

They stepped inside. In spite of the warmth of the evening, the place was cold as a catacomb. Water seemed to be everywhere, dripping from the roof, glistening from the sides, oozing up from the spongy track. Puddles gleamed in the torchlight. Something scuttled away in the darkness. Something else swooped towards them, parting Kate's hair.

She half-screamed.

'Shhhh,' he told her, holding her hand.

'Rats, bats and buckets of blood,' he said, to give himself courage.

His uncle, an enormous man with polished riding boots, used to say such things. Happily there were no buckets of blood so far but he wouldn't count on it.

'I can't go on,' said Kate.

She told him she could feel the tons of masonry, the earth and the rock pressing down on her.

'We have to,' he said, though he could feel it too.

They half fell down a strange pothole that suddenly opened up in the track.

'No one would know if we fell,' she said. 'What if we broke a leg? We'd lie here till the rats got us.'

He tried to think of the tunnel as a wondrous piece of engineering, though a small enough feat by the standards of the Victorians.

'This is a hundred years old at least,' he said. 'Imagine the men who built it. Just picks and shovels and the sweat of their brows.'

He thought of the navvies, mustachioed men in braces; where were they now, and their wives and sweethearts, pretty girls with soft brown hair, and their children, the dear little babbies? All gone under the hill.

A great white thing flapped out at them whoo-whooooing like something out of a ghost train so that he almost dropped the torch and cried out.

'Just an owl,' he said, to reassure her.

Kate was in a bad way, quietly sobbing beside him.

Was it an owl? Or a familiar? Weren't the Cotswolds still centres of witchcraft? And if it were an owl, couldn't owls go for your eyes and blind you?

They tripped over something – a wire? a long bony hand? – and fell in stinking mud . . .

'Oh fuck,' he shouted, in fear and vexation.

'Fuck fuck fuck fuck fuck,' replied echo.

The torch was broken.

'I'm not going any further,' said Kate in her strange coldy voice. 'I don't care what happens. I'm not going on.'

But far away in the distance he could see, without the torch, a faint glimmering of evening.

'Come on,' he said. 'It's the end.'

'It's the end,' she repeated.

'End, end, end,' said echo.

They stumbled towards it like souls of the dead towards the light, trammelled as they go by things that would stop them. There was one last ordeal to be undergone. As they hurried forward into the pearly twilight, thankful to be rid of the dreadful place, a brick fell from the arch above the entrance and struck Duncan on the shoulder, knocking him to the ground.

Kate cried out again. He rose slowly, feeling his injury, flexing his arm to test for a fracture. It appeared there was nothing broken.

'It'll be a bruise,' he said. 'I was lucky, another inch and it would have been brains for supper.'

Kate sat by the trackside, white-faced and shocked.

'My God, look at us,' he said.

They had come into the tunnel with all their city gloss. They had emerged looking like survivors of a disaster. Kate's dress was torn and mud-stained. Her shoes were no longer shoes but mud-hods. As for him, his grey trousers were blackened and his jacket, where the brick had fallen, was torn and slime-stained. Both of their faces were streaked with mud and lichen.

He stooped and examined the brick or half-brick as it turned out to be. Did it fall or was it thrown? He inspected the roof. There was no sign of a brick missing along the parapet.

Once again, he said nothing to Kate. She did not look as though she could take any more.

'I want to go back to the hotel,' she said.

They were in a steep cutting, and vulnerable to any attack from above.

'We'd better move on now,' he told her. 'There was a stop just down the line. Rollright Halt. There'll be houses there. We can call the police and phone for a taxi.'

She rose wearily and followed him. All the stuffing seemed to have been knocked out of her. It was plain to see she'd never had survival training. In a few hundred yards, the cutting became shallower and a mile further on they came to the halt. It was, however, a halt without houses.

'We'd better follow the lane up the hill,' said Duncan. 'There's a village at the top.'

'I'm so tired,' said Kate.

'Just a little way,' he told her.

It was growing darker now. The very light mist he had noticed earlier had turned almost to hill fog as they climbed towards the top. Behind them they heard a car coming.

'Let's stop it,' said Kate. 'I can't go on.'

The car, without lights, was coming very fast. Indeed as they stood and waved, it appeared to be driving straight at them.

'Bloody idiot,' cried Duncan. 'Look out.'

He flung himself at Kate and pulled her to the side as the car swept by. It was a red Peugeot. Duncan caught a glimmer of a coppery head bent low behind the wheel.

'That was my car,' said Kate.

'Did you see who was driving it?' he asked.

But he knew who it was. Above them, they could hear the yelp of tyres and racing of engine as a car was turned round at high speed and came down the hill towards them again.

'Quick,' said Duncan, 'over here.'

He grabbed her hand and led her past a gate, down a path and into a field beside the lane where huge standing stones appeared; some leaning attentively, strangely human in the mist. They sheltered behind one, looking back towards the road.

'What are they?' asked Kate wonderingly.

'The King's Men. It's a Bronze Age stone circle. They always come to a different number when you count them.'

She didn't seem inclined to try.

'What are we going to do?' she whispered.

'Follow me. We'll try to make our way up to the farm across the field here.'

They began to cross cautiously, from standing stone to

227

standing stone, peeping round each one to make sure the coast was clear.

'She's probably gone down to the wood the other side,' whispered Duncan, as they came to the last stone before the paddock.

'Wrong,' said a hard voice in his ear. 'Did you learn nothing from me, Duncan?'

Kate started crying.

'Stop that,' said Jo, putting a gun in her back.

So, thought Duncan, I was right. We never had a chance.

'Walk back to the car, both of you,' said Jo. 'And don't try anything. I'm quite prepared to use this. Not that I need to.'

They walked back towards the road, praying for traffic, but nothing stirred. Great Rollright was a quiet place on a summer evening.

'Get in the front, both of you. Let the woman drive. I'll keep you covered in the back.'

'Where are we going?' asked Duncan.

'We're going where you wanted to go, Duncan, remember. We're going to seal island. Your fate is sealed. Remember?'

Kate had stopped crying, but seemed glazed as if on automatic pilot.

'Snap out of it,' said Jo, brutally, 'and wipe your face, you look like a guttersnipe.

She handed Kate a cloth.

'Spit and wipe, go on, you dirty little whore. You too, Duncan. I don't want you looking like vagrants. We don't want to be stopped until we get there, do we?'

Thirty-Nine

They drove all night beneath an elderflower moon, Duncan taking turns with Kate at the wheel.

Jo sat in the back, gun in her hand, occasionally passing them a thermos top of lukewarm coffee – just in case they were thinking of throwing it at her, she said. They were famished, but all she had was digestive biscuits, better than nothing but not much. They stopped only once for petrol, outside Cardiff. Jo made Duncan do the filling while she sat with her gun in Kate's back.

'You try anything, Duncan, and I'll blow her backbone in half.'

The look Kate gave him persuaded him not to try anything.

It was past three in the morning and the dawn was just breaking when they drove through St David's and took the little road past the cathedral that looks as if it's sliding down the hill, towards the sea. They drove for another two miles, branched right down a track that petered out above a cliff, and stopped. Jo told Duncan to reverse the car into a cranny sheltered by overhanging branches where it would be virtually invisible, and then she ordered them out.

Kate and Duncan were by now exhausted, but Jo appeared to be her usual cool self.

'Down the steps,' she told them, 'and into the boat.'

'Where are we going, Jo?' Duncan asked.

'Over to Selsey,' she said. 'Where else?'

Selsey was where he had been thinking of taking Kate anyway. It was where Booth had set up his seal-watch. Why was Jo taking them over when Booth would be there?

As so often before, she read his mind.

'Mr Booth – Alec – has met with an accident, Duncan. I've been staying with him now and then, you know. He really liked me. I was so sorry about his fall. I had to take him in to hospital. He's got bad concussion, I'm afraid. The cliffs can be very slippery in wet weather. But it's all right. I told them I was working with him and would look after everything.'

So Booth had fancied his chances with Jo, had he? Duncan didn't know whether to laugh or cry. The poor old chap had certainly been heading for his fall.

He followed Kate down the steps to the boat which was moored to a little jetty at the foot of the cliff.

'Get in,' she said. 'And don't think of diving overboard. It's ebb tide and it empties out of the Irish Sea at something like six knots here. I read that somewhere. See those rocks over there?'

They looked where she was pointing. A ridge of white foam seethed around a half submerged reef that extended like trolls' stepping stones from the island to the mainland.

'The lifeboat ended up there sixty years ago. Everyone was drowned. All right? Now sit down and shut up.'

She started the engine – a sturdy old inboard – and cast off. The boat, equally sturdy, butted out into the current. It was going to be a beautiful day, thought Duncan – only from the point of view of weather, of course. But it was impossible to be absolutely downcast, tired though he was, at the spectacle the morning presented.

The great expanse of moving water shimmered and shimmied like a billion sequined backsides, the low morning sun catching the tops of the waves and throwing light about in a positive carnival of iridescence. To the left and behind, the towering grey cliffs were sombre, in shadow, but beyond, to the south, the islands showed intense viridian, russets, yellows – and brilliant whites where the gulls nested among their guano.

The island they were heading for, Selsey, was one of the largest, covering some fifty acres. It had been inhabited, farmed, sometime in the past, but now it was deserted, apart from uncountable seabirds, an over-run of rabbits and a substantial colony of grey seals from which, according to some, the island derived its name – though others preferred the derivation from the Norse 'säl' meaning holy, for there were prehistoric burial mounds on its two summits and at one time the island boasted two chapels. One was dedicated to St Justinian, apparently St David's confessor, and the other to St Dyfanog, an early Celtic missionary. All this Duncan could remember, for he had spent many days around St David's in his childhood, kicking his heels while his mother (and father when he was around) went nature-watching.

A pity, thought Duncan, that he had taken against nature at the time. It was a tendency, he supposed, of many small boys to resent their parents' interests. Hours spent watching birds could seem better spent at the cinema. For him especially, though, nature was already a threatening affair, hedged about with instructive images of pain and death and little heaps of feathers that Father had filmed.

He looked over at Kate. She seemed to have gone into a kind of hibernation, a huddle of resignation he had seen on the faces of South American Indians facing the devastation of their homes by a mudslide.

He reached across to comfort her.

'Cheer up. It's not so bad,' he whispered.

But Jo heard him and disagreed.

'It *is* so bad,' she said. 'And worse.'

They could see the tidal race quite clearly now, the ebbing water bottled up by the line of rocks, a couple of feet higher one side than the other, and the sea going mad as it tried to force its way through. All around, swirls and eddies showed the counter current of the thwarted water, and whirlpools appeared, licking round the timbers of their boat.

'Don't you think you should steer further away?' suggested Duncan.

'What does it matter?' said Jo, though he noticed she edged the tiller sharply towards her.

Duncan thought, I could take her now. She's concentrating on the boat, I could knock the gun into the sea. And then he saw she'd tied it to her belt. She would do that, wouldn't she? She never made mistakes, did Jo. He comforted himself with the reflection that, in the struggle, the boat would have hit the rocks and killed them all. It wasn't much comfort, but it was comfort of a kind.

They were nearing a little stone quay now.

'Get ready to hang on,' Jo said to him. 'And no funny stuff.'

She brought the boat in expertly. Was that another thing the boys had taught her?

'You'll never get away with this,' he said, rather limply, as she tied up.

'You'll never get away at all,' was her unsettling rejoinder.

She made them walk in front of her as she directed them towards the stone house which Booth had rented. A couple of outbuildings, a yard, and a small enclosed garden showing scratchy grass completed the farmstead. It was all the human habitation there was on Selsey. He noticed a television aerial on the chimney, but no sign of a telephone.

Inside, the house was cheerless, though it need not necessarily have been so. Booth was not a domestic man, and Jo had wasted no time on charming touches. She had come here because there was business to be done.

Duncan did not know whether he was more tired than hungry or more hungry than tired. Kate did not look as though she cared. Jo settled the issue.

'If you eat now and then sleep, you'll wake up hungry again, and I've only food for one meal. So you can sleep now.'

She pushed them upstairs and showed them into two separate rooms in each of which were two beds and a sleeping bag.

'Separate rooms,' she told them. 'None of that filthy stuff even if you were feeling like it, which I imagine you're not.'

Kate slumped into sleep as soon as she sat on the bed, then Jo took Duncan into the other room.

'Look, Jo,' he said, 'I'm sorry, but you know I had to do what I did. I had to get away. You wouldn't have respected me if I'd become utterly dependent. You know that.'

'You cheated on me,' she said. 'You are a filthy man. I gave you everything and you had to go creeping about in other women's cunts.'

The word shocked him. Jo had never used words like that. She hated that sort of language. His face must have registered his surprise.

'You taught me foul language, Duncan, by your foul behaviour. Which is worse?'

'I've said I'm sorry.'

'You're not sorry. You've more or less admitted that you'd go back and do it again. But when I've finished with you, you'll wish you'd known what was good for you.'

'Look. Can't we just go back and forget it?'

'Go back? You mean, together?'

'Well . . .'

Duncan's mind raced. If he said yes, there might at least be a chance.

'Go on,' she told him.

'We could try to start again. Give it a chance.'

'You're pathetic, Duncan, d'you realize that? What sort of idiot d'you think I am? I wouldn't give you a second chance if you were Jesus Christ himself. But to me, Duncan, you're more than just you. You're the whole idea of men. So-called intelligent humans ruled by a whistle between their legs whose tune they have to dance to. God didn't mean that when he created mankind. I'm visiting the sins of the fathers on you, Duncan, and the cousins and the brother and the uncles – especially the uncles . . .'

Duncan tried another tack. All this talk of God had given him an idea. Did she have some kind of religious mania?

'I don't think you're very well, Jo, that's the thing. I'd give anything to help. Why don't you let me take us back to the mainland?'

He moved towards her, but in a flash the gun was out.

'Good try, Duncan, but I taught you all you know, remember. You won't catch me napping. Make your peace with yourself now, and rest like your little whore.'

'At least let Kate go,' he said. 'She has nothing to do with all this.'

'Nothing to do with it?' Jo blazed. 'Oh Duncan, you're so blind. Remember what King Lear says, Duncan? "The gods are just, and of our pleasant vices make instruments to plague us." She was your pleasant vice, Duncan. Don't you think she's guilty, too? She has a lot to answer for, that one. Sleep now. I want you in good shape.'

She left him and went downstairs. Duncan could hear her moving about and tried to guess what she was doing. Some kind of preparation seemed to be afoot, but it could wait for the moment. No doubt he would discover its meaning soon enough. He lay there, waiting for sleep, but tired as he was, it would not come. Surely there was something he could do? What was the weak link in Jo's armour?

To soften her in the past he had used humour, but she seemed to have no propensity for that now. It was perhaps one of the first clinical signs of madness, he thought; loss of sense of humour. But what did one do about it? Plying her with jokes would be like offering colours to a blind man.

The trouble was, in his heart he still could not believe she would go through with whatever she was planning. At the last moment, she would relent. But suppose she didn't. Who was going to save them then? Someone at the hotel must have called the police by now. Their bags would be still there. A description of Kate's car would be circulated. If they could only hold out long enough, there was a chance someone would find the Peugeot, and the police would come looking for them across the water.

The trouble was, Jo did not seem to be planning for a long stay on the island. One meal, she had said. How on earth were they going to stretch that out?

There was the sudden sound of wind against the roof. He looked out of the window. Clouds had come up. Beyond the barn he could see the water out in the bay beginning to show white horses. He remembered his excitement as a child when his mother said 'White horses in the bay!' He loved to see the huge waves and think: If someone offered me £1,000, would I be brave enough to dive in? He knew the answer to that. Luckily, no one offered the money.

'Perhaps there'll be a shipwreck,' he would think, or a tidal wave. Even then, he had a well developed sense of possible disaster . . .

Why could he not sleep?

He remembered the Henry Newbolt poem he'd had to learn when he was ten. It was called 'He Fell Among Thieves'. He lay, as the wind drummed in the roof, recalling the story. An Englishman had been captured by brigands in some remote piratical part after a struggle in which both sides had received fatalities. The Englishman had sportingly suggested that they call it quits, but the brigands had other ideas. 'Blood for our blood, they said.' So the hero had asked to be spared for one more night so that he could see the sunrise.

To this they had agreed, and left him with his thoughts, as Duncan himself was now left to his. In the poem, the hero had thought of his childhood, his father 'calling him down to ride', his school, his university and 'the College Eight with faces merry and keen', the steamer taking him out to this godforsaken corner of Empire to bear the white man's burden . . .

How different it was now! There was nothing left of honour or uprightness or any of those virtues it was customary – almost obligatory – to mock. Only a mean and watery liberalism now passed for a code, and try drawing on that in your hour of need! The soldier's pole had fallen all right . . . But what had he, Duncan, done to keep it upright? No doubt about it, he had skulked. It had been easier that way . . .

It was with such dispiriting conjectures that Duncan finally fell asleep. And when he woke, it was not with a sense of thankfulness for creation, as Sir Henry's hero had done, but with a keen sense of waste. He rose hurriedly and ran downstairs. Jo was putting some tired lettuce round a plate containing three pork pies and a tomato. A stack of brown bread slices and some Flora margarine also made an appearance.

'Not much good beating cholesterol if I'm not going to live long anyway,' he said.

Jo looked at him.

'It's not how long you live, it's how you live, Duncan.'

The extraordinary thing was, the more he saw her now, the more he admired her. She had something of the stuff of a Newbolt.

'It's like some sort of Greek tragedy,' he told her. 'The end is inevitable and terrible; once started it has to end that way. And yet, you can sympathize with the humans who are caught up in it – even respect them, as I respect you, Jo.'

She responded to that idea although it did nothing to soften her resolve.

'I'm glad you've come to that, Duncan. Because when we die together, we shall be close again. Death will cleanse all the faults, all the filth that, living, I can't forgive you for. Then we shall be as we were.'

It was true; she was like some retributive force beyond nature; but that didn't mean he wanted to die.

'Would you shoot me if I tried to escape?' he asked.

'You know I would,' she said. 'And then I would shoot her, and then myself. But I don't want it to be like that. Please, Duncan, don't let me have to do that.'

It was the first time she had begged anything of him. Although it seemed hopeless, it gave him heart.

'Come,' she said, 'eat, it will give you more courage.'

'What about Kate?'

'She won't wake for some time yet,' she said. 'I put something in her coffee. I promise you, Duncan, she is better off asleep.'

He did as Jo suggested, and polished off the pie, limp lettuce and all. Salad cream sachets from the Journey's End Café added to his sense of unreality.

'What about you?' he asked.

'I ate while you slept. Come,' she said, 'the tide is right. I want to show you something. No time to waste. We're not in the Old Brompton Road now.'

'"I wasted time and now doth time waste me",' he said.

Jo smiled for the first time that day.

'Oh, good, Duncan. That's better. Now you're beginning to understand.'

Forty

She led him down to the jetty.

'Get in,' she said.

He settled himself in the stern and waited for her to join him. Even here where the boat lay, sheltered by an encircling arm of protecting wall and rock, he could feel the uneasy bump and lurch of the rising sea.

'Hold on to the jetty now,' she told him.

He leant across and grasped the side while she clambered aboard and started the engine.

'Where are we going?' he asked.

'I want to show you something.'

'Isn't it a little choppy? The wind seems to be getting up.'

'I've been out with Booth in worse than this. It'll be more sheltered when we round the point.'

'I hope so.'

He wasn't the best sailor in the world.

'Cast off now.'

'What did you want to show me?'

'Sea . . .'

At least that's what he thought she said, but the wind took the word and spun it round like spray as the boat headed out into the channel.

'Sea?' he shouted. 'I've seen the sea.'

I joined the Navy to see the world, and what did I see? I saw the sea.

'Seals,' she shouted back. 'Seal with an l.'

He thought of suggesting that they go and see them another day, but the limited supply of food in the house seemed to indicate that another day would be a day too many. The sea thumped and flopped at the old boat. Fortunately, it was a following wind and tide so they were spared the worst of the weather. Even so, he was getting wet. What would it be like coming back? He comforted himself, as another sheet of spray flew past, that Jo, ever since he had met her, had always seemed to know what she was doing.

'"And everyone cried, 'You'll all be drowned!'",' he shouted.

He had introduced her to Edward Lear during her literary phase, and hoped perhaps the gentle poet-painter would exercise a benign influence. Indeed, there seemed to be some response.

'The Jumblies,' she shouted back with something of the old Jo in her tones. 'Give us another one.'

But he wanted her to concentrate on navigation rather than literature.

'"What little sense I once possessed has quite gone out of my head",' he yelled.

That would fox her, and it did, as well as being peculiarly relevant.

'Um,' she said. 'Um. Give up. Whoops!'

A quantity of ocean landed in his lap.

'The Dong,' he bellowed in alarm and irritation.

'The Dong?'

'The Dong with the Luminous Nose.'

There was something magnificent about her, though, as she sat by the tiller with her red-brown hair blown by the wind, looking like something out of the *Ring* cycle. Why did she want him to see seals? Why all this procedure? Surely Kate could have come too, rather than leaving her to wake alone in the farmhouse?

No vestige of his former feeling for the girl remained – Jo

239

had effectively killed that – rather in the manner of Winston and Julia in 1984. There was a hymn too, how did it go? 'Through many deeds of shame, we learn that love grows cold.' Love was very cold now, cold and soaking, but he still felt sorry for Kate. He blamed himself for getting her into all this.

Still, he comforted himself, he knew Jo. Her moods did not last for ever. She would come round, apologize, and the harm done – though considerable, indeed actionable if Kate wished to take it that far – could perhaps be limited.

A particularly large comber raced by, making the boat twitch like a filly at her first race, but Jo held her steady as they rounded a little cape and made for the western shore of the island. This was the side that, sheltered today, normally took the full force of the prevailing westerlies from the Atlantic. Here storm beaches had been thrown up; little coves crammed at the neck with boulders and pebbles delivered by the breakers and built up over countless centuries so that, in the end, the beaches lay above even the fiercest storms and the highest tides.

It was here that the Atlantic grey seals, Duncan knew, would have their young any time between September and January, starting again on their cycle of copulation and birth within a very few weeks of pupping. It was here, too, that the mothers would keep their pups for the vital days before they learnt to swim.

Already Duncan could see a little clutch of young seals at the edge of one cove and Jo pointed out a couple swimming further down the bay. What was it Booth had said about the rogue female? Some outlandish tale that he had rather discounted, knowing Booth's complicated relationship with himself. No doubt there were occasionally rogue females. But did they really bite the males' members in the way he had described? Or was it Booth's fantasy? It was news to Duncan that seals had a bone in the penis like a dog or an otter as he had said; but then it was news to him that dogs and otters had them too. Nature was full of such surprises.

'Where's the rogue female?' Duncan shouted.

Jo made a sign; enigmatic, hieratic. He would have to wait. He hoped it wouldn't be too long; he was getting wetter. The boat plunged and bucketed round another point, and the sea diminished a little. A stretch of desolate cliffs was revealed in which a row of sea caves showed up like holes in a grey cheese.

'The tide's just right,' she said. 'Just past halfway.'

It was towards one of these caves that Jo now steered. Duncan was relieved to think that the journey was nearing its goal at last. No doubt they would approach, peer in, spy on a seal, and pass on to the next cave. What was cave in Latin? A funny word, the sort of Latin word you didn't forget, even after all that time. Spelunca! They would pass on to the next spelunca. But not a bit of it. He suddenly realized what she meant to do. Oh my God. She actually proposed, in this uneasy sea, to take the boat right into the spelunca, under an overhang only a couple of feet or so above their heads.

It seemed incredibly dangerous, but there was nothing he could do to stop her. The matter was out of his hands. If he had attempted to wrestle the tiller from her they would have ended up on the rocks.

He ducked hurriedly as the swell lifted the boat under the overhang, almost scraping the bow as it passed underneath. The cave stretched away into the darkness, resounding to the disconcerting lop-lop of water when the noise of the engine died. There was a dank, frightening smell of seaweed, ooze and dead fish. The boat wobbled uncertainly in the squeezed-in water.

'Is it quite safe?' he asked, his voice sounding too loud among the echoes.

'Quite safe,' said the echoes.

Jo smiled mysteriously.

'Listen to the echoes,' she said.

And then he asked the question that had been troubling him.

'Halfway what?' he said, his voice cracking with concern.

'Sssh. You'll disturb the seals.'

'Halfway what?' he whispered urgently.

'Halfway what do you mean?' she asked.

'The tide,' he almost squeaked with the seriousness of it. 'You mean it's halfway down, don't you?'

'Out, Duncan. We speak of the tide being out.'

'Well is it? Is it halfway out?'

She laughed now.

'Don't be silly, Duncan. Why do you think we're going in without any power? The tide is coming in, Duncan. It's easy to see you're a landlubber.'

This was ridiculous. She was mad. They were going to be trapped in here. All his claustrophobia rose gaggingly, leaving a bitter taste in his mouth.

'Turn round,' he shouted.

'Shhh,' she cautioned again. 'The seals.'

'Damn the seals. We have to get out. We're trapped.'

Jo smiled and shook her head at him.

'Oh, Duncan, you are an old panicker. There's a storm beach at the end here. It's above all but the very highest tides. I've waited on it till high water myself, and watched it turn. It's fun. Come on now, Duncan. This is the adventure, remember.'

She was reverting more and more to the old Jo now. Jo in her smiling and reasonable mode. If he went along with her, she might in a few more minutes become entirely herself again. He had to do what she suggested at the moment, though every instinct in him rebelled against it.

This was the fear that had loomed ahead of him all his life; his sense of impending horror had been but a pre-echo of these terrors to come. Hadn't that been the way of it in *The White Hotel* in which the central character had had the same sense of doom, had even been psychoanalysed for it, only to discover that her presentiments were well-founded, but it was the *future* and not some childhood trauma that had been haunting her.

So it must be with him. If only he had gone for psychoanalysis instead of taking up self-defence, this would never have happened! Some rabbity little psychoanalyst would never have taken him into a sea cave and scared the pants off him. Of course, talking of pants, Jo had provided other attractions, but what use was that now? It was mere expense of semen, a capital talentlessly obtained and meaninglessly dissipated.

He realized with a shock that the boat was grounding.

'We've hit the bottom,' he shouted wildly. 'We're going to sink.'

Why did Jo not show any concern?

'Calm down, Duncan,' she said.

His eyes, acclimatizing to the darkness, now perceived that they had reached the end of the channel. Before them lay a small beach such as the ones he had seen outside, with boulders and pebbles piled high to the back, accumulated by God knew what wrack and hurricane.

'Quick,' said Jo. 'Jump.'

She indicated a boulder as big as a small car and he prepared to do as she ordered. The situation could only get better if he did exactly what she said. Scrambling up from his half-crouch in the boat, he sprang onto the stone, slipped, grazed his knee, skidded, and just stopped himself falling off the other side.

'Clumsy,' she smiled.

She was doing something to the boat's engine, turning off the fuel or something of the kind; and then she stepped nimbly out to join him.

'So,' he said. 'Where's the seal?'

His teeth chattered in spite of himself.

'You must be patient,' she said. 'I should have thought you'd know that.'

They sat down on the pebbles a little higher up and waited in the gloom. Duncan tried not to think of the entrance slowly closing. The water, noisier now, began to lap succulently at the storm beach, not just at the edges but it seemed right underneath them. The boat bucked and ducked and wriggled. Duncan could hear the wood complaining as it ground against the rocks.

'The wind must be shifting to the south-west,' said Jo. 'They said it would.'

'Is that better or worse for us?'

'It doesn't really matter,' she said.

'Shouldn't we tie the boat up?'

'It'll be all right. It's not going anywhere. Better if it's not tied in a place like this.'

Marine matters were not his forte, but he couldn't help feeling her attitude to her craft was wrong. He walked across the beach and looked back towards the entrance to the cave, eighty yards or so away, and was just in time to see it, even now, disappearing under a comber. The sight of it swept him with a wave of horror stronger than anything he had known. The realization of where he was, trapped in this deep vaulted cell, unable to escape, with a rising tide outside and an equally implacable force of nature within, suddenly unmanned him. He knew, at a stroke, that Jo for all her apparent reasonableness was not going to melt this time.

She noticed his wild-eyed look as he came back across the beach, slipping again on a stone that the rising waters had splashed.

'What is the matter, Duncan?' she asked.

'I'm frightened,' he said. 'I don't mind telling you.'

He saw no reason why she shouldn't know.

'Oh, Duncan. You were always frightened.'

'Yes, I was. And now, it seems, with good reason.'

'It didn't have to end like this, Duncan.'

She kept talking about the affair as though love still meant something, as though their lives weren't in danger.

'Sometimes,' he said, 'you just have to face that the thing's finished.'

'That's what I'm saying, Duncan. It didn't have to end like this.'

But what was this? Her gesture, after all, seemed to embrace the cave, not their affair. Perhaps he had misinterpreted her. What a horrible thought!

'You don't mean . . . the end,' he said. 'What do you mean? End? We can go, can't we? When the tide turns. When we've seen the seals . . .'

'There are no seals here, Duncan. The families don't use this cave.'

'B-but you said they did.'

'I was fibbing, Duncan. Like you . . . deceitful . . .'

'Why? Why don't they come here?'

But he knew the answer already.

'Because this cave gets flooded by the sea at neap tides. It would kill the young pups. It's only the rogue female that comes here.'

Now he saw; she had brought him here to die. He tore off his jacket, ripped off his shoes, and scrambled to the water's edge, poised to plunge.

'Where are you going, Duncan?'

He turned. She was holding the gun again.

'I don't need to use this,' she said. 'You'd never get out. I know how you swim. You told me yourself you hated putting your head under water. Better to stay, hm? Face it together. See, I've brought a bottle of wine for you. Your favourite . . . Châteauneuf-du-Pape. Didn't you say it always makes you feel better? Let's have a glass together and drink to the future.'

Of course. She had been bluffing about the neap tide. The water in front of him looked the most unpleasant place in the world – dark and hungry – with who knew what creatures with nuzzling beaks and long prehensile arms lurking under the rocks. It was the sort of water you didn't go in unless you were being flogged with a rattan cane air-flown from Singapore.

He came back, sat beside her and opened the bottle of Vieux Telegraphe '86 that she had extracted from her bag along with a couple of glasses.

'Only plastic, I'm afraid,' she said.

The mundanity of the apology contrasted strangely with the surroundings. He sipped and felt the wine coursing through his optimism system. The taste was excellent, a long wine with plenty of fruit and tannin. If there were anything in the world that could reconcile him to a vigil, waiting for the tide to turn, this was it. He soon began to feel a great deal better.

Putting the glass down beside him, he asked her about her knowledge of the coast in general and seals in particular. She told him she had come down to see Alec on various occasions when she had actually said she was going to Barnard Castle. She had always been fascinated by the sea. Alec had shown her round the island, taught her how to use his boat, and talked endlessly about the film he was making.

'I'd done a sea cadets course, Duncan. You didn't know that, did you?' she said. 'And then I did some training with a guy I knew who was with the Specials.'

He didn't know that. And he certainly didn't know, before she told him, that she had come down here after the cellar business.

He avoided the topic of Mel's death. There seemed no purpose in raising it, it might upset her. He didn't want her upset. They sat and talked like old friends, although the knowledge that she had killed someone sat ominously at the corner of his mind. It would be the thing, he felt, that in the end would decide everything.

Meanwhile, he still hoped that – if he worked on it, brought back the camaraderie of the past – she might yet relent. Camaraderie in a dank cave with the tide lapping at your toes is not an easy thing to evoke but how he did work! Stories, anecdotes, little jokes they'd shared, expeditions they'd gone on ... No stone of the relationship was left unturned, no wriggling little worm, no shrivelled strand of memory was left unexamined, for he supposed that – mad or not – she was bound to have an escape plan up her sleeve. What else had she impressed upon him from the start of their business relationship.

'Get off the line, Duncan. Safeguard your exit.'

And as his old headmaster used to say: 'Example is better than precept.'

Of course she would have a way out.

With thoughts like this, and conversations like that, and a glass or two more of the good red wine, the time passed. And then he realized that the water was more than three-quarters of the way up the little storm beach, and still coming on. Outside, it seemed there was a near gale blowing. A big sea was humping up the water and throwing it at the cliffs in liquid bombardments whose dull boom-boom could be heard here, deep inside, in the heart of the rock.

In here, the water slopped and sucked and gurgled against the grey boulders and against the cavern roof with great speleological sounds of hock and thock and glog as if it were itself animate, more alive than all the things that lived in it.

Now, it was brought home to Duncan, after so many alarms and false self-comforts, that this was the end of a road. The world had come to this: just Jo and himself and the grey boulders and this monstrous lapping sea.

The boat, he saw, was half-submerged, its hull stove in by the continuous battering it had suffered, caught between rock and surge. Seeing it like that, so wantonly destroyed, a symbol of life and order, the craft of man, made him panic again, and ask another question whose answer he did not want to hear.

'It is an ordinary tide today, isn't it? It's not a neap tide, is it, Jo? This water, it's not going up to the roof? Is it, Jo? Is it?'

She smiled slowly and looked at him with love.

'Duncan,' she said. 'How many times do I have to tell you?'

'I didn't sleep with her, Jo,' he said. 'That time I took her out. I didn't sleep with her.'

'You slept with her in your mind,' she said without rancour. 'You weren't to be trusted any more.'

247

A particularly large tongue of water licked at her shoe but she didn't move. The curtains in his mind were lifting now. Yes, this was the scene. He had been here. The gloom, the suck and flop of the water, the booming of the cliffs like gunfire, no light but the faint day transmitted through the water in a dim, dun, soggy fibre-optic effect . . . No hope of anything but a slow and horrible death as the water, rising implacably, first banged and scraped, then tore and fractured their heads on the roof, and then drowned them like cats in a bag.

'We could still make it,' he said. 'The tunnel's not so long.'

She shook her head again, and smiled once more. It was the smile that told him everything was lost.

'We'd be broken on the rocks, Duncan. Don't fight it, Duncan. Go with it. See? It's easy.'

And still the water rose.

They climbed to the back of the cave where the oozing roof – fractured, striated and unstable – sloped down to meet the pebbles. There was no way out; no tunnel, no fault, no chimney to climb, no ledge to grip.

'This is the end of the road, Duncan,' she said.

When the first slurry of foam, thick with the gleanings from more moderate tides, flowed round their feet, she gripped his hand.

'No,' he cried out. 'No, no. Come on. Let's go!'

He held on to her hand but he could not move.

When the water reached his groin, she reached out with her other hand and gently touched him.

'Poor old man,' she said. 'Everything will be washed.'

'We're going to die,' he said.

'I couldn't teach you how to live, Duncan. Let's see if I can teach you how to die. A bad life can be redeemed by a good death, you know.'

'That's rubbish,' he cried. 'It wasn't all bad.'

'That's what you think, Duncan.'

He had thought before that he understood in some degree

how he had offended, even hurt her, but now at last he realized that the offence was mortal.

'You see, Duncan? Now you know what you did to me.'

'Let me go,' he shouted. 'Let me go. I'll be better. You'll see.'

The first dark wave tilted his head back, almost lifted him off his feet. Somehow she was still holding on to him, still exuding confidence and strength.

'No need,' she told him. 'Death cancels everything. And I believe, Duncan, yes I do believe, that then and only then, we can start again . . . at a different level, perhaps, Duncan . . . not 10 or any level that we know . . . but we, we two, we two will be the same.'

Another surge broke around them, almost smothering her as she spoke, but still it seemed she was the master.

'Goodbye, my darling,' she said, 'just for a very little while. Look for the light.'

She kissed him, and the extraordinary thing was that, as she did so, all fear left him. He truly believed that they would in some unfathomable way soon be together in perfect happiness and harmony, and that all this . . . the heaving waters, the ominous cave, the monstrous rumbling and thundering . . . was but a womb from which they would shortly emerge, kicking and spluttering, into a blissful new creation.

Even as he surrendered to this notion, however, he experienced a sudden intense pain in his calf, his legs were knocked from under him, and he felt himself being dragged rapidly backwards through the water in the direction of the light. It was not at all what he had expected from death.

He heard one despairing cry.

'Duncan!'

And then the waters closed over him.

Forty-One

He was conscious of being in a tunnel that rapidly grew lighter. He could not breathe. Fluid was everywhere; in his mouth, in his nose, in his eyes, in his throat, in his lungs. But the light dominated everything now, and he opened his eyes and saw an infinity of white-grey; and there was pain; and he felt himself being slapped about . . .

As full consciousness returned, however, he perceived that he was not in some kind of celestial maternity ward but was, in fact, being rolled about by the waves at the very top of a rocky shore, under impassive cliffs and beetling crags, along with an assortment of shoredrift. As he dragged himself out of the waves' clutch – no easy matter – he noticed that he was bleeding from what looked like a dog-bite in the leg.

He looked round dazedly for any sign of Jo, but all he could see were two large seals being chased by a smaller one out into the white horses of the bay. The significance of this was lost on him for the moment.

He set himself to climb the cliff since it seemed there was no other way satisfactorily to escape from this desolate place . . . Luckily here a fault in the rock had left a crumbling slope beyond which he could see a scaleable route leading to the summit.

When he had climbed a little way, he stopped. It had all been instinct up till now. Now he must make sense of all this. Jo must still be inside the cave. How had he escaped? Slowly his mind began to piece together the evidence; the wound in his leg, Jo's talk of the rogue female whose cave it was, the seal chasing the others out to sea ... That must be it. He had been attacked by the rogue female defending her cave, presumably selecting him not Jo on the grounds of sexual discrimination (and, thank God, not intent on crippling him in the way that Booth had suggested). He had then been duly jettisoned by her when she saw two other potential intruders.

He had been nearly killed by one rogue female and coincidentally saved by another. But was Jo rogue? Hadn't the fault been his? After the experiences in the cave, he couldn't help but feel more rogue than she. He had to go and find her.

He stood up helplessly, looking at his bleeding leg and at the raging sea. He didn't stand a chance. But that wouldn't have stopped Jo. She would have done anything for him.

He climbed down the cliff again and started to swim out. A wave took him and hurled him back against a rock, cracking his head. He tried again and again he was thrown down. Three times he tried ... and then he thought groggily, this is stupid, she's a murderess, if I save her, she'll go to prison, she wouldn't be able to bear that, I can't see her surviving in prison ... poor Jo.

So he gave up and slowly climbed the cliff again, wiping from his face salt water that seemed to be coming from his eyes.

Half an hour later, he had crossed the island and the farmhouse was in view.

He was surprised to see smoke coming from the chimney. He quickened his step and hurried up the path as best he could – his leg was already beginning to stiffen.

Inside, Kate was up and making tea.

'My God,' she said. 'Where have you been? You look as though you've been in a shipwreck.'

'I have,' he told her, dully. 'You could say that.'

How could he ever have thought that he loved her? It was to mistake baked beans for a banquet.

'Jo's dead.'

'Dead?'

She couldn't believe it.

'Thank God,' she said. 'Well done, Dunc.'

He hated to be called Dunc. Jo never called him Dunc.

'Well done?' he asked incredulously. 'Well done?'

'Yes,' she said, 'that makes two of us.'

'Two? Two what?'

'I killed Mel, you see. It was a mistake. She came back and said she was getting married and wanted to live in the flat again. I was livid. After all I'd done to the place. Why should she have it? We had a row and I followed her out and hit her where you showed me . . . the seventh vertebra, Dunc. I didn't think it would do it, but she just fell over.'

'Fell over?' repeated Duncan, dully.

'Of course you all thought it was Jo, that was the lucky part. Sorry about putting your card on Mel. I just thought it would put them off the track, and it did, didn't it? And now she's dead, so everything's all right.'

'No,' he said, shaking his head which felt as heavy as a moon of Jupiter. 'Not all right.'

Not for Mel. Not for Jo. Not for anyone.

'But for us it is,' she said. 'For us, we're in the clear.'

'We?' he repeated.

'Let's make love,' she said. 'I feel incredibly horny. Do you know, there was something about Jo, the way she looked. I think she was pregnant . . .'

Duncan sighed. He could feel tears beginning to form, involuntary as desire.

Outside, halfway across the channel, a large motorboat came into view. Even from this distance he could tell that there were a couple of blue uniforms on board, and that the vessel was heading for the island.

It was giving a wide berth to the Bitches.

Somewhere out there in the multitude of waters, Jo was floating out to sea. All her skills were no use to her now – the jab and the stab and the lightning reflex. The copper curls were dulled, the breasts no longer buoyant.

Her strangeness had become familiar, at one with all dead things.

He could feel the onset of delayed shock; and there was something else; something he did not feel; something he had imagined from time to time, over the last year with Jo, that he had shed but which had a horrible habit of returning.

He did not feel fear any more. This time it was gone for good. No need for the stomach to sink or the heart to lurch or the hedge of topiary humour he had planted around himself to be maintained.

He was free.

It was an alarming prospect, like sudden riches.

AUTHOR'S NOTE

Sticklers for accuracy may notice that I have slightly stretched the facts in certain areas that suited me: the geography of northwest Oxfordshire, the coastal islands of Pembroke, the beauty of girls who work in advertising agencies, certain tendencies of the Atlantic grey seal, the habitat of meerkats, the behaviour of dinghies in hurricanes . . . This, I hope, is excusable in fiction. On the other hand, in terms of the oddity of humans, I have probably underplayed the situation.